BY THE SWORD DIVIDED

'I came to take my last leave of you,' Anne said, releasing herself from his arms. 'As a Fletcher, and owing obedience and loyalty to my husband, according to my marriage vows, it seems I am now your enemy rather than your child.'

Sir Martin held her at arm's length, surveying the face he loved, now grown so hard and set. 'How cruel and unnatural that sounds. The thought has cost me many sleepless nights, be sure of that, Anne. How many more devoted families throughout this land must find themselves from now on divided by the sword? And all because a group of cunning and ambitious men of Puritan persuasion have roused the people and defied the King.'

.

By The Sword Divided

MOLLIE HARDWICK

Based on a BBC Television series
by John Hawkesworth

SPHERE BOOKS LIMITED
30 – 32 Gray's Inn Road, London WC1X 8JL

First published in Great Britain by
Sphere Books Ltd 1983
Copyright © 1983 by Egret Productions Ltd

Set in 9/10½ Compugraphic Century Textbook

Printed and bound in Great Britain by
Cox & Wyman Ltd, Reading

This book is based on the television serial
BY THE SWORD DIVIDED created by
John Hawkesworth and made as a Co-Production
between BBC Television and Consolidated
Productions.

The author wishes to acknowledge that in writing
this book she has drawn extensively on material
from scripts by the following writers: Alexander
Baron, John Hawkesworth, Jeremy Paul and
Alfred Shaughnessy.

By The Sword Divided

CHAPTER ONE

On all the tree-strewn landscape, which to a pensive onlooker would have appeared as limitless as the cloudless dark blue sky above it, nothing moved save two horses. Nodding companionably flank to flank, they trudged without need of guidance along a trackway flattened for them by many years of other hooves and wheel rims, their tired feet lifting scarcely clear of the dry ground.

They had walked a hundred miles and more in the summer heat, and before that had lurched and staggered to stay upright and unharmed in a sea crossing; and before that, how much marching, and galloping, and charging, and rearing up, to wheel, and retire, and turn to charge again. They were jaded nags, and knew it with their horse-sense, which told them also that the men astride them were bearing down extra heavily because their strength, too, was all forespent.

Under the dust and general grime which stained their leather jerkins and breeches and hid all but the most obvious outlines of their faces, both men would have been found to be young, in their twenties, with bodies spare from hard living and complexions weathered from constant outdoor exposure. If well scrubbed, they would have emerged as obviously of differing types and degrees, the tall, fair young man's features more finely delineated and his eyes more alert and enquiring than his stocky companion's stolid, earthy look of the born son of the soil.

Master and man they were: Thomas Lacey Esquire, son and heir of Sir Martin Lacey, Baronet, of Arnescote Castle, in the County of Warwickshire, and Will Saltmarsh, son of the blacksmith of Arnescote Village, his loyal though not invariably humble servant. And a long way they had come, because until a week ago they had been in the Low Countries, fighting Spaniards for what had been the Protestant cause when the long war had begun, but had since become part of a conflict of political rivalries.

For the last mile or so the trackway had been showing signs of gentle upward sloping. Now it suddenly steepened, causing the tired animals to snort and labour harder, pressing their worn hooves harder against the ground and nodding their heads more deeply with every step. It was a long ascent, curving round a great hump of hill coated with tall trees. When either animal flagged his rider automatically reminded him with a prick from a star-shaped spur, keeping him moving until there came at last the blessed relief of the summit and a reining to a halt.

'There, Will. Did you ever see fairer sight than that?' said Tom Lacey, stirring himself to swivel his gaze from side to side of a spectacular panorama of fields, crops, hedgerows and coppices, laid out before and below them like a patterned carpet that stretched as far as eye could reach.

He swung down from the saddle, eagerness overcoming fatigue, and stood, hands on hips, staring down on the many-hued vale.

'Aye,' Will agreed, getting down to join him in contemplation. ''Tis a change from bogs and dykes.' He looked silently for some moments, then added, ''Twould be grand cavalry ground, too.'

Tom frowned and turned his head almost sharply.

'The war's behind us. It were better to leave war-talk where it belongs.'

The servant shrugged, making a rueful, dusty smile.

'They was always on at a man to use his eyes and spell out the ground for himself. Habits die hard.'

'Well, that's one you won't be needing longer, like a few others that soldiering's taught you, my lad.'

Will grinned openly.

'It'll be quiet living.'

'Quieter than the Low Countries, but not so quiet as the grave. Be thankful for mercies.'

'Aye, master. There's that.'

They feasted their eyes in silence for some time, while the

2

unattended horses cropped the sweet untrampled grass at the track side.

'You're right, though,' Tom admitted at length. 'A sweep of good horse could carry the whole plain.'

'And a few cannon up here could wreak fair havoc.'

'On the other hand, a company of muskets, concealed in that wood over there . . .' Tom Lacey banged his thigh, raising a small dust cloud. 'Enough of this, you pernicious coxcomb! You're tempting me into it. I tell you, we're done with war, both of us. By God's grace, I can hand you back to your kin in a single piece. As for myself . . .' A hand stole to his side, under his ribs, and he winced a little. 'There's a little less of me than went from here, but nothing that need signify.'

His companion nodded, in more sober mood.

'There was sights a man must thank his Maker he'll never see in this land.'

'Amen. The Spaniards will be unlikely to try to come here again. What with losing their whole Armada last time, and the cost of these present wars, they could never find the resources. So you turn your mind to the smithy, Will Saltmarsh, and stick to the weapon you carry in your breeches, assuming you can find some wench game to tussle with you.'

'Oh, as to that I've my notions already, master. Three year we've been gone, which means that a wench I've kept in my mind's eye should be perfect ripe for harvesting about now.' The servant's leer changed to a grimace as he added, 'That's if no rogue's gone and cropped her already behind my back.'

Tom laughed out loud.

'Only one way to find out — get on your way. Come, Jasper!'

His horse, trained by long service, moved obediently to obey him. But when he had mounted he sat still for quite a minute, his eyes still ranging the landscape, so empty, so many-coloured, so English and secure — so utterly unimaginable in any association with war.

Soon the Castle would come in sight, a grey-gold mass of stone standing serene on its height, the church a little below it, Arnescote village nestling at its foot. The Conqueror had begun its building; to his day belonged the great gateway of the Keep, and the Great Hall within. Two huge round

CHAPTER TWO

At the very instant of Tom Lacey's jerking the rein, to command Jasper to resume his weary plod, Anne Lacey sat up suddenly from the greensward on which she had been lying under that same sky. A shiver shook her slim body.

John Fletcher sat up, too, tossing aside the stem of grass he had been sucking.

'What is it, Anne? I saw you shiver.'

'I . . . I thought I heard Tom's voice, calling to me.'

John peered about, then placed his arm round her, drawing her close.

'Then your hearing must be matchless. Warwickshire and The Hague are not exactly within calling distance.'

He kissed her ear, but it was dutifully done and she did not respond.

'It is so with twins sometimes. Often our thoughts have matched, and we have communicated without even a word spoken.'

'In that case, I hope what he is telling you is how much he approves his sister's marrying his best friend.'

'No fear that he wouldn't. But I hope all is well with him, John. I have worried ever since I woke one night with a stabbing pain in my side, enough to make me cry out and bring my maid running. They were for fetching the doctor for me, but I knew it was no infirmity of mine own. It was something concerning Tom.'

'Has he mentioned nothing in his letters?'

'What letters? I sometimes wonder whether that university you and he attended even taught him to write his own name.'

John laughed and pressed her tight to him again.

5

'I won't deny that he's only half the scholar that your future husband can claim to be. The lawyer's gown would never have suited him. All the same, a man could envy him his wit and charm and courage — and I can assure you he can write his name and a good deal more.'

'Then he would do well to condescend to do so more often. Three years away at the wars, and scarce a score of letters from him in that time — and such poor lame notes when they come. I do believe the only time he filled more than two pages was after grandmother died, and that was mostly explanations why he could not come home.'

'Considering that he was under siege somewhere or other at the time, you were lucky even to have his letter.'

Anne sighed. 'I suppose we must take the same view as regards our wedding. I wrote to tell him as soon as the contract was sealed, but never a word, of course.' Her fair brow clouded again. 'I pray God he is safe.'

'Amen.'

They sat there on the grass, in the little hollow they had chosen for the picnic they had brought with them from Arnescote Castle. With great grumbling, because it had interrupted her long preparations for the espousal banquet two days hence, Mrs Dumfry had put up for them a basket of pasties, ham, pickles, cheesecake and a bottle of rose petal wine of her own making. They had ridden here, and turned their mounts loose to wander where they would, while they ate the food and drank the wine and then sank down side by side to stare up at that blue infinity, thinking their separate thoughts about what lay so soon ahead of them.

Twenty-four years was the age shared by Anne and her absent twin brother. She was handsome without being beautiful, brown of hair, her complexion unmarked by any of the poxes which, unlike so many other children of her time, she had survived unscathed. Her fine eyes were her best feature, reflecting the determined nature which had enabled her so effortlessly to supervise her father's household since her mother's death sixteen years ago in childbirth.

John Fletcher was no more than a year older than she and her twin brother, his old Oxford University friend. He could well claim intellectual superiority to the more dashing Tom, and it was typical of the difference between them that whereas Tom had chosen to take himself off to fight as a mercenary in the long, muddled conflict which history would later term the Thirty Years' War, John had continued his legal studies and looked forward to the day when he might get himself elected a Member of Parliament. In these ways he was proving himself a dutiful son to Sir Austin Fletcher, whose only child he was. Sir Austin was a former Hull ships' chandler, who had won his way upward to a fine house in London and an impressive counting house, in which his many clerks and overseers pored over ledgers concerning Barbadian sugar, Virginian tobacco and a range of other commodities in which Sir Austin had built up interests. He knew the value of thrusting ambition, did Sir Austin, who had deliberately set his intention on a knighthood for himself, which he got, and a sound profession and a well connected bride for his son, which he was on the verge of achieving also.

That Anne Lacey had become the chosen one was owed to Sir Austin's having bought land at Swinford not far from Arnescote Castle and having an ancient mansion redesigned by that most highly regarded of architects, Inigo Jones. As a matter of expediency, Sir Austin had got himself appointed to the local magistracy, placing him thereby on equal terms with such born gentry as Sir Martin Lacey. Assessing the material advantages of this, in the manner that his shrewd mind turned towards any set of promising new circumstances, Sir Austin had recognised that his only son and heir and the elder of Sir Martin Lacey's two daughters were of almost matching age and that marriage between them would be a tidy affair with useful potential. Even so, he had conducted the negotiations like any other transaction.

'One thousand pounds,' he had said, in his plain Yorkshire accent, as he faced Sir Martin across the document-strewn table in the steward's room at Arnescote. Present alongside their respective masters were Nathaniel Cropper, Sir Martin's steward, and Master Mabbutt, his counterpart in Sir Austin's employ, an alert, middle-aged man who noticed with keen pleasure the two men across the table from him exchange a glance. Mabbutt and Sir Austin had come there that day conscious that they were about to engage in

7

business off their home ground and in castle surroundings which would have overawed most self-made merchants. Both knew, however, that the younger Lacey girl, Lucinda, was also being sought in marriage at this time, and they had made a point of learning the figure of the dowry Sir Martin had agreed for her.

'I must concede,' replied the castle's owner, looking his visitor directly in the eyes, 'that the jointure you propose is a generous one: a life annuity of eighty pounds, and, in the event of widowhood, four hundred pounds per annum in perpetuity. But a thousand pounds . . .' He made a clicking sound with his tongue and teeth.

Sir Austin held his gaze, as he asked, 'What's your figure, then?'

'I had put it at eight hundred.'

'Ha! Sell your girl short, would you?'

Sir Martin frowned and the lean fine-featured face framed by his long curled ringlets flushed pink.

'Whatever that remark might mean, I take it to be scurrilous, sir.'

'In plain meaning, Sir Martin, it is that I know you to have settled one thousand pounds on your child-daughter to the Earl of Walmer, and that what is sauce for the gosling ought surely to be sauce for the gander.'

Though levelly delivered, it brought Sir Martin to his feet, Cropper following suit. 'That is a private matter!' Sir Martin barked. 'Any negotiations which may or may not concern my younger daughter carry no bearing on this present question, which, I would remind you, is of your own raising.'

Sir Austin remained seated, riposting coolly, 'Nobility's worth more than trade, in other words?'

'Those are your words, not mine.'

The two masters glared at one another, chins jutting. Their men of business exchanged dutiful scowls. It was the Yorkshireman who sought to douse the mutual anger.

'You must forgive my lack of manners, sir. A plain man. Have to take me as you find me.'

'If it were not a question of my daughter's happiness, I would not choose to take you at all, sir.'

'Aye, aye. Let's not forget the children. Come, sit down and let's talk on.'

Satisfied that he had gained some little ground, Sir Martin sat slowly, explaining, 'To be frank with you, it is precisely because I have just agreed a portion for my younger daughter that . . . that I now find myself in somewhat straitened circumstances. If you are under the illusion that you are dealing with a wealthy man . . . ?'

Master Mabbutt, who had been glancing round, was about to put in a remark that he saw no evidence of penury. His master forestalled him.

'What I see, Sir Martin, is a man who is, for all his family trappings, in his way as plain as me. Enjoys a little cut and thrust on principle.'

'Eight hundred and fifty,' was Sir Martin's immediate response. 'A fair portion for a young woman of old family to wed a lawyer . . .'

'Of none? Come, gather up, Mabbutt. We'll waste no more of this gentleman's time.'

Sir Austin was on his feet, gesturing to his man to collect their documents. Both principals knew now that each had made the point he had brought with him to the meeting, and that it behoved them to be frank from here on.

'*Two* weddings!' Sir Martin almost wrung his hands. 'Expenses of church and banquets. Guests to put up. Villagers to feast. And all the time the King ready to drain my purse with his taxes.'

Not so artlessly as it might have appeared, Sir Martin had touched on a grievance near to his adversary's heart. From past conversation he knew that Sir Austin Fletcher bore little respect for His Majesty King Charles the First. As a blunt man, who knew what he wanted and went after it looking neither right nor left, Sir Austin despised the King's vacillations and chronic inability to keep his word. Even more, he resented his habit of levying taxes without Parliament's consent, yet still allowing the country's economy to decline, with dire effects on the import-export trade which represented Sir Austin's fortune.

Sir Martin himself, although a loyalist of the old school, was not wholly in favour of the King. As a Member of the recently dissolved Parliament he could not approve of a monarch who preferred to rule without parliaments, or to ignore and override them as he saw fit. He sought to play on the Yorkshireman's sympathy for a fellow financial sufferer.

'I'm stung all round. Under siege.'

'The King bites deep into my apple, too,' Sir Austin was quick to remind him.

'Yes, yes. But you are a man of large business. You can play the City games with the rest of them. I am merely a landowner, prey to the climate as well as the King. What — will you have me sell my land to accommodate you? Think of the two hundred pounds difference between us as acres of land. What is two hundred pounds to you, compared with my acres to me?'

'There is no comparison, sir. But there is one between my son's wife coming cheaper to him than the Earl of Walmer's. How would my standing be, as a neighbour and fellow Justice, if word got round as to that?'

'With all respect to yourself, sir, to equate your son's standing with the Earl of Walmer . . . Why, you overlook that I should be giving you the privilege of marrying into an historic line.'

'And I offer you a marriage into wealth!' Sir Austin snapped back. 'My boy may not be an earl, and only a fledgling yet at the Inns of Court, but he has his father's ambition and his own brain. He will be a Member of Parliament . . .'

'If there ever be a Parliament again.'

'The King must call it back. He must. But that is by the by. I put it to you that when I am dead and my John inherits he will make your girl ten times richer than any noble sprout could ever dream of. Wealth for her, and a cosseted old age for you if you outlive me, and yet you quibble now over a mere two hundred pounds.'

Seeing his host waver, the Yorkshireman had come round the table to take him by the arm and lead him away down the chamber, past the great iron-bound chest which housed the deeds and documents pertaining to Arnescote Castle and its estate properties, away from the hearing of the rival stewards. In a lowered voice he confided, 'See here, my friend, I have a proposal to put to you. You know me for what I am and what I'm about. I'm too clumsy, or too honest, to disguise it. I wish to be a gentleman. I was not born one, only the proud son of a poor Yorkshire chandler. Give me a leg up in the world, and in return I'll put you to rights in the world of commerce, which is where my name counts for something.'

Sir Martin searched his features. He was no snob and did not instinctively dislike this man, although there was something almost studiedly blunt about him. He did not dislike the notion of John Fletcher becoming his son-in-law, either. He was Tom's old friend, which was recommendation enough, and Anne appeared to like him well, though if there was much love between them it was not very apparent in John, who had always struck Sir Martin as rather too consciously clever for his own good.

Sir Austin's friendly grip was still on his arm.

'Pay over the thousand pound I ask, and let it be known about. That way my boy will be on a par with yon young nobleman in the matter of a dowry from you. In return, I'll place the money in my company, for you to share the profits from it half-about. Thus, all will be knit up in pragmatic style and everyone benefits.'

He leaned closer. 'As to the marriage, I'll have my ships at Bristol unload as many barrels of Spanish wine from Cadiz as you and your guests and all your villagers can fill their bellies with.'

Sir Martin Lacey raised one eyebrow.

'*Spanish* wine?'

They roared with laughter together and clasped hands. Behind them, at the table, the stewards gave each other a nod and thin smile and reached over for a dry handshake.

So Anne Lacey became betrothed to John Fletcher on the fifteenth day of May, Anno Domini 1640; and as they knelt on the grass and stowed away in the basket the remnants of their picnic, they looked well matched and cosily domestic, which was as should be with a young couple only two days away from their wedding ceremony.

CHAPTER THREE

Anne's twin was nearer than she knew. Not half a mile from
Arnescote village, where woods clothed a hillside, the two
horses and their riders emerged into a clearing, dominated
by a gallows-tree. The grim iron frame dangling from it was
empty of its usual burden.

Tom looked up. 'No one on the gallows. Has my father
gone soft, Will?'

Will shook his head. 'Not likely. I warrant there'll be
someone in the stocks at least, master.'

Their nags picked a careful way down the zigzag path that
led to the village, emerging on the tidy green, surrounded by
cottages. A number of their occupants were gathered round
a point of interest, which, as the riders drew nearer, proved
to be, as Will had prophesied, the occupied stocks. As they
dismounted, those on the fringe of the crowd left it and came
to greet them. First came Sir Martin's tall head gamekeeper,
Walter Jackman, his face alight with pleasure, hand out-
stretched.

'Master Tom, sir. Home from battle! God save you, sir.'
They shook hands, and Tom laughed, pointing to his tired
horse.

'Limping horse, Jackman. It was never thus with Caesar,
alas. How's my father, and all the household?'

'All in fightin' trim, sir — nothing changed.'

'Cropper? Goodwife Margaret? Old Minty? Mistress
Dumfry? The same caterwauling in the kitchen?'

'At each other's throats, day and night, same as ever, sir.'

The raised, shocked voice of Will made them turn. He
stood by the stocks, staring down at the occupant, a plump,

12

baby-faced boy, cheeks blubbered with tears, shifting unhappily on the hard narrow bench, his feet trapped in the holes cut in planks which stretched between two posts. They were whipping-posts, and they had been well used. At the foot of one of them, drops of recently shed blood flecked the ground. The boy in the stocks lifted his head as Will approached. His doublet was splattered where someone had thrown a rotten potato at him, but otherwise he had got off without the usual pelting of filth.

'Brother Will?' he said faintly, his face contorting with tears.

Will stared, unbelieving. 'Sam boy — what you done?'

The boy shook his head helplessly, and began to weep. Will hurried back to Tom's side.

'Master, 'tis my brother Sam in the stocks.'

'Sam? Never!'

Jackman broke in. 'Aye, it was I locked him up. Your father's made me a constable now, sir. The lad got drunk at the Mayday dance, called the parson a Papist pig and blathered out against the bishops and the King.'

Tom made a shocked face. 'Against the King? Now there's some mischief, Will.'

'But he wouldn't, not Sam, sir,' returned Will vehemently. 'He's the mildest fellow — he's an idiot, almost. He hardly knows who the King is.'

'Maybe he's had some educating since you've been gone, Will,' said Jackman; 'bad thoughts from them travellin' Puritans who come and preach, then shift off fast.' They were by the stocks now, the little crowd backing off at the approach of Tom. He asked sternly, 'Now, Sam Saltmarsh, what's this misbehaviour?'

'Oh sir,' the boy moaned out, 'master — sir, I swear as God's my judge I know not what I done.'

'You have some quarrel with the King?'

'His Majesty? No, sir, I'm as loyal a subject as there is in the land. I'd die in battle for the King — and Sir Martin and all the bishops if they ask me. I were led on, sir, by Ned Willowby, the shoemaker, and a gang of 'em. First they filled me up with ale, then all I knew was rough-handlin'. Then they dropped me in a barrel in the cellar of the inn and left me. I was there for a whole day, sir. Then the — the court, sir,

13

orderin' twenty strokes of the birch . . .' He hunched his lacerated shoulders, and Will saw, with pity, the blood-stained cuts in the white skin. He picked up Sam's frieze jacket, lying on the ground beside him, and placed it over his back; but as the boy winced and cried out he let it fall again.

'My father's court, was this?' Tom asked Jackman.

'No, sir, the church court — the Archdeacon's court, sir.'

'Aye, sir,' put in Sam, 'wi' the parson waggin' his finger at me. And now I'm here till I apology. But I can't apology for what I don't know I done.'

A girl at the front of the crowd called out 'You were soused, that's why you don't know!' Tom turned on her. 'Hold your tongue!' Then, full of authority, an echo of his father, he addressed the wretched Sam.

'You have a grudge against the parson? You dispute some point of doctrine? At the dance, you made some theological point on church procedure?' The crowd laughed obediently, not understanding. Sam stared blankly, understanding even less, and muttered something.

'You were drunk,' Tom told him sternly. 'That's not in dispute. And you caused offence. You deserve your punishment.' He strode back to his horse and mounted, leaving the onlookers murmuring agreement, as they were expected to do. But the girl Rachel, her venom suddenly turned to pity, ran to the village pond nearby, dipped the corner of her apron, and wiped Sam's streaming face. She worked in the kitchens of the castle, where beatings were not uncommon, but a public lashing was a different thing, and she had a soft spot for young men.

The crowd melted away, tired of the poor sport. Aching and increasingly miserable, Sam sank into apathy, a numbed half-sleep. The ring of hooves on the cobbles aroused him. John Fletcher had reined in his horse and was looking down at him, not as Tom Lacey had looked but with compassion. After a moment he turned the horse's head from the direction it had been taking, and headed towards the church.

The parson, Michael Butterworth, proved adamant. 'The boy is a blasphemer and a heretic, sir. I only did my duty, as Christ is my judge.'

John's voice was calm and reasonable. 'I've no doubt you did, Vicar. The lad's a fool and deserves the chastening, but

14

with my wedding so near, and Mistress Lucinda's, and guests descending on the village, Sam's wretchedness will be an eyesore. I think we have a case for clemency, don't you?' A slight jingle of coins drew Butterworth's eyes to a purse, held significantly near an offertory box.

'Clemency? Has Sir Martin indicated, then . . . ?'

'I have not spoken with him. It was my wife-to-be, Mistress Anne, who was uppermost in my thoughts. It would be a shame to scar her happy days.' Very unobtrusively he turned and left the church. The purse now lay beside the offertory box. The vicar picked it up, a smile spreading across his face.

He was still in a good mood that afternoon, when Anne and Lucinda came to sit before him in the front pew, to receive his statutory instruction on the duties of a wife, always administered on the marriage-eve. He enjoyed intoning this litany to wide-eyed virgins ready to be suitably terrified by the vast authority of Man, and he always wore his best cassock for the occasion; though, to tell the truth, neither of the present brides-to-be exactly conformed to this ideal. The elder, who was sitting up very straight and regarding him intently, had a look in her eye which was less than meek, and the firm set of her mouth betokened a shrew in the making, he thought; while the younger girl, small, and fair as her brother, looking scarcely more than a child, sat comfortably, even sprawlingly, at ease, and had already yawned once with only the barest attempt at concealment. Butterworth raised his sonorous voice.

'As your humble priest, I say unto you, take heed of the first wife, Eve, who in her nakedness drew her husband into folly and temptation, and the world was punished therefore. The prime duty of a wife, as I perceive it, is subjection and obedience. Call your husband Lord, and serve him as humbly as you would Christ Himself . . .'

Lucinda fluttered her hand prettily. Displeased, he stopped.

'Yes, child?'

Her blue eyes were certainly wide, but he saw naughtiness lurking in them. 'You would have us lie like spaniels at our husbands' feet, then?' she asked. Anne cast her a sideways reproving look, and the parson stared.

'Spaniels?'
Innocently she recited:

> 'A woman, a dog, and a walnut tree,
> The harder you beat them, the better they be.'

'Is that your meaning, Vicar?'

Anne broke in. 'I think my sister means that you would not have us surrender *all* our liberty and become man's slave?'

As this was exactly what he had meant, Butterworth gaped and thrashed about in his mind for an answer. Out of the corner of his eye he saw someone enter the church and kneel at the back. It was John Fletcher. A praying man might be expected to shut his ears to anything but his own intercessions, but the vicar decided to take no chances.

'Slave?' he echoed. 'By no means, child. That word is not used of wives in the Bible.'

'But we are slaves in law, sir,' Lucinda said pertly. A reluctant smile twitched at Anne's lips.

'You mistake my meaning, ladies. I stress only the need for vigilance. Your husband is controller of your fate, and the solemnisation of Holy Matrimony commits you to the sacred duty to love, honour, and *obey* him, so long as ye both shall live.'

'I thought . . .' Lucinda began. Hastily he told the girls to kneel, muttered a prayer, and hastened off into his vestry. He was not fond of awkward questions. Before Anne could reprove Lucinda as she felt she ought, however strong her silent agreement, she saw John coming towards them from the back of the church. At her hurried whisper, Lucinda left her and ran out, leaving the betrothed pair together.

'Well, was the advice useful?' John asked, reading the answer in her face. 'I had no intention to interrupt, but I wished a private word with you, on another matter — a small thing, but best cleared up between us.'

Anne nodded, puzzled.

'That man's prating through his nose, dressed up like a hobby horse at a fair,' John went on. 'And all this.' He waved a hand towards the church in general. 'The trappings of this place — the pulpit, the cross, the painted glass above the altar — does it not smack of Rome to you?'

'Rome? Why?' Anne was even more puzzled. She had never heard such intensity in John's voice before, or seen such agitation in his usually calm face, and she was worried by it.

'Babylonish, even!' His voice was raised to the pitch of a ranter at a street-corner. 'It's a growing mood in this country. Archbishop Laud tyrannising over the church — a Catholic queen on the throne of England . . . Anne, we're being drawn into the clutches of Rome. Don't you sense it?'

Anne, who did not, shook her head. She hoped John was not sickening for something, so close to the wedding.

'I would wish less pomp and ceremony at our marriage, Anne,' he said solemnly. She laughed.

'You'd have me call you Puritan, would you? Well, my love, I would honour your wishes and remove everything that offends you' (it would take some doing, she reflected, if it included the removal of the church windows) 'but my father would scarcely be pleased. Our family has worshipped here since the third Edward's time with no thought of Rome.'

John considered for a moment, then took the hand she held out to him, and smiled, reverting to his normal manner. 'I stand rebuked. Let it be as the majority will have it.'

'Spoken like a true Parliament!' she said. Arm in arm, they left the church. As they passed the green, John noted that the stocks were empty.

Anne was thinking, as they walked the short distance to the castle, of the conversation she had had with Tom on the day he came home. Even after a long separation they had fallen at once into their old intimate relationship, through the thoughts behind the words. He had said, as though it had only just occurred to him, 'So you are to be wife to John Fletcher.'

'Yes. It pleases you?'

'Puzzles me. You've known him seven years. He could have plucked you in your bloom. Is it a love match, or were you bundled into it by our anxious father?'

Anne heard her own voice, almost stridently defiant. 'Shame on you! I believe I am in love.'

Tom had fixed her gaze with his own. 'Does he love you?' When she made no answer he said, 'It's a canny catch for the Fletchers.'

17

Her head went up. 'I am not a pawn, in the Fletchers' advancement, or anyone's.'

'Ah. Then all is well. You are in love, both.' He nodded, as though satisfied, and gave his attention to the arrangement of his deep lace collar.

Anne turned her shoulder on him, angry. 'I knew you'd face me with this. You are a beast!'

'I read your mind, you see, even when I'm far away. It's nature's trick with twins.'

'I read yours, too. I hear you sometimes, whispering...'

'Words of caution? I'm most probably drunk at the time.'

Anne shrugged. 'Most probably. I ignore you, in the main. Have you something against my husband?'

'Nothing much. I like him — as a man likes his opposite. I could never settle to books at Oxford — he often did my work for me.'

'While you taught him games?'

Tom answered, with mock pedantry, 'I drew him to a certain appreciation of the game which otherwise his nature, I think, would have denied him.' Make what you can of that, his eyes said to her.

'Well, perhaps that's why I grew fond of him,' Anne said. 'I had a surfeit of games with you, remember? He has some of your mischief, which I enjoy. And a seriousness and serenity which I admire.'

'Then you have got yourself a man. Be happy, Anne — I need you to be happy.'

She kissed him. 'Dear Tom, there shall always be two men to make my life complete.'

Now, going home, she wondered how much of what she had told her brother had been true. She did indeed admire John's intelligence and maturity — was rather dazzled by them, perhaps. Far from the rôle the parson had mapped out for her, she saw her future self not as John's slave, but as his helpmeet, his partner; together they might go far. And yet — did she fully comprehend him? His outburst in the church had struck her as something quite foreign to his nature as she knew it, the sort of feverish stuff a man might let out in delirium. Rome, indeed, what nonsense! She glanced back at the square grey tower of the church, nestling securely among trees green and blossomy with May; the church where she had been christened and would be married, with all the familiar rites, in old, beautiful surroundings, the bones of her ancestors under the stones at her feet, their names on the walls. The bright-painted tomb of her grandparents, he in formal ruff and robe, she in her huge hideous heart-shaped coif and great sleeves, their hands pointing to heaven: could these be Romish?

Yet John was very wise. It could be that John was right.

Preparations for the wedding banquet were at their height. Under Margaret Goodwife's supervision the tables were laid with cloths of white damask and linen, and set with dishes of silver and fine pewter; before Sir Martin's place stood a huge, magnificent bowl of silver-gilt, his particular pride. Finger-bowls, napkins, knives and spoons stood at each lesser place, and where the bride and bridegroom would sit, at the centre of the high table, a double-handled loving-cup of silver.

Menials scuttled about like mice, followed by scolding directions, and from the kitchens floated rich smells. A boar's head, whole, jowls of salmon, whole carp (pray God it was not too far on the turn, but the sauce would disguise it), rabbits and pullets, chickens roasted, legs of new mutton, a great quantity of sparrow-grass, freshly cut, young peas and potatoes, pigeon-pie with a bird atop of each, arranged very lifelike though unmistakably dead, and quantities of pies made from fruits kept in spices and sugar from the previous summer. Huge cheeses, golden, red and white, gave off their savour; and yet none of these things would be eaten until the following morning, after the couple had gone to church and come back. With so much to prepare, nothing could be left until the last minute.

Nathaniel Cropper, Sir Martin's steward, was accompanying his master round the tables, inspecting the seating arrangements, when they were interrupted by the arrival of a well-dressed messenger, bearing a letter. Cropper took it from him.

'From the Earl of Walmer, sir,' he said.

'Ha.' Sir Martin opened and scanned it, his features creasing into a deep scowl. 'The young Lord Ferrar travels here with the Earl's steward, to pay court to my daughter Lucinda and conclude the marriage contract. They should be here within two hours. God in Heaven!'

Anne, who had heard, ran forward. 'They cannot come now! They'll spoil my preparations!'

Sir Martin's craggy face was still furrowed with a frown. 'Is not one wedding enough in a week?'

Lucinda, at Anne's side, had turned pale. Her voice trembled a little as she said, 'I am willing to delay, father . . .'

He was not listening. 'Intolerable intrusion,' he snapped. 'Send them away, Cropper.'

'But it's the Earl of Walmer, sir. I fear we shall offend . . .'

'You're right — we shall offend. Very well. Margaret, stop that and take Lucinda to her room and make her presentable.'

But Lucinda did not want to be made presentable. Mulish-faced, huffing with impatience, she held on to one of her bed's posts as Margaret drew up the embroidered petticoat, laced the under-bodice tightly to push up the young bosom, and straightened the locket, containing her betrothed's picture, which hung round Lucinda's neck.

'Stand still, child, now — don't move or you'll disarrange yourself. I'll fetch your gown and the new lace collar, if those lazy sluts have pressed it yet . . .' She hurried out.

When she came back, the gown over her arm, the room was empty, and the locket and chain lay discarded on the floor. For hours they sought in vain, in the house, in the grounds, even the lanes round about. Nobody dared suggest dragging the deep duck-pond, but some of the servants eyed it thoughtfully. Maidens take strange fancies.

It was after storms of temper from Sir Martin, furious disclaimers from Margaret, and much questioning of the bemused servants, that Tom was sent after night fell to find his sister, with his father's words ringing in his ears: 'I'll have the wanton back if you have to drag her by the throat.' While he searched, the breathless Cropper intercepted Lord Ferrar's coach, and turned it back, after a lame explanation that there was infectious sickness at the castle. A pity, such a handsome and civil young man as Lord Edward was, but women and their whims could play the devil.

Tom found Lucinda where he expected to find her, in an old hiding-place of theirs, a cranny behind the altar-tomb of that Sir Thomas Lacey who fought at Creçy. She was cold,

20

dusty and frightened. Putting his lantern down on the tomb, he said gently, 'Never fear, Lucinda. I come as a friend, with food and warmth.' He opened the basket he carried, and put a blanket round her shivering shoulders. 'Well, this is a chilly place, among our ancestors.'

'Whom I shall presently join!' she declared.

'Foolish talk, foolish talk. Have some of this.'

'No. I would rather be found dead beneath the altar than brought dead to it — with one I do not love. Oh, Tom!'

He held her close. 'There, gently now, gently.'

She clung to him. 'Oh Tom, I'm afraid! Good Margaret says, "Be always with your hourglass in your hand, measuring out your little span." It isn't death I fear, but that I shall go to Hell, my sins not pardoned. Oh Tom, will *you* pardon me?'

Tom laughed. 'I fear it would carry little weight with the Almighty, but I'll pardon you on earth if you'll confess the reason you ran away.'

'You will take me back. I know that. It's your duty. If you do, you kill me as surely as if you pierced me with your sword. There, so do it now!' She tore ineffectually at her bodice. Tom put her hand away and drew her cloak together.

'I've seen enough of death, my dear — you must find another executioner. And this is all play-acting, Lucinda — let's talk sensibly, as we have not since I returned. This husband you say you do not love — how came you by him?'

'I met him at a masque, not six weeks gone. How could he love me? He could not even *see* me in my vizard.' She scrubbed at a tear on her cheek. Tom, smiling, dried it. 'Then, within two days, Father asked me if I found him agreeable. I said politely "Yes", as I would say of many.'

'Ah. And on that slender thread . . . ?'

'I'm informed of the contract, measured for new gowns, primped — and told how much it consists with my interest to become one day the Countess of Walmer.'

'So he aroused in you not one tiny spark, this masked wooer?'

'I'd rather take a dozen from the village than bed with him!' Lucinda flared, to Tom's outright amusement.

'There's spirit, woman, if not prudence. Well said, lusty lass!'

21

'In truth, there is no lust in me. I am not woman yet.'

He smoothed her tumbled hair. 'No. But it behoves young girls to grow and shed their dreams, and to obey their parents.'

'And was it so for Anne?' she said angrily. '*She* disdained every suitor till this one, while I am bartered like a prize animal at a fair. You're no friend to me, Tom — you speak with Father's voice.'

'Sister, we're all but chattels of our parents, for them to dispose of how they wish. You plead a solid case, and I would plead it with you. But I fear it founders on necessity. And skulking here in a fit of the sullens — this leads not to liberty, but shame on all of us and the lash for you.'

Lucinda rose stiffly, and blew out the flame of the lantern as if extinguishing her own last hope. Like the heroine of a Webster tragedy she declaimed, 'Then lead me to my fate, my death, for I have no wish to live in chains!'

Tom's broad smile was invisible to her. 'Come, then,' he said, taking her cold hand. But she threw herself against him, trembling and weeping again. 'Oh, Tom, I'm not feigning, I'm sick in the belly — leave me here and say you have not found me.'

'They know you're here, child.'

'But I'm ill . . . Oh, must I face them?'

'*We* shall face them.'

'Then truly — you're my executioner.' She fell limply into his arms and hung there, a dead weight.

———————

When, at night, a merry party of guests and musicians conducted the bridal couple to bed, Lucinda was not there to join in the traditional bawdy revels. Tom was almost the last to leave; Anne went into his arms and they kissed solemnly. He held her away from him.

'I guarded you for four-and-twenty years, and now I must relinquish you. Cherish your lawyer, Anne. We shall need him if Lord Walmer sets about us.'

'Lucinda will not marry, then? I hoped she might have changed her mind.'

'Not of her own free choice. She's set and stubborn.'

'Oh, Tom, take care of her when I'm gone . . .'

John, nightgowned and solemn, was waiting pointedly for Tom to leave. Tom released his sister, putting her hand in her bridegroom's.

'I leave you in safe hands, Anne,' he said. 'Goodnight.'

The house was quiet when Sir Martin strode to Lucinda's bedchamber, a birch rod in his hand. When he entered she was sitting on her bed, clad in her night-robe, a picture of meekness. As he stood flicking the rod she slipped to the floor and knelt, her back to him, holding tightly to the bedpost. Again and again the rod was raised, and fell on her unprotected back, until at last Sir Martin was satisfied and she was allowed to rise. She had not uttered one cry.

'Am I pardoned, father?' she whispered.

'You are. You took your punishment well, like a Lacey. I'm proud of you.'

Lucinda pressed home her advantage. 'And I need not marry my lord now?'

He had not expected such a question. Faced with it, he could only say lamely, 'You need not marry.'

Then he strode out, confused in his mind, angry with Lucinda but more angry with himself. Such a to-do, and all for nothing, the wench getting her own way instead of yielding to his will. It had done him no good to wield his authority. He had beaten his wife, once, and only once. She had not cried out, either, but there had been a look in her eyes when she faced him afterwards which had made him feel less than a man.

He sat by the fire with Tom for a long time, saying little. At last Tom raised his goblet. 'I drink a toast — to Master and Mistress John Fletcher — to you, sir — and to me. To family unity and the continued happiness of this most blessed household.'

Silently, his father drank.

CHAPTER FOUR

In the year that followed Anne's marriage England had drawn nearer and nearer to Civil War. King Charles could not see how dangerous was his insistence on the use of the new Prayer Book by those who violently disapproved of it, particularly the obdurate Scots. They were determined to hold out against him, and his own Parliament backed them. In that August of 1640 a Scots army crossed the Tweed, defeated the King's army, and took two key towns. In June the next year more, and serious, trouble was brewing for him over the Border, while in London, Parliament seized on the King's weakness and mis-government to sweep away the Star Chamber and other courts, and generally set its face against the Crown. There was strife hanging in the air, like the first rumblings of a thunderstorm.

Tom Lacey's year at Arnescote had not been entirely happy. Though a deep well-spring of affection lay between him and his father, Sir Martin's intractability (not unlike the King's, Tom sometimes thought) warred constantly against his son's new-fangled notions of managing the estate. Little differences constantly arose: the feeding of cattle, the borrowing of horses, trivial matters, but fraying to the temper of both. The day came when Tom, quiet but resolved, told his father, 'I'm going to stop managing the estate with you, sir. You and I don't run well in double harness.'

Sir Martin sighed. 'True, Tom. My fault. I'm a selfish old dog who can't learn new tricks; we seem to squabble more than King and Parliament.'

'Well, it *is* your estate, father. You ran it well enough without me.'

'It will be yours one day to do as you like with.'

'Not for many, many years, I hope,' said Tom, and meant it. A wintry smile rewarded him. It would be a relief to be without Tom and his modern ways, but his father liked to feel that Tom felt love, as well as duty.

'What will you do,' he asked, 'when you go from here? There's a good house on the Welsh estate.'

'It rains in Wales, and the country's not kindly, like our Cotswolds.'

Sir Martin was visited by inspiration. 'Then go seek your fortune in the Americas, lad! We have a stake there, through old Austin Fletcher, part of Anne's endowment. Think of it! Ranting crop-eared Puritans and man-eating Indians — that should be challenge enough for a brave young man.'

Tom laughed. 'I think I can forgo it, father. And I'll not be exiled — I'm too fond of you and Arnescote. I'll to court, to offer the sword of an old soldier to the King.'

'He's in need of one, by the sound of things. It can't be long before the Parliament dogs are baying for his blood, damn them all . . .'

Cropper appeared, and handed his master a letter. 'This came for you, sir. A summons from the Exchequer.'

Sir Martin unfolded and read it, growling. 'Damn the Exchequer! Why should the High Sheriff be a tax-gatherer? The King will squeeze us till we crumble. Why, the pound's worth half its value ten years ago — the King has no gold left and Parliament won't give him any. It's the same old complaint, Cropper, this country's going to the dogs. Well, needs must — I'll to London, and have it out with them, for what good it'll do.'

When Anne rode into the castle courtyard the next morning the family coach was standing at the door, loaded up with Sir Martin's personal luggage. So she was in time. She made her way to her father's bedchamber, where, surrounded by would-be helpers, he was irately finishing his dressing for the journey and issuing instructions.

'That gardener, Cropper — if you find him fiddle about his work, throw him on the dung heap. And you, Margaret, lock the maids in their attic at night — that new boy in the yard's a stoat if ever I saw one, and the village has enough bastard children in it already to make a regiment.'

25

Lucinda giggled, and her father turned on her. 'And don't *you* snigger, child, your time will come. Mind, while I'm away you'll spend one hour a day at your mathematics with Mr Cropper, before any playing! I'll con the book when I get back. And you'll keep at your sewing and needlework with Margaret — a new cover for this chair wouldn't come amiss.'

Lucinda made a disgusted face, then changed it quickly into a serious one, as her sister entered the room.

'Lord God in heaven,' Sir Martin exclaimed, 'it's Mistress Fletcher.' There were embraces all round, and a visible lightening of Sir Martin's temper at the sight of his favourite daughter.

'But you've come untimely,' he told her. 'I've been sent for to go to London, to be bullied by the Exchequer.'

'Your clerk in Swinford told me so, and the news brought me here — I pray you'll take me with you, father. I have luggage for the journey loaded on a packhorse — my groom is putting it into the coach.'

Sir Martin exploded. 'Is he now? And have I said you may go? What do you want with London, woman? The plague is raging like a forest fire, and all the Roundhead 'prentice boys and the general rabble of Puritan puck-eared rascals are rioting and screeching their heads off. What have you to do with London?'

Anne met his gaze calmly. Since her marriage she had gained a new authority of manner; she was mistress of her own house now, not to be bullied by her father.

'John is in London at my father-in-law's house,' she said, 'and they have much company and need me.'

'I hope it's good company,' he growled.

'Some of the best. Master Pym and John Hampden. They have formed a good opinion of my husband's worth.'

'Have they so? I hear your John speaks well enough in the House of Commons, but some of the meat of his discourse somewhat smells of the rotten arguments of Master Pym and his gang of rebels against the King.'

Anne's face said nothing, nor her still hands.

'The King needs taking down a peg, that I'll grant: to rule without Parliament was plain folly, but those Puritan cur-dogs are snapping over-close about his heels. Killing his friend Lord Strafford was wrong, and done against the law of England.'

'It was necessary for liberty. Strafford was an impeached traitor.'

'Hm. Liberty. It's a word can cut both ways. It's not for liberty they defy the King, it's for money. All that crew have companies in the Indies and in America, and they want to force the King to use his fleet to save their gold from the Spanish.' He raised his voice. 'Their God is Mammon, not Liberty. You ask your father-in-law — you ask Sir Austin. They can push the King too hard, beyond breaking-point.'

Anne said nothing.

In the coach, jogging on their way, he relaxed against the squabs of the coach seating, hands on knees, and looked at his daughter, straight-backed and demure. There was a certain plainness in her dress that had not been there before, and a straight line to her once curved mouth. Both had come with marriage, but it was not Sir Martin's way to see what he did not wish to see.

'Let me look at you child,' he said. 'It's too long since I saw that sweet face of late. You've grown so like your dear mother.'

She took his hand and held it, smiling composedly.

'You're happy and content. Yes, I can see that. Not yet with child?'

'Not yet, father. Be patient — you'll have a grandson soon enough.'

'I miss you,' he said. 'I miss you almost as much as I missed your mother.' She had died so young, had fought so hard to live, with all her small strength. If she had lived, he thought, he would have been a milder man today, and a happier one. And yet, and yet ...

'You have Tom and Lucinda,' Anne was saying. 'Isn't that enough children round your table?'

'Nay. Tom's not yet found his course — he's like a ship without a wind. Gadded up to London yesterday, to Court, to sniff round the highborn whores that flock around the Queen — much good that will do him. And Lucinda's but a wilful child ...'

The wilful child, at that moment, was accepting meekly enough a music lesson from Hugh Brandon, who acted as

27

valet to Sir Martin and singing-boy to the household. He was a pretty boy, and he blushed easily. It amused Lucinda to arouse that blush, and to practise the art of flirtation on him, quite without serious intent. She played the lute perfectly well when she liked, but it was quite entertaining to pretend otherwise, so that Hugh's long delicate fingers would place her own correctly on the strings.

She played the prelude to the song she was learning without a mistake, one of the fashionable Italian ballads, and drew a compliment from him, at which she fluttered her lashes becomingly.

'You're a good master, Hugh. Now, while I play you shall sing the words.'

Hugh's voice, that had once been so high and flute-like, had broken into a light tenor which had a manly charm of its own. It suited the pretty Italian of the love-song. Lucinda thought of herself as the King's beautiful tragic grandmother, Mary of Scotland, making music with her courtier-secretary, David Rizzio; only Rizzio had been an ugly little dark man and Hugh was only eighteen, and comely. She struck the final chord and translated the verse from the music-sheet.

' "Oh, beautiful eyes, that I adore, do not make me so sad. I long for those bright eyes that I worship, as I serenade you, O my joy." Are *my* eyes beautiful, Hugh?' She let him have the full benefit of them. He turned scarlet, from white throat to white brow, and stammered that indeed they were.

'Now you blush. Oh, Hugh, I'm sorry — only ugly girls fish for compliments, but you play-act so well.' She riffled through the sheets of music. 'All these songs are about eyes, or lips like two budded roses, or skin soft as the down of turtle dove — poets seem to think of nothing else.'

'They are all about love, Mistress Lucinda.'

'Why don't they write about battles, or — or dogs; something real, something important?'

'Battles and dogs don't sound well to the lute.'

'No . . . and music is supposed to be the food of love. Though why love needs food, who can tell? Can *you* tell, Hugh?'

'No, I cannot tell,' the boy said, turning away his face as another blush rose in it.

'Why, are you in love, sweet Hugh? You are, you are, you are!' Lucinda bounced joyfully up and down. 'Who is it? You must tell, I command it, and if you lie you will shrivel up in hell-fire.'

Hugh, deeply embarrassed, squirmed and eyed the door. 'I cannot speak of it.'

'You must, Hugh! Secrets are evil, they rot inside like canker in a rose. I must test you by rote. I know, by the alphabet. I love my love with an A ... is it A, Hugh? Ah, I see it is. A. Who can A be? Ah, I have it. Anne, my sister Anne. Can you deny it?'

Hugh shook his head violently. 'Never speak of it, I beg you. Mistress Anne must never know of it. It — would not be proper. I beg you, mistress, not to tell her, even as a jest.'

'She shall not know of it,' said Lucinda magnanimously. 'Poor Hugh, to go forever unrequited. Still, you are beautiful, and there are girls aplenty. What does it feel like to be in love?' she enquired, her head on one side like a robin sizing up a plump worm.

Hugh picked up the lute and appeared to be examining the strings critically. 'A kind of tingling ... in the heart.'

'Oh. Kiss me, Hugh — just once, for me to try it.'

Hugh obliged, to get the matter over with, but very chastely. Lucinda pondered on her reactions. 'Hm. I think there was a little — just a little tingle.'

In case she decided to repeat the experiment, Hugh struck a chord on the lute and presented her with a new sheet of music. 'Now this farandole, if you please,' he said. He very much hoped that before long Mistress Lucinda would find out for herself what being in love was like, and how painful it could be.

In a stately room of Whitehall Palace Sir Anthony van Dyck was at work on his massive picture of the royal family. The great painter's hand moved slowly, meticulously. His bearded face was furrowed with intense concentration, and also with weariness and pain. Only forty-two years old, he knew that before long he would look into the eyes of Death, just as now he looked into the dark sparkling eyes of England's Queen, Henrietta Maria.

Mary, her adoring husband called her, but she would never appear other than the Frenchwoman she was, Henriette Marie, royal daughter of France. She sat for this portrait in a chair of state, her small son James in her arms, his elder brother Charles, Prince of Wales, beside the chair. He was eleven, tall for his age, dressed up in velvet and lace to match his mother's splendour, with a miniature sword at his hip. His face was plain, swarthy and good-humoured. He smiled readily enough for the painter; they all did. The Stuarts were a united, loving family, the Queen proud of her two young sons.

Puritans, who hated her for her Catholicism, derided her as ugly. In fact, she had the pointed face of a charming squirrel, fine eyes and lustrous dark ringlets, a formal row of curls dancing on her brow. She was a little creature, matching the small King, but seated she looked majestic enough, the rich silk of her dress flowing about her, the fashionable lace collar setting off her graceful shoulders and drawing the eye to the single string of huge pearls round her neck. On the table beside her was a small crown, also pearled. In the background of the picture Sir Anthony had sketched Windsor Castle, that other proud royal residence, though it was more than twenty miles away.

Tom Lacey, wearing his best clothes and appearing the complete courtier, stood with a few more young men as elegant as himself. Near the Queen two ladies-in-waiting, Lady Carlisle and Lady Sutton, hovered, ready to arrange the Queen's dress if it were disordered, to bribe the small dogs at her feet into staying still, and if necessary to remove young James and hand him over to one of his nurses. Van Dyck would be glad when he had finished painting James and could dispense with him altogether.

Because sitting for portraits was a boring business, the Queen had commanded the poet Edmund Waller to read to her while she sat. Tactfully he had chosen a poem in her own praise, which he declaimed eloquently.

> 'Well fare the hand, which to our humble sight
> Presents that beauty, which the dazzling light
> Of royal splendour hides from weaker eyes,
> And all access, save by this art, denies.'

The Queen clapped, echoed by all the company.

'Elegant,' she said. 'We thank you for your compliments, Master Waller.' She had a thick French accent and she preferred to speak her own language. The toy spaniel at her feet had made itself a bed on the trailing folds of her skirt, dragging the silk out of line, and was now sleeping in an unpaintable ball. '*Ah, comme je suis ennuyée de ce petit chien* — Sutton!' The handsome attendant lady darted forward and removed the dog, as James, who had been fidgeting, broke into a howl. Charles took this as a cue to relax, yawning and stretching. The sitting for this day was over.

As the Queen stepped down from her daïs to inspect the painting, Waller rushed forward to help her; van Dyck rose, with difficulty. She inspected, carefully, admiringly, the portrait of the absent King, which occupied the other half of the canvas, a slight figure in diamond-buttoned doublet and breeches frilled at the knees, the new falling ruff making his head appear detached from his body; a prophetic image which none in that company could have seen, in their worst nightmares, as ever coming true. Sad dark eyes, gentle mouth, trim pointed beard, he seemed more scholar than king.

'*Qu'il est beau*,' said the Queen, stroking a painted cheek lightly. '*Mais — moi, un peu triste*, Sir Anthony.'

'Not sad, Your Majesty,' the painter protested. 'Strong, and serious.'

Waller leapt in with another apt slice of poem.

'The gracious image seeming to give leave,
Propitious stands, vouchsafing to be seen;
And by our Muse saluted, mighty queen,
In whom th'extremes of power and beauty move —
The Queen of Britain, and the Queen of Love.'

Her Majesty smiled her sweet, rather toothy smile, and gave both poet and painter her hand to kiss. Then she moved away, towards her private apartments, followed by the courtiers and two priests who had been on the fringe of the company.

Lady Sutton, who had caught sight of Tom, hung back. The two of them were left alone, but for van Dyck, who was wearily collecting up his paints and brushes, helped by a page-boy.

'Well, well,' she said softly. 'Tom Lacey, by all that's wonderful.' They studied each other in silence, these two who had known each other so long, first meeting when Tom was a lusty but callow youth and she a lovely young girl married to a cloddish husband. She had taught him all any boy could wish to know about sex and the way of a woman with a man. From her, too, he had learned enough of woman's nature to understand his sister Anne, and was the better friend to her afterwards. Now he was no longer callow, but still lusty, and since the end of the war he had lived chaste but for the occasional village girl. And she was almost thirty but as beautiful as ever, more full-blown, perhaps, with the same beckoning look in her eye.

'Grown up somewhat, I think, my handsome soldier boy,' she said.

'That is in the way of things — we all grow older. Is his lordship at court?'

'No. He's with his hogs in Suffolk. My apartments are where they were — you'll be quite safe, my pretty cavalier.' With a nod she scurried off in the direction the others had taken.

Her apartments were comfortable, even luxurious. Many candles in silver sconces made her dressing-room a place of golden light. She sat before her dressing-table, languorous as a painted Venus, while her maid released her hair from its twisted ribbons and pearls, and brushed it out with a soft swishing sound. The beautiful face reflected in the silver mirror smiled lazily at Tom, as he reclined clad in a satin robe embroidered all over with small flowers, bees and butterflies. Her own robe was of ivory, of the same tint as the shoulders and bosom of which it gave generous glimpses.

They had been talking idly — yet not altogether idly, for such matters were becoming deadly serious — of the troubles between Parliament and King. Tom was used to his father's violent opinions, but now he heard the truth of how things stood in London, from one at the heart of them. It was not reassuring.

'So,' he said, 'all is not healthy with the body politic.'

'It is riddled with worms,' said the rosy reflected mouth.

'Not a game I would ever want to play.'

'Your father plays it — as High Sheriff.'

Tom laughed. 'A son need not inherit all his parent's vices — my father is a slave to duty. You yourself play politics fair enough, by the way.'

'I have to, my dear — to survive.' She dismissed the maid, and turned to face Tom. 'There are things it's not wise to say before servants. Pym and his Puritan gang have spies, even in our bedrooms.'

'So? Then they must hear things that turn their crop-ears red.'

But she was serious. 'Believe me, one is not safe from them anywhere.'

'Is he so bad a ruler as they say, this king of ours? Certainly he's not greatly loved; he has not the common touch.'

'Poor man. He has no great skill in choosing counsellors. Because he's slow and somewhat serious, a flashy wit pleases him, and he's more inclined to hear than hearken. For my part, Tom, I think him not the worst but the most unfortunate of kings.'

'Unfortunate? It was not fortune but folly made him marry a Catholic princess, and let her flaunt her Papist ways for all to see. He lets the Queen rule both head and heart — that's his main folly.'

'Not his head. In certain matters he's a secret obstinate man, impossible to move. He believes God has set him above other men to rule this kingdom. Anything he does is justified by God.'

'Then he needs no Parliament?'

She shrugged. 'He tried to rule without it, but he failed. He couldn't find the gold he needed to make an army, without Parliament. Now the Irish Papists are in bloody rebellion, and still the King has no army to stop them, while Master Pym has managed the Parliament so cunningly that he has shorn the King of all his rights and privileges.'

'Is it to be King Charles or King Pym, then?'

Shaking out her hair, she tied a ribbon round it. In that style, the years slipped away and she was once more the girl who had first charmed and then seduced him. He watched her with growing desire, tired of the conversation. But she said, dropping her voice a little, 'The King is a great dissembler, Tom. He enjoys a double plot.'

'A double plot?'

She was examining her face in the mirror, touching it with a hare's foot. 'Is that rouge enough to suit your taste?'

'You've no need of it. What did you mean just now?'

'Nothing,' she said hastily. 'Those words never passed my lips. I blab worse than the Queen, my mistress.'

Tom's rising passion made the subject seem unimportant. He went to her, turned her towards him, and took her in his arms. Smiling up at him, she let the ivory satin robe slip from her shoulders, lower and lower, until she was half-naked, like a mermaid, and as seductive. A sweet musky scent came up from her, alluring his senses. He thought it came from her skin, not from any of the porcelain jars on the dressing-table. He stooped his head to kiss her shoulder, then her throat, feeling her shudder with delight. She pulled him closer, her eyes glowing with a desire as keen as his own.

'I find you,' he said deliberately, 'a most beautiful and desirable creature — far more so than I ever remember.'

'Fie, fie. I believe you're become a greater dissembler even than the King, Master Lacey.' Her fingers were working on the buttons of the embroidered robe, until it was open to the waist, and her warm seeking lips were against the pulse that hammered at the base of his throat.

'Come,' she murmured, 'let's see what tricks of love the Flemish mares have taught you . . .'

CHAPTER FIVE

Tom spent much time in London that summer and autumn, deeply infatuated. While his mistress remained at Court, and her husband in Norfolk, they were free to indulge in all the amorous play they desired, though they were careful not to flaunt their connection. The King, a loyal and devoted husband, looked coldly on licence. Only when harvest-time came, and news that Sir Martin's new estate manager was sick of a malignant fever, did Tom reluctantly take himself back to Arnescote.

The months had seen more trouble between King and Parliament. News of it reached Arnescote by every traveller who called there. Charles had gone to Scotland on a placatory mission, which had gone disastrously wrong; rumours spread that he was buying enemies to his side with part of the Crown Jewels, which he had taken in his baggage. The great collar of rubies had certainly been pawned in Holland. Then rebellion had broken out in Ireland, which had dissolved into anarchy. The native Irish had risen against the Protestants of Ulster, with terrible slaughter which would never be forgotten, and which rebounded on Catholics in England.

Tom heard with alarm that the Queen's chapel had been closed, her priests dismissed, and her confessor sent to the Tower. He sighed with relief that his mistress was a Protestant, and so would not lose her post at Court. He was impatient to see her again, and to be in the thick of whatever was brewing in London, but first he must join in the Christmas festivities at Arnescote. There was an uneasy feeling about them, as though peace on earth and goodwill

35

toward men were in shorter supply than hogsheads of ale and fat geese.

After the turn of the year Tom could stand it no longer. Though his father frowned, and Lucinda begged, he rode off to London four days before the revels of Twelfth Night: and so was there when the storm broke.

On 3 January 1642 the King's new Attorney-General appeared at the bar of the House of Lords and presented articles of Parliament of high treason against five leading members of Parliament and one peer. They were Denzil Holles, Sir Arthur Haselrig, John Pym, John Hampden, and William Strode, of the Commons, and Lord Kimbolton of the Lords. The charge against them was that they had traitorously endeavoured to subvert the fundamental laws and government of the kingdom of England, to deprive the King of his royal power, and to place an arbitrary and tyrannical power over the lives, liberties and estates of His Majesty's liege people.

'It's more or less true,' Tom said to Mary Sutton. 'The Commons *have* overstepped the mark. Henry the Eighth would have had all their heads before this. Well, now we'll see who is the stronger. They're to present themselves for arrest at two of the clock today, in the House.'

'Excellent,' she said. 'May they leave it in chains, the villains.'

'I shall go, of course,' said Tom. 'How could I keep away from such a putting-down? Though I doubt it's the wisest thing His Majesty can do . . .'

When he saw her next, that evening, her dressing room was a flurry of silks, satins, and laces, being crammed into boxes and chests by her maid, while she packed with jewels a velvet-lined coffer embroidered in stump-work. He stopped at the door, taken aback. It had meant this too, all that business at the Commons.

'You're leaving?'

'I must. The King is going to Hampton Court, with the Queen and the children. Tom, what happened? Rumours fly round this place like bats.'

Tom sat down, helping himself from a flask of wine.

'Well. There were three or four hundred of us with him; he'd told us to stay still at the cost of our lives. Then he went

36

into the Chamber while Lord Roxborough held the door. We could hear through it, but not see. He said, "By your leave, Mr Speaker, I must borrow your chair a little." Then, when all had risen to him, he said something like, "Gentlemen, I am sorry for this occasion of coming to you. Yesterday I sent a sergeant-at-arms to apprehend some that at my command were accused of high treason ... I am come to tell you that I must have them, wheresoever I find them." '

'But were they not there?'

'No. Not a sign. So he demanded of the Speaker where they were, who answered that he had neither eyes nor tongue, but as the House directed. Then the King said, very quiet and bitter, "Since I see all the birds are flown, I do expect that as soon as they return, you will send them to me." Then he left the Chamber, and they shouted "Privilege! Privilege!" after him.'

She flung a heavy pendant into the coffer. 'Folly! Folly and betrayal. It was the Queen urged him to it. I was told she cried out "Go, you coward, and pull the rogues out by the ears, or never see me more!" '

'That was folly,' Tom said. 'Where was the betrayal?'

'That whore-bitch Lucy Carlisle, two-faced as a coin. She's Pym's cousin, did you know? I've warned the Queen of her many a time, but she wouldn't hear — poor stupid woman. Carlisle went to them and warned them. And the worst of it is that creature will get off scot-free. I warrant she's safe in hiding with Pym and the rest.'

Outside, in Whitehall, the shouting and chanting was growing louder, a mob with but one head, it seemed. The King has lost London, Tom thought. This is the end of something, and the beginning of something. He watched his mistress packing, flurried and angry and beautiful, and his heart was heavy for his own loss as well as the King's. 'And you?' he asked.

'I'm to go home, to Norfolk, and wait for a summons to meet the Queen at Dover. She is to go to Holland, on the pretext of taking little Princess Mary to meet her Dutch bridegroom — but in truth to pawn these.' She opened a large, iron-bound coffer, full to the brim with jewels, points of coloured fire that sparkled in the candlelight, the milky sheen of pearls, the glint of gold and silver settings. Tom stared.

37

'The Queen's?'

'Some hers, some mine. We've divided them between us to buy guns and an army for the King. He will not go with us; he travels north, to York — and he has sent for Prince Rupert.'

'But Rupert's in prison still — in Austria, surely?'

'Not now. Those in high places thought he would be more useful free. So he's to travel to England, to escort the Queen and her family to meet his, at The Hague, then to come back and join the King.'

'I see.' So King Charles was calling in reinforcements from his own family; his sister Elizabeth, widowed Queen of Bohemia, and her sons, most particularly Rupert, the dashing, handsome, twenty-three-year-old, a fearless soldier and a magnificent swordsman.

Tom looked round the room where he had spent so many nights and days of sensuous enjoyment. Now it seemed like a toy room in a baby-house disordered by a child; wraps, robes, scarves thrown about and bundled up for travelling, the dressing-table bare of paints and rouges and scents, the pretty, erotic classical pictures gone from the walls, the ivory cupid from Italy wrapped up in a cloak, only his curls showing. Tom would never come back to this room, or, possibly, the woman who was leaving it.

'Are you safe?' he asked her, 'quite safe?'

'Yes.' She came to him and they kissed, a long kiss.

'Goodbye, my valiant lover,' she said. 'May God have mercy on us both and this poor country.'

Six months passed; months of worsening strife and rumours ever more disturbing. But Lucinda, in the pride of her youth and the most beautiful flowering time of the English summer, was not thinking of wars and troubles as she rode out on her young chestnut mare. The Cotswolds were lovely in their ethereal green which is misted with blue shadows, a background by a master painter for sturdy houses of honey-coloured stone that seems to have drunk in sunshine for centuries.

She was on the outskirts of Chipping Campden, its square church tower topping the roofs of Campden House and the charming small look-outs Sir Baptist Hicks had built for his pleasure. Soon she would turn towards the town and ride up its handsome street to the shop down three steps where they sold striped ribbons and little phials of flower perfumes which were better than the distillations Margaret and the maids prepared (though it would never do to let Margaret know that shop-bought stuff was preferred to her own making).

She whistled up the two dogs, which had strayed off and were romping together, big rough-haired gazehounds rejoicing in their freedom and the exhilarating airs of the morning. Obediently they stopped playing, and ran back towards her, and another dog ran with them.

If indeed it were a dog, for she had never seen one like it. It was white, covered in small tight curls, and ran on slender fleet legs. Against its white fleece its eyes were singularly dark — and, strangest of all, it wore a blue collar studded with silver. As it ran, its long ears streamed like banners and its black nose twitched with eagerness. A dashing dog, a Cavalier of a dog.

From the other direction a rider was cantering towards her. 'Boy! Boy!' he called, and the white dog turned and flew towards him, barking joyfully. Lucinda surveyed the rider with approval. Even in the saddle she could see that he was exceptionally tall, broad of shoulder and slim of waist, the dark flowing hair beneath the plumed hat proclaiming him Royalist, the rest of his clothing rich and splendid, a great scarlet cloak over black and silver. As for his face, she had never seen one so handsome; dark-skinned, lean, high of cheekbone and thick of eyebrow, with 'a sort of frowning look to it', as she told her maid later, that quite turned one's heart over.

Reining in his mount, he swept off his hat in a courtly bow. 'I hope my dog has not troubled you, madam.' She noticed that his accent was not English, but of a foreignness quite charming to the ear.

'No, indeed not,' she said with her prettiest smile. 'But what kind of dog is he? I never saw one like him.'

'He is a poodle. He came from Vienna — I don't think there are any in England.'

'Is he fast? As fast as my gazehounds?'

39

'Yes. He would show you if he caught sight of a hare. Are there hares hereabouts?'

'Not many. But I must see Boy run. Look, that oak tree on the hill — I'll race you to it and the dogs can chase.'

The dark eyebrows rose slightly. He had lived in England before, but the great freedom of English ladies' manners had slipped his memory. He decided to let himself be amused by it, and nodded affably. At her sign, he jerked the reins and the two horses were off, galloping over the green turf, Lucinda's ringlets flying in the breeze like Boy's ears, her companion's cloak blowing like a flame behind him. To his surprise, she reached the oak-tree first. From the crest of the small hill it stood on she looked across the shining valley to a distant view of Arnescote, a pale golden vision, and wondered if she could find an excuse for taking her dashing companion there.

'Well done, madam,' he said graciously.

She bent towards the dogs, panting and fawning at the horses' feet. 'And well done, Boy. Well done and well run. My name is Lucinda Lacey, sir.'

He paused for a fraction of a moment before saying 'And mine is Rupert.' Though he had expected a start, a blush, perhaps a dismounting and a curtsey, she continued to look at him as though he were a quite ordinary person. 'Have you come far?' she asked.

'Quite a long way — from Holland.'

'Oh. What were you doing there?'

'Nothing very much,' he said, straight-faced. 'Staying with my mother. But before that,' seeing she expected excitement, 'I was in prison.'

'How horrible!'

'Oh, it was not too horrible. I had him for company,' he nodded towards Boy; 'and there were tennis-parties, and hunting, and quite a few visitors. Oh, and the Governor's daughter was extremely pretty.'

Lucinda's eyes were like saucers. 'What a strange prison. Our prison at Swinford is not of that sort at all. I am sure my father, who is a magistrate and the High Sheriff, would not allow dogs — or hunting or tennis — or . . .'

'No. But I was a war prisoner; I was captured in a battle.'

'I see. Then that of course is quite different. My brother, Tom, was in the foreign wars.'

'Yes, I know him,' said the astonishing Rupert. 'It is him I have come to see, at Arnescote Castle. I was on my way there.'

Lucinda's face was a study in realization, shock, and embarrassment. 'Rupert,' she said under her breath, 'Prince Rupert.' And aloud, 'Oh, your Royal Highness!'

'That is right,' he said graciously. 'I am Prince Rupert.'

Lucinda tried simultaneously to straighten her hair, pull at her skirt which had wound itself round her ankles, and compose her face into a dignified expression, but only succeeded in appearing even more gauche and young than she was. She stammered an apology, he must forgive her for her forwardness, she had not known . . .

'There is nothing to forgive,' said Rupert, looking kindly down at her from his immense height. He was only twenty-three, but his sense of royalty, as the King of England's nephew, and his easy, happy bringing up in a large, beautiful family, gave him enough confidence never to need to put anyone's pride down. 'It was a fine meeting,' he said. 'You have a kind of — what in German would be called *glanz* — a sparkle, about you, Mistress Lacey, like your brother's. Will you show me the way to Arnescote Castle?'

'That's it,' she said, pointing. 'It will be a pleasant . . . it will not take us . . . oh look, Boy has run away.' She heard herself babbling, but before long, she knew, she would be quite composed in the presence of the first Prince of the Blood she had met. And as they rode, she let herself wonder whether it was her fate, her future, that had come to her that morning, with a white dog for its herald.

When they reached Arnescote she tactfully vanished. Sir Austin Fletcher was with her father, she knew, busy dealing with a petition from the local people to the King and Parliament; they would not want women's chatter.

Both men had signed it, over some reasonable talk. Sir Austin, appending his signature, summed up his feelings.

'Everyone's agreed that we can't have the King at York and Pym in London sitting growling at each other. They must meet and talk, as you and I have talked, Sir Martin. Oh, we don't see eye to eye, not by any means, but we sit together on the Bench and we deliver judgement impartially together. You are for King and Parliament, and I am for

Parliament and King. We run this countryside in harmony — we could run the whole country so.'

'I wish we did,' returned Sir Martin with a grim smile. 'No, my dear old friend, at the heart of this sad confusion in the kingdom we have two men, both hard and arrogant, both believing God is with them, both jealous and greedy for power, both unyielding. That's the rub of this particular game, and I doubt a thousand petitions will change their courses one notch.'

As Sir Austin opened his mouth to answer, Tom entered, to be greeted with a frown and a dismissive wave by his father. But he said, unwavering, 'An important visitor.'

'You receive him, Tom.'

'A royal visitor.'

At this both men sat up straight, staring. Sir Austin said 'Not the King?'

'Prince Rupert of the Rhine. He is here and awaits.'

Rupert received them as though the Great Hall of Arnescote belonged to him. Sir Martin was delighted, Sir Austin overcome, for all his Parliamentary sympathies, by this proud young Royalty. To Sir Martin's warm invitation to stay at Arnescote, 'a place not worthy, but poor,' Rupert replied that his usual bedroom in war was a tent or barn, to which Arnescote would seem a semi-paradise. From there he would go on, he said, to join the King at Nottingham.

Sir Martin was startled. 'Not York.'

'No. The King is to raise his standard in Nottingham.'

His three listeners exchanged glances. Sir Austin voiced what all were thinking. 'Then His Majesty is determined on a war?'

'Sadly, my uncle has been provoked beyond any endurance. These fractious Puritanical men in London have rebelled against the Crown, and I am come to help my uncle raise an army to put them down.'

'God save the King,' said Tom. Both echoed him. Then Sir Martin came back to the present moment, and the duties of a host, inviting the Prince to take some refreshment. But the visitor, uncoiling himself to his full height, requested to be shown to his room, turning at the door to tell Sir Martin, 'I will steal your son, sir, if I may. He knows more of soldiering than most men of my acquaintance, and we shall have a hard time to knock these peaceful English gentlemen into some fierce and able shape.'

When he had gone, escorted by Tom, the two left behind said little, both shaken by the sudden reality of civil war. Sir Martin poured a glass of wine for each of them, but no toast was drunk. Seeing Sir Austin lost in thought, he unobtrusively unlocked a drawer, took from it a large key, and left the room with it. In the passage he encountered Cropper.

Very quietly he told the steward, 'Take a message by your word of mouth to Master Pike at Boyton. Request him on my account that he goes into Swinford as quietly and privately as may be, and brings half the powder, match and bullet shored in the armoury there to this house, with all the expedition he can manage.'

The steward took the key. He understood perfectly. Prince Rupert's loud confident tones had carried beyond the walls of the Great Hall.

———————

Next morning in the kitchens, the servants were gathered in an interested knot, watching the white dog as he happily devoured pie from a large wooden dish. Mistress Dumfry, the cook, regarded him with disfavour.

'Well,' she said, 'I never thought to see the day when a dog would feed off my best venison pie.'

'Ah,' said Will Saltmarsh, 'but that's no ordinary dog, Mistress D., that's a royal dog. They say the Grand Turk himself wanted such a dog. Why, I've seen him take a Polack's arm for his dinner, before now.'

'I'll warrant it tasted not half as good as my pie.'

'I've heard say that dog is the Prince's familiar, and keeps him proof from bullets in the battle,' said Will.

'Sleeps on the Prince's bed, I know that,' put in Hannah, the prettiest of the maids. 'And you've no need to look at me like that, Will Saltmarsh, I seen the dirty paw-marks on our best sheets.' With a toss of her head she left the kitchen, followed by Will, with a tray of food intended for the Prince's servant-bodyguard, Ludwig, who was engaged in cleaning his master's sword. He received the food with gratitude, squeezed Hannah's arm, and bestowed a heavy German wink on her. She pulled away, but not too quickly — Ludwig was a large imposing man with awesome moustachios.

'I won't have none of that now, Master Ludwig,' she said, and Ludwig grinned as though she had accepted his advances eagerly. Will explained. 'He don't speak English, but he does speak the language of love — that I do know, Hannah, frequently, not to say often, and 'specially with comely serving wenches.' The buxom Rachel, behind Will, edged forward with a provocative wriggle of her ample hips, and the German's eyes rolled towards her. Will saw that he was going to have to use all his fascination to get anywhere with Hannah, so long as Ludwig was about Arnescote.

A shout from Mistress Dumfry summoned Rachel back to the kitchen to scour a filthy pot that was needed for serving the Prince's dinner. Will followed her idly. Drawn by an unusual sound outside, he climbed on a bench to look out of the high window. What he saw drew a long surprised whistle from him.

'Well, well. We'll all be off to the war soon,' he said. Mistress Dumfry looked up.

'War? What's all this talk of war?'

At Will's beckoning, she hoisted herself up beside him. Out in the courtyard two men were unloading barrels from a cart, and rolling them into a shed, watched by Sir Martin and Cropper, who was making an entry in a ledger.

'What's in them?' the cook asked.

'Powder, match and bullet. That's not just to practise popping our pistols — there's enough powder in those barrels to blow up this house twice over.'

Rachel squeaked and Hannah shivered. But Mistress Dumfry, scrambling down from the bench, snorted. 'Who's going to blow up this house, I'd like to know? The only enemies this kingdom's got are the Frenchies and the Spanish, and I ain't heard of either of *them* coming across the sea to make a war.'

A bundle that had been crouching on a stool by the fire suddenly raised a raddled face. Old Minty had been about the kitchens of Arnescote as long as anybody could remember, though what her precise function was nobody could have said. She had acted at times as midwife, inflicted her ideas of primitive medicine on sufferers (who usually became worse), and fancied herself as a prophetess, much given to solemn pronouncements. She made one now.

'There's a pestilence in the country's blood. It's over-hot and violent — a great carbuncle with many heads has come up and will burst, and rain pus and blood on all the land.'

'Oh, have done, you old hag!' said the cook. 'Ought to have your tongue cut out, that you ought.'

Undeterred, Minty went on. 'Pus and blood'll drown all the fairies and Robin Goodfellow, and there shall be no more dancing round the maypole.'

'Ha' done, will you?' Mistress Dumfry raised a wooden spoon threateningly. But she was more shaken than she would admit, and the girls were openly frightened. Rachel asked timidly 'What's war like, Master Saltmarsh?'

'Well, speaking for myself, if I'm cunning enough to keep off the pikes and guns, which I am, it means a full belly and good loot.'

'But I mean what will it be like for us here?' Rachel persisted.

Will did not answer at once. Into his mind had flashed pictures of the effects of war he had seen in his campaigning, and they were all terrible. Burned homesteads, churches pillaged, cattle wantonly slain, infants in arms murdered for sport, maids, wives, even old women brutally raped, not by one man but many; innocent householders who tried to defend their property cut in pieces and fed to dogs. He could not bring himself to speak of such things to women. He said only 'For you, Rachel, it could mean a full belly of a different sort.'

The cook turned on him, outraged. 'We'll have none of that sort of talk in my kitchen! Out, out, I say, and take that dog with you, Prince or no Prince.'

Minty was still muttering. 'When the flame of war breaks out in the tops of the chimneys, the smoke will cover the whole land . . .'

Sir Martin lost no time in preparing his family and staff for

45

the realities of war. In the stableyard a rough target was constructed, of boards nailed together with the outline of a man chalked on them, life-size. All the male servants in turn were instructed in the art of wheel-lock pistol-shooting by Will, watched by their master and Lucinda, while Prince Rupert and Tom talked, out of earshot.

'It's decided,' said Rupert, 'that I am to be the General of the Horse, in absolute command, only answering to the King himself, with no old fuddy-duddies of generals to pish and haw and stop the action.'

Tom, for all his admiration of the Prince, feared that he had no conception of the true situation he was faced with, coming as he did from countries that had been battlefields for centuries. He tried a warning, without much hope that it would have any effect.

'The English are not used to war, sir. They will be very green, like unbroken colts.'

'All the better — they will have formed no bad habits. I've seen the English hunt, and they have good brave hearts and strong fast horses — all we need. I tell you, Tom, give me four thousand horses, and riders armed with pistols and sword, and I will give England back to the King within the week — and every spike in London town will boast a rebel's head.' He strode into the circle of Will's pupils and took over the instruction of Lucinda, who was about to fire the pistol. The lean brown royal hand guided hers into the right position.

'Firm but not too tight, and don't hang on the aim — ready — fire!'

The bullet flew straight to the heart of the chalked effigy, and a round of spontaneous applause came from the spectators.

'Well done, Mistress Lucinda,' said Rupert. 'You'd make a fine soldier.'

She looke up at him adoringly. 'I wish I could fight for you, sir. I wish I were a man.'

'He gave her one of his rare smiles. 'Before long, I think there will be many men right glad that you are a maid.'

Lucinda blushed. Not only the effigy had lost its heart.

CHAPTER SIX

Ten men sat round the refectory table in the Great Hall of Arnescote, Sir Martin at the head, Tom on his right. The others were neighbouring gentry, squires, landowners, men who had seldom if ever met before in one room. One, Charles Pike, was a friend of long standing, another, rich old Robert Capel, Sir Martin disliked personally, as he did sour Master Ayres. In the interests of their common cause it was necessary to sink past differences. Together, at the foot of the table, sat Sir Austin Fletcher and his son John.

Sir Martin looked round the faces, watchful, non-committal, apprehensive, according to their natures.

'Gentlemen — old friends and neighbours. Our poor country is rocked on a sea of dangers and distractions. I have called you here because I have received the King's Commission of Array, in which His Majesty, being well assured of the cheerful compliance and loyalty of the greater number of gentlemen hereabouts, does call upon each one to take a commission in his army, and form troops and companies from his loyal subjects to come to his aid.'

'God save the King,' said Pike, and others, although not all, echoed him. Ayres, who had come prepared to dispute, asked keenly 'For what does the King seek our aid?'

'He asks aid to put down those rebellious parts of his Parliament that seek to overturn the state.'

Ayres tittered. 'I think this King could no more manage an army than he can manage his wife. Or his own councillors, who are feeble, fractious and corrupt. The only army he's like to get, for all his fine Commission of Array, is an army of Papists and debauched nobility and gentry, broken-down

47

servants and tapsters and the like, the lewder rout of people.'

There were murmurs of disagreement round the table. Tom half rose, but his father motioned him down, saying civilly 'I am sorry for your opinion, Master Ayres; it shall be noted.'

John Fletcher and his father exchanged glances. Then John said 'Father-in-law, gentlemen. I am lately come from London with orders from Parliament to muster militia and trained bands in these parts, to join my Lord Essex to fight for King and Parliament.'

Nobody spoke, but the silence was eloquent; a serpent was in their midst. Capel looked frightened. In his fine house he had furniture, tapestries, gold and silver, paintings, that might easily be lost to him if the countryside were filled with brawling scavengers.

Tom laughed. 'Trained bands! You go beat your drum outside the Town Hall in Swinford, John. Though you scatter gold on the street you'll get no more than a few loutish butcher boys and roguish Roundhead apprentices running to your call.'

'Peace, Tom,' his father said. 'John Fletcher has his orders; let him obey them, if that is what his conscience dictates. I am to tell you further, gentlemen: the King requests the loan of the powder, match and bullets stored in our local armouries.'

'Our local armouries?' Ayres almost shouted. 'May I ask on whose authority half the powder, shot and match belonging to this part of the county was removed from Swinford to this castle?'

'On mine, Master Ayres, as the King's High Sheriff for the County.'

'It is stolen, then, without consulting us,' Ayres said triumphantly.

'No. It is here for the better safety, and that it may be well guarded.'

Capel put in querulously 'The powder is paid for by us, with our money — it is ours, for our defence. I hope, Sir Martin, you will not disarm the county at such a time of danger?'

Patiently (he had come to the table determined to keep his temper) Sir Martin answered 'I say, we loan that part to the

48

King that is held here at Arnescote, and the half we have in Swinford we keep for our own defence.'

'I will part with all my blood,' cried Ayres, 'before I let the King have one corn of it!'

Tom shot to his feet, hand on sword-hilt. 'And I will part you from some of your blood now, Master Ayres, if there is any left in your disloyal and shrivelled-up heart.'

Ayres too was on his feet. 'This is the house of a known malignant,' he shouted, 'who harbours a Papist Prince under his roof. I say we should tumble the lot out of the windows!'

'Don't be a fool,' said his neighbour Barlow, 'sit down, man.'

Before a brawl could develop another voice spoke, clear and loud and foreign. 'You may throw me out of the window if you can, but I won't be dubbed a Papist by you nor any man alive.' Prince Rupert had heard the whole discussion hidden in the shadows of the gallery. He leaned now on its balustrade. 'My father, the King of Bohemia, lost his whole kingdom in the Protestant cause in Europe, and I have been near to losing my life for it.'

Ayres, crimson-faced now, was almost grovelling. 'Your Highness — your Royal Highness — I do most humbly beg your forgiveness.'

'You have it — and you should beg Sir Martin for his, for your unseemly behaviour.'

But Sir Martin had raised his hands, and his voice, to quell the angry murmurs round the table. 'Gentlemen, gentlemen, put away your swords — this is not child's play. You are guests in my house and we have serious business.'

When they were quiet, he continued, very seriously. 'It seems we are divided; so be it. The great God who is the searcher of my heart knows with what sad sense I go into this service. We are all upon this stage, and must act out the parts that are assigned to us in this tragedy. Let us do it in the way of honour, and without personal animosities. And let us pray to the God of peace that He will give us a short end to this war without an enemy.'

Nobody spoke. As Sir Martin rose, they came to him, one by one, to shake him by the hand. Last of all were the Fletchers, Sir Austin visibly moved as he said, 'Goodbye old friend.' Both men knew that it might well be goodbye indeed.

To John, Sir Martin said, 'Look after Anne.'

Tom had stood aloof from the farewells. He advanced to shake hands with the Fletchers; their leave-taking was wordless.

Lucinda was hovering on the staircase as Rupert left the gallery. She had grown skilful at finding out where he would be, and waylaying him, a manoeuvre which he understood perfectly. He had grown familiar with it when he lived at Whitehall, much pursued by the pretty ladies of his aunt's court. To Lucinda he was kind and courteous, loyal and charming child that she was, but he was no squire of dames, and would have agreed with that Cavalier poet who wrote that the mistress he chased was the first foe in the field. He was a natural though quite unintentional heartbreaker.

Lucinda gazed up at him appealingly, almost touching his sleeve, where the brocaded cuff fell back to show a deep ruffle of lace.

'Did you hear what they said, sir? Is there any hope of peace — among our neighbours, I mean, those who disagree with my father?'

'None, I fear. One made me a grovelling apology for some harsh words, but it was all humbug.'

'John Fletcher — did he not seem at all inclined to bend?'

'Far from it. An obstinate rebel if ever I saw one.'

'Alas. Poor Anne. No, stupid Anne for clinging to such a stick as him and going against our father! How can two sisters be so different in sympathy? I would shed blood for the King — and you, sir.'

Rupert felt it would be inappropriate either to chuck her under the chin or slap her on the back in hearty dismissal. Instead he did as he had always done when one of his sisters had been over-demanding; he kissed her hand, very gracefully but quite coolly.

And Lucinda understood, or feared she did.

When he rode away from Arnescote, Tom at his side, gallant in half-armour, a figure of chivalry, he wore a red rose she had given him beneath his collar. As the two horsemen grew smaller and smaller in the distance her misted eyes brimmed over with tears. Her father saw them fall; for the first time since her rebellion over her betrothal to Lord Edward Ferrars he wished he had exercised his parental authority firmly, compelled her to show herself that night, insisted that the wedding take place. She would most likely have come round in no time to cherishing that personable young man, eager as she was to give her heart to somebody. Instead, her father had let her run away, then beaten her, like a disobedient puppy.

He sighed and returned to his castle, now a place preparing for siege.

Russet leaves were falling from trees mellow with September as Anne's carriage rolled along the drive towards the Castle. She looked out of the window (and how pleasant that coaches now had glass windows, unlike the draughty uncushioned boxes of her girlhood).

'Look,' she said to her maid Emma, a plain respectable young woman, 'here it is, my home. Arnescote.'

'What a fine place, ma'am. A proper castle, isn't it?' Emma was a Welsh girl, unused to living in anything grander than a cottage. To her, Arnescote was indeed magnificent, with its gatehouse and twin towers, as grand almost as the palaces of the Strand, which she had seen in London; and in such great grounds. To Anne it was home, more so than her own comfortable but modest house, and she looked on it with great affection.

Until, as the coach entered the courtyard, she saw that all was changed from what she had known. It was crowded with horses and men — horses of all sorts, from cobs to hunters, being exercised by men she recognized as workers on her father's estate. Some were neighbouring farmers and some the Castle's servants, such as Jackman, the gamekeeper, and William Broad, the old head groom. Jackman was calling the roll for twenty or so men raggedly lined up. John Moresby, the huntsman, was acting as trumpeter and finding the instrument more difficult to master than the familiar horn. But for the clumsiness of the men, and their motley clothing, the scene could have been a barrack-yard. Anne's face darkened. She scrambled out of the coach, Emma behind her, and made her way to the entrance, not looking aside or greeting anyone.

The hall was empty and quiet after the bustle of the court-yard. On the landing above the staircase they met Hannah, laden with a basket of logs. Anne, much out of temper, addressed her without a greeting.

'Where is your master, Hannah, and Master Cropper? Is nobody about today?'

Hannah dipped a curtsey. 'Save you, Mistress Anne. You'll find them in the steward's room, making ready for the war.'

'The war, the war! There'll be precious little talk of peace in *this* house, that I know. Well, find Margaret Goodwife and send her to my bedchamber. Make haste, girl!'

The bedchamber that had once been hers had been closed up since her departure. The bed where she had spent her last night of maidenhood, the chairs and dressing-table, were all shrouded in sheets, the heavy curtains drawn. It was like a room where someone had died. Impatiently she pulled the curtains.

'This place is like a tomb. Open that press, Emma, and take out everything that's in it, hats, dresses, coats, body-linen, everything. Then lay it out on the bed, fold and pack all.'

'What in, if you please, ma'am?' Emma was timid of her stately surroundings and her mistress's sharpness.

'My trunk, girl, what else? And should you ask where it is, I hear Jeffreys now, lumbering up the stairs with it. Come in,' she said, in response to the coachman's knock. He entered, weighed down by a small travelling trunk, which he put beside the bed, puffing as he did so, Anne noticed.

'Was there no manservant about to assist you with the box?'

'The men are all about the courtyard, ma'am, recruited for the war.'

'They are indeed. You'd best go down and guard our carriage, lest my father press it and you into service with the King's army,' Anne said grimly. 'We'll be away from here before nightfall, come what may.'

When he had gone she flung herself into folding and pack-ing, determined not to be distracted by the military sounds outside. To deaden them, she shut the window. Another knock at the door interrupted her, and the voice of Margaret Goodwife.

'Come in!' she cried. 'Margaret, dear old friend. Let me embrace you.'

Margaret let herself be embraced, standing stiffly, making no return gesture and looking straight ahead. Then she said, coldly, 'My attendance was required, so I came. What is your wish?'

Anne sensed the coldness, and in her prickly state resented it. Icily she said 'My father-in-law has lately gone to visit his properties in the Americas, leaving us more room in Swinford. So I'm come to remove what is left of my belongings out of this house. My maid, Emma, is here to assist me.'

'Then what should *my* task be, Mistress Fletcher?'

'Can you not call me by my name? It is Anne, if you remember, and has been so ever since you washed and clothed me as a child.'

'Aye, so it has,' answered Margaret unsmilingly. Anne dropped her haughty pose.

'I have no special task for you, Margaret — I only sent for you to greet you, to enquire after your health and pass the time of day, and to learn what news there may be of my family and my home. From your expression one would guess that every member of the Lacey family is either dead or dying, and the servants, to a man, down with the plague — were it not for all the clatter of war out there below the window. What of my father? Is he well?'

'He is well enough, Mistress Anne, and attending to important business with the steward.' She glanced at the clothes on the bed. 'Those collars will need attention. I'll press them for you if you wish.'

'I do so wish,' Anne snapped back. 'See to it, if you please.'

Margaret laid the loose collars aside, and began to fold a dress. A silence fell between them. Emma, working at her packing, made herself as inconspicuous as possible. Then Margaret said, 'You'll be in need of looser bodices and skirts before the year is out, I'm thinking.'

'How so?' Anne's tone was cold.

'When the good Lord sees fit to bless your union with Master Fletcher — if he hasn't done so already.'

Once there would have been confidences, and kisses. Now Anne merely said, rebukingly, 'Such secrets will I and my husband keep, until the time is ripe. In the meantime, no stranger should indulge in idle tittle-tattle.'

Margaret straightened herself, meeting Anne's eye. 'Your tongue is sharp and hurtful, Mistress Anne — to dub your old devoted nurse and friend a stranger!'

'Did you not yourself receive me as a stranger just now, when I greeted you?'

Margaret answered like her old self. 'If only you could know, my dear child, how much it grieves us all to see you pledged for life to one who stands against all that your father and your ancestors have held so dear! It brings me close to tears, even to think of. What a dreadful time we live in . . . oh, my child.' She was weeping, the tears out at last. Anne put an arm round her, the woman who had been all but mother to her.

'Dear Margaret, don't weep. Can you not see how I am torn, as our family and all of England is torn? But we must follow our true beliefs, whatever shall be the cost. Dry your eyes, now. God in His wisdom will decide, not kings or parliaments, how our country shall be ruled.'

Margaret, comforted to be in favour again, composed herself. She would dearly like to have said that in her opinion Anne was following her husband's true beliefs, not her own; but it was no use stirring up more trouble. Before she could be tempted to say more Lucinda was in the room. She wore a mutinous expression Margaret knew well; in her hand was a staff bearing a silk standard, embroidered with the Lacey arms.

Coolly she asked 'Is my long-lost sister receiving visitors?'

Anne looked up, glad to see her. 'Come in, Lucinda, but forgive us if we continue our packing — I must return to Swinford before nightfall.'

Lucinda glanced about the room, making no move to approach Anne, so that Margaret said sharply 'Where are your manners? Embrace your sister, child.'

Lucinda dropped a dutiful kiss on Anne's cheek, then displayed the standard, waving it proudly. 'Look at our flag! Margaret and I made it. It's called a cornet, the cornet of Lacey's Troop. It will be carried into battle by Peter Crane, and *he* is also called the Cornet — isn't that strange? And Charles Pike is to be the Lieutenant and all the men from the estate are . . .'

Anne interrupted sharply. 'I don't wish to know the details, Lucinda. And I advise you, in your childish innocence and foolish pleasure in the sight of fighting men, that there is no glory in war.'

Lucinda laughed. 'No glory? Sister dear, I would give my life to ride out to battle with those men, and follow our family's standard, and fight beside Prince Rupert against those cruel Parliamentarians.'

'It's for men to slay each other, if slaying there must be, not puny girls. Better for you to learn how to comfort men with severed limbs and stumps that bleed and fester.'

Lucinda spun round, fingers in ears. 'I won't listen to you.'

Margaret shook her head at Anne. 'Don't distress the child. Such talk is not for young ears.'

'Not too young to hear the truth.'

Lucinda took her fingers out of her ears, and sailed to the door; she had a parting shot to fire. 'It may please you to learn that Bess and Dido are requisitioned for the troop.'

Anne gasped. 'My horses! No. I'll not permit it.'

'They're already mustered. Look out of the window — Dick Skinner has Bess, and Laking the falconer has Dido.' Lucinda flounced out, clutching her standard. She had been sorry about the two mares, and said goodbye to them before they were taken out of the stable, but it had been very satisfying telling Anne.

The news she had just heard did not make Anne's greeting of her father particularly cordial.

'I came to take my last leave of you,' she said, releasing herself from his arms. 'As a Fletcher, and owing obedience and loyalty to my husband, according to my marriage vows, it seems I am now your enemy rather than your child.'

Sir Martin held her at arm's length, surveying the face he loved, now grown so hard and set. So this was what had come of the match he had striven so hard to make, bargaining pound for pound with Sir Austin; this was the result of letting the girl pick and choose her suitors, passing over those he had selected for her with such care, to settle on an upstart of a London lawyer, a Puritan at heart all this time. Well, it was done.

'How cruel and unnatural that sounds,' he said. 'The thought has cost me many sleepless nights, be sure of that,

55

Anne. How many more devoted families throughout this land must find themselves from now on divided by the sword? And all because a group of cunning and ambitious men of Puritan persuasion have roused the people and defied the King.'

Anne flared up. 'Not so, father!'

'Hear me out. These devils have invoked the natural passions of the mob, and challenged the authority of God Himself.'

'Speak no more of this, Father, I beg you! In God's name, let us not embroil ourselves in politics.' Her voice softened. 'I am your daughter come to say farewell to you and to my home. I grieve enough to find this cruel, foolish war is come between us. Let us at least part in friendship and love for one another.'

They embraced, each happier for what had been said. Then Anne broke the bond. 'There is the matter of my two horses...'

'I gave the order for their requisition. We need strong horses, Anne.'

Angry protest sprang to her lips. Suddenly she checked it, and made a gesture she had not expected to make, earlier that day, in her resentment of what was happening at Arnescote. The horses mattered, but her relationship with her father mattered more.

'No,' she said. 'I'll not complain. As you once gave them to me, so let me give them back to you in gratitude for all your love and care for me over the years. I'll not be mean and petty over such a trifle, at a time like this.'

And so their parting was fond, as in past days, before the sword came.

———————————

The troop had grown from a ragged, chaotic confusion of men and horses into something far from perfect, but spirited enough to give Sir Martin some cheer. Towards the end of October news came that the King, encouraged by the Parliamentary leader's dallying in Worcester, felt encouraged enough to march south to Edgecote, only a few miles from Arnescote. Lord Essex's troops gave chase, and encamped themselves in the valley where lay the little town of Kineton. Rupert was urging his uncle to action — there must be a battle soon, any day now.

On a still moonlit night Lacey's Troop prepared for leaving. Lucinda, against all orders, crept out at midnight with a pot of broth Mistress Dumfry had grumblingly prepared for her. It would bring some warmth and comfort to some of the men, and she could not resist her last chance to be near to the troop, to savour the exciting atmosphere of preparation and let herself imagine that she was going with them. Rupert was at Kineton: if only she could imitate those heroines of ballad and story who borrowed a man's clothing and fought by the side of their loved ones, unrecognized until the battle was over. There she would lie, wounded, beautiful, pale, and Rupert would order someone to unloose her corselet, and so discover her womanhood and her identity. Perhaps she would die, romantically, or, better, he would have her tended until she recovered, single her out for bravery, perhaps make her his princess . . .

'Halt! who goes there?' The voice of Peter Crane the Cornet startled her almost into dropping the pot. When she answered softly, he recognized her.

'Forgive me, Mistress Lucinda. But my orders are to challenge any intruder to the horse lines after nightfall.'

'And if they refuse to stop?'

'To draw my sword, challenge, and if need be, fire my pistol. Our men and horses are on active duty now, as in the field, and must be well guarded day and night.'

'Spoken like a good officer. I have some broth here to warm the guard.' Crane thanked her, and gave the pot to Trumpeter Moresby to carry to the sentinels. She strolled towards the horses, Crane at her side. Some of the mounts slept on their feet, others whinnied gently and shook their bridles. Lucinda stroked soft noses, murmured names: Bess, the gentle Bess, and black Dido. 'I think I shall not sleep tonight,' she told the Cornet. 'The moon is so bright, and the thought of tomorrow — oh, how I envy you tomorrow.'

Since young Crane privately thought his own situation anything but enviable, he was a little puzzled by this enthusiasm.

'Are you not proud,' she went on, 'that when the dawn comes and first light breaks you are to carry my father's colour at his side, and ride out from here to fight for our King?'

'In truth, Mistress Lacey, I know but little of the reasons for this war. My fear tomorrow will not be so much of facing cannon shot and sword cuts, but the dread of killing fellow countrymen. Would it were the French we must fight against, or some other foreign force. But to charge and kill Englishmen . . .'

Lucinda had heard her father and others say this, and it was certainly an unpleasant thought. But compared with the glory of war, it did not trouble her overmuch.

In his chamber, at his prayer-desk, Sir Martin knelt in the moonlight, and prayed to Almighty God for a blessing on the coming day, and especially that his sovereign lord King Charles might have protection in the fight.

After the troop had ridden away at dawn, to the cheers of those left behind, a great silence settled upon Arnescote.

All day Lucinda wandered about, longing for action of some kind, for news, for anything.

Kineton was only some three hours' ride away, but might have been across the seas, so remote did it seem. Until, about mid-afternoon, a distant booming was borne on the air, and the sharp crack and clatter of muskets. The terrified maids huddled together, too afraid to scatter to their work; and Lucinda walked, and listened, and was not quite so filled with pleasurable excitement as she had been. It was the longest afternoon she had ever known. She was relieved when dusk began to fall; surely the battle could not last much longer. But then there came a sinister light in the sky, to the north-east, like a glow from Hell, causing the servants to pray frantically.

Lucinda climbed up to the highest room in one of the castle's twin towers. From there the road could be seen — and yes, there were figures on it, discernible in the dusk, men walking slowly, as though tired and lame, and two carrying something between them on a litter.

Margaret had joined her at the window. 'What do you see? Your eyes are younger than mine.'

'Men, moving very slowly. Soldiers.'

'Ours or theirs?'

'I cannot see. Now a rider. And a waggon — I think a waggon, not a coach . . . They're passing the end of our road — so they cannot be ours. Oh!'

'What is it?' Margaret peered over her shoulder.

'A horse, riderless, look. It's galloping towards Arnescote. Quick, Margaret, downstairs.'

When they reached the courtyard the horse was already there, its snorting and puffing loud in the gathering darkness. Lucinda reached its side at the same time as Old William, the groom, and both recognized it with alarm.

'Oh God, my father's charger! Is he wounded, William?'

Patting and soothing, William gently felt the frightened animal's body and legs. 'Only scratches, as I can see — but look here, mistress.'

The saddle was soaked with blood, the blood of the rider.

CHAPTER SEVEN

The waiting that night was harder than it had been in the day. Hour after hour went by, with no news. At last Lucinda told the servants to go to bed and sleep as best they could, while she kept watch upstairs in her chamber, and Cropper remained below, near the front door, ready to rouse up hastily at any noise.

She had not meant to doze, tense and afraid as she was, horrible visions of her father slaughtered and mangled chasing themselves through her brain. So much blood, it must have come from a mortal wound. She cursed herself for not overbearing Cropper and the groom and riding to the battlefield while some light lasted, to search for her father's body. They had said it would be useless, and dangerous to herself. 'Here is where news will come,' Cropper said. Of course he was right; but it was cruel to have no choice but to sit and wait, on edge with anxiety.

Yet her eyelids had closed, and she had slipped sideways in her chair, when the clangour of the bell brought her upright with a start. She rushed down the stairs, meeting Hannah and Margaret on the way. They found Cropper already at the great oak door, unlocking and unbolting. As it creaked open the three women crowded behind him, staring into the darkness.

Outside were no soldiers, no heavily-laden litter: only a single figure in the shadows. Cropper raised his lantern, showing the visitor to be a woman, young, dirty and bedraggled, and unknown to any of them. Cropper, disappointed in news of his master, addressed her roughly.

'What brings you to Arnescote at this hour?'

Her voice was timid, humble, not quite educated, with a slight accent that was not of Warwickshire. 'We are in search of shelter for the night, my mother and I, sir.'

'How so, when there are inns and hostelries a-plenty in Swinford and Banbury?'

The woman moved closer. 'We are relatives of Sir Martin Lacey, escaped from the rioting and affrays of London, seeking refuge in this house until the war is over and London calm again.'

Lucinda said 'My father and my brother are both at the war. You say you are relatives — how so?'

'Why, through my father, lately dead, who was only brother to Lady Lacey. Have you not heard of Henry Protheroe?'

Lucinda looked enquiringly at Margaret, who shook her head. But Cropper remembered something. 'There was such a person came here once during my time as steward — at the time of Sir Martin's betrothal.'

The woman was almost inside the door now, clearly confident of being invited within. 'My father,' she said, 'died in penury some five years since. His trading failed in Bristol, but he was too proud to ask his well-married sister for a favour. Thus they never did meet or exchange word from the moment that my aunt, Kitty Protheroe, entered this house as Lady Lacey.'

'It's true enough,' Margaret said. 'I had not recognized the name, the way she spoke it. Lady Lacey was indeed a Mistress Protheroe, and she did tell me of her brother's misfortune, and of his child, a daughter.'

'That daughter am I.' The voice was now less diffident and humble. Lucinda went forward impetuously.

'Then we must welcome you at once. Come indoors.'

'My mother . . . She lies ill in a cart — I have dragged her all this way. She is sick unto death, I think.'

Cropper peered into the roughly-made hand-cart. The old woman crouching in it, in dirty blankets, was a loathsome sight, emaciated to skeleton thinness, her face a mass of running sores. He shuddered. What he murmured in Margaret's ear caused her to say urgently to Lucinda, 'To bed, dear child. This is a matter for older, wiser, counsels.'

'But these ladies — my aunt and cousin? They must not be sent away like ailing animals!'

Margaret led her away, protesting. Then returning, she sent Hannah to rout out Minty, and summoned Susan Protheroe indoors, none too welcomingly. Meekly, wordlessly, as silently as a snake she glided in.

The three of them, Margaret, Cropper and Minty looked down at the body of Mistress Protheroe, laid out on a straw pallet in the barn. It was only a body now, the eyes glazed and the mouth fallen open. Minty shut the staring eyes and pulled a blanket up over the face.

'The plague,' she whispered, 'the black plague. She must be under the earth by dawn.' Cropper and Margaret looked at Susan, who sat motionless near by, showing neither shock nor grief, however much she may have felt. Minty half urged, half pushed her out of the barn towards the outbuilding where laundry was done, and, carefully not touching her, got her into a laundry tub filled with hot water, giving her a cake of soap to wash with, and copious draughts of ragwort and lentil to ward off infection. Body and face were clear of spot, she saw; the plague had not taken hold. If it had, the old woman would by strength or cunning have kept the sufferer away from the house, caring nothing for what might happen to her. The mother's body must be earthed, with or without the Reverend Butterworth's services, every shred of clothing burnt of both mother and daughter, cart, blankets and all.

So Susan Protheroe spent her first night at Arnescote, unobtrusive, grateful to all and especially to Lucinda, who was ragged-nerved and weary after an almost sleepless night, and not minded to take much heed of the story of her cousin's poverty-stricken life. She listened to the tale with half an ear, aware that her cousin, now washed, combed and dressed in some garments Margaret had found, was reasonably comely, large-eyed and fair-faced, buxom of figure — much older than herself or Anne, but young still, no disgrace to Arnescote in appearance.

'If you will let me stay,' Susan was saying, 'I will repay your Christian kindness with hard work. I am a practised seamstress . . .'

The clanging of the bell broke into her words. Lucinda

leapt up and rushed to the door, the first to reach it. A young Cavalier officer stood there, dusty and battle-stained, seething with impatience. Lucinda knew him at once, and was amazed, but to him her looks meant nothing, for he at once asked if she were one of the family.

'I am Lucinda, my Lord Ferrar,' she said. For this was the chosen bridegroom she had scorned, hidden from, and forgotten. Yet, seen again, he was handsome, so handsome as to put Prince Rupert out of her mind, and gallant, and with a great charm about him.

'Lucinda Lacey!' he exclaimed. 'In truth you have changed — forgive me. But I have brought Sir Martin home...'

'Alive?'

'Alive, but with a bad wound in the thigh, and swooning with pain. Bring him in, lads — carefully on the steps — so.' The two carters who bore Sir Martin between them were conducted by Cropper towards the stairs, Lucinda watching apprehensively.

'How did he get the wound?' she asked Edward.

'In the first charge down from Edgehill to Kineton. The King himself bade me bring him back home. Now I must go back.'

'How did the battle go?'

'Who can say? The fight was ended by six of the clock, when darkness made it impossible for men to see each other. There had been much slaughter — I have never seen aught like it, even in the foreign wars. Half of all who fought on both sides either dead or wounded, I heard — but all ended in confusion. Old Sir Edmund Verney, the King's Standard-bearer is killed; all we found of him was his hand still gripping the broken shaft, with the ring still on it containing the King's portrait.' His hearers shuddered. 'But the King and Prince Rupert are safe, though they fought in the thick of it. His Majesty has withdrawn to Edgecote and Essex is gone to lick his wounds at Warwick Castle, they say.' As he turned, Lucinda saw that his right arm was bloodied, a rough bandage wound round it.

'But you're wounded yourself!' she cried. 'Come in, and let them clean and dress it for you.'

'No, no, it's well enough, I thank you. I am needed with

my men — farewell, Lucinda.' With a bow and a wave of his hat he was gone. Lucinda stood, looking after him, for a long time.

———————

Sir Martin's wound was grievous, a thigh-bone shattered; but between Margaret's good nursing and Minty's strange-smelling lotions, he would recover completely in time, though always with a limp. And Tom was safe, unhurt, and able to tell them how the battle had gone, which was certainly in favour of the Royalists.

'The King refused Prince Rupert's plan to march direct on London,' he said, 'so now the Prince goes off in anger, snapping at Essex's heels, and the King and army will make for Oxford in God's good time. What a chance wasted. Well, our troop did bravely. I must away, back to my duties. Mend quickly, Father, for we need you.'

Sir Martin smiled thinly. 'I'll not fight again, Tom. You must defend the honour of the Laceys on the field of battle.'

———————

The year 1643 had brought changing fortunes to both sides. In February the Queen arrived from Holland, bringing with her eleven transports filled with ammunition and stores for the King's army. Her arrival caused much joy among the Royalists; she had been an unpopular figurehead at Court, but now she seized the chance to become a heroine, with a price on her head. Calling herself 'She-Majesty-General-issima', she ate her meals in sight of the army, camp fashion, joked and flirted with the soldiers, magnanimously pardoned an enemy on his way to be hanged, and generally gave new heart to the Royalist cause.

By July she was in charge of her own army, leading it from Newark to Stratford-on-Avon. A reunion with the King took place at Edge Hill, which he thought of as the scene of his first victory, and poets broke out in songs of praise.

When gallant Grenville stoutly stood
And stopped the gap up with his blood,
When Hopton led his Cornish band
Where the sly conqueror durst not stand,
We knew the Queen was nigh at hand.

When great Newcastle so came forth,
As in nine days he scoured the North,
When Fairfax's vast, perfidious force
Was sunk to five invisible horse,
When none but ladies stayed to fight —
We knew our Queen was come in sight.

Dashing, daring, romantic, she was all her husband should have been and was not, the fatal flaws in his character eating away at his Cause. Now he had no other advisers but her, and she, alas, was poor in judgement. Yet, this summer in Warwickshire, their love for each other and high confidence gave hope to all their followers.

For Parliament, one Oliver Cromwell, a man of Huntingdon, had risen to the position of second in command to Major General the Earl of Manchester. Some new leader was needed, for John Hampden, that brave, popular, highly principled statesman and soldier, had died of wounds got at Chalgrove Field, still urging measures which might have ended the war cleanly and quickly. By such accidents as the flight of a bullet is history made.

Now the King and Queen were at Oxford, holding court and gathering their forces — and money. Silver and gold came to them, the gift of generous and loyal supporters; ostensibly lent but in fact given freely, without any serious expectation of repayment. The Laceys were among those busily collecting up all they could find for the Royal treasury. Lucinda's silver-backed hairbrush and trinkets, the steward's chain of office Cropper prized so dearly, bequeathed to him as it had been by his father, handed down from generations of Croppers who had served Laceys. With these went the family silver: dishes, flagons, standing-cups wrought with strange monsters and garlands, salts, ewers and basins, beakers and tankards, porringers that had been christening gifts to the children, punch-bowls and monteiths.

All these craftsmen's works, each emblazoned with the Lacey arms, would literally go into the melting-pot. Cropper was for hiding some, just a small portion, in the cellars, but, as Sir Martin pointed out, what was the use of saving anything to be sniffed out by any Roundhead pack of curs that might one day fall on Arnescote?

Lucinda, with her father and Cropper, was in the secret room of the cellarage, where the silver was concealed.

'But who is to remove it all to Oxford?' she asked.

'Will Saltmarsh. He must return tonight to set off in darkness.'

'Alone?'

'Cropper and I were on the point of choosing one other to accompany him,' Sir Martin said.

Lucinda's eyes lit up, and she clasped her hands. 'Oh, let it be me! There is no other . . . man you can spare. Let it be me, Father!'

Sir Martin laughed, a genuine laugh of good-natured derision. 'You, child? Lame as I am, I'd rather go myself.'

'You cannot,' she flashed. 'and Cropper cannot — you need him here. There is no one else, I tell you truly.'

Cropper suggested 'Hugh Brandon, sir?'

It was Lucinda's turn to laugh. 'Hugh? He has a weakness of the heart that comes upon him with too much exertion, or he would have been at the wars with Tom. No, I have twice his strength. And we're much of a height — I'll dress in his clothes, as a young Cavalier.'

Both men looked shocked. Cropper shook his head. 'The highways are full of danger.'

'Then we shall avoid them, and find a way through woods and hedgerows. Is Tom still at Oxford?'

'Believed to be,' Sir Martin answered, broodily eyeing his headstrong girl.

'Then I have a double mission — to convey the silver, and to urge him to do his duty and return to defend his home. Does he not shamefully neglect us?'

Sir Martin had thought himself a man not to be moved, once his mind was made up. But his daughter was a match for him in resolution, and he was more than a little proud that she should want to undertake such a daring venture. Before long, between argument and pleading, she had got her own way, and was gleefully studying a map of the country she would have to cross.

Parson Butterworth was seriously alarmed by the rumour that a Roundhead troop had been seen approaching Arnescote. Trembling, he came to Sir Martin in search of protection; which, apart from the bleak promise to blow the church to smithereens from the castle ramparts, should it be occupied by the enemy, Sir Martin declined to give. It lay out of his power, garrisoned as Arnescote was with a handful of women and a few men unfit for war. Instead, he suggested that the vicar hold a service in the Great Hall.

'Young Hugh can lead us in a rousing chorus that will put the fear of God into any skulking Puritan — scare the breeches off 'em. What do you say, parson?'

Meekly Butterworth agreed, though it was not what he had hoped for. The silver voice of Hugh Brandon, betraying in its sweetness nothing of the resentment he felt in having parted with his best suit of clothes to a girl, was raised above a feeble quavering chorus in Psalm Fifty-nine.

> 'Deliver me from mine enemies, O God: defend me from them that rise up against me.
> O deliver me from the wicked doers: and save me from the blood-thirsty men.
> For lo, they lie waiting for my soul: the mighty men are gathered against me . . .
> They go to and fro in the evening: they grin like a dog, and run about the city.'

Lucinda, in the lowest of the vaults with her father, Will Saltmarsh, and Cropper, looked up at the sound, smiling. She was the very picture of a dashing young Cavalier, Hugh's doublet belted tightly in round her waist, his breeches and high boots disguising the pretty shape of her legs, and her ringlets serving as well for a boy as a girl.

Will was busy moving the last of a number of wine-casks, leaving the wall behind them open to view. Sir Martin gave one of the largest stones a smart rap with his cane. Slowly, grittily, it slid aside, revealing a dark hole.

'This chamber,' he said, 'has lain hidden since the days of King John, known only to the head of the house and his

67

steward. In time past it sheltered fugitives and priests. Now, in the chamber there is a small door going to a passage which leads directly to the crypt of the church. Cropper has cleared the rubble from it.'

Cropper glanced down ruefully at his clothes, which gave evidence of contact with a great deal of very old dust. Lucinda shifted impatiently, anxious to be gone.

'It's a cunning point for escape,' said her father. 'Search parties are diverted by the wine, and, with good luck, render themselves insensible to their duties. But we delay — we must take advantage of Butterworth's presence in the house. Will, do you have the horses in position?'

'Aye, sir.'

'Rations and provender?'

'Enough for three days' journey, sir, hidden in bushes just beyond the church.' He took hold of two heavy canvas bags which Lucinda had been trying in vain to lift, and thrust them into the hiding-place, stepping in after them. Lucinda threw her arms round her father, enjoying to the full the dramatic situation she had forced on them all.

'Farewell, dear father! You always wished for a second son — now you have one.'

He shook his head. 'Child, I beg you make not light of this matter, and beware of carelessness. Lie low in daylight — obey Will in all matters . . .'

She began to protest that she, not Will, was the officer in the enterprise, but Will was impatient to be gone. Sir Martin, with a parting blessing, watched them disappear into darkness lit only by the flickering flame of the candle she carried, then replaced the stone and with difficulty began to move back the casks to hide the entrance to the escape-route.

Upstairs the small congregation was still singing.

'As for me, I will sing of thy power, and will praise thy mercy betimes in the morning: for thou hast been my defence and refuge in the day of my trouble.

Unto thee, O my strength, will I sing: for thou, O God, art my refuge, and my merciful God.'

Alone by the fire, picturing the stages of Lucinda's

journey, and the perils she might encounter, Sir Martin did not hear the soft approaching footsteps, until one of the dogs at his feet awoke and growled. Susan Protheroe stood beside him, smiling, a steaming tankard in her hands.

'Not yet in bed, uncle? See, I have brought you a drink.'

He took it, not wanting it, and thanked her. Still she lingered. 'It's a chilly night. Shall I fetch a blanket for your shoulders?'

'No. The fire and the drink suffice. Thank you.'

She caught sight of the book on his knees, and tried to read the title upside down. 'What is your book? I should be pleased to read aloud to you.'

He shut the book with a bang. 'It was merely to pass the time. Go to bed, niece.' But she had sunk to her knees beside him, and was looking up into his face with large innocent eyes.

'Dear uncle,' she said, 'I know the reason for your wakefulness. Lucinda is not in her chamber.' At his startled look she added 'Trust me. She has gone to Oxford with the silver. How brave of her — and braver still of you to send her. But uncle, I am so much in your debt for harbouring me that I should willingly have gone myself, had you asked me, and spared you the anguish of parting with her.'

He hardly heard what she said, still shocked. 'Does the whole house know, then?'

'Just I and Margaret. I've put word out that she has a sickness, to explain her absence.'

''Tis more like I who have the sickness — to send a fragile daughter on a soldier's mission.'

'Such are the sacrifices,' she murmured, 'in these treacherous and lonely times.' She took his hand and held it to her cheek, in a daughterly gesture. He disliked such demonstrations, but let it stay there. At least the girl was company; her chatter kept him from the worst imaginings about Lucinda.

Who, at that moment, was riding speedily towards danger.

CHAPTER EIGHT

The two travellers, with their mounts, pack-horse and bags of treasure, had got safely through their night's journey, and found what seemed the ideal place for their first halt, a half-derelict barn in a lonely situation. Will, reconnoitring, found only some chickens below, pecking among straw, and what seemed at a glance an empty hayloft. Lucinda gazed round disparagingly.

'This is a foolish place —' she began, but found Will's hand over her mouth.

'Talk in whispers or not at all,' he hissed.

'Why — are we not alone?' He made no answer, busying himself with unpacking provisions for their meal. Lucinda was not used to being ignored by servants. Angrily she whispered, 'I trust you will not forget your place. My father will surely ask me for an account of your conduct.'

'For every tale you tell, mistress,' he replied philosophically, 'I'll have one to match it — for your brother's ear.'

'Villain!'

'Aye, of long standing.' He shared out the food. 'Here, eat, then get some rest. We're but a third of the way.' As she began to eat, he moved to the one small window and stood at it, pistol cocked.

Lucinda had been looking forward eagerly to the food, but it tasted not over-pleasant, overwhelmed as its savours were by the strong smell of hens and old straw. She was uncomfortable, too; Hugh's breeches were a bad fit and her thighs were rubbed and sore from riding astride. The enterprise began to seem less romantic than when they had set out; it seemed strange, somewhat distasteful, to have

70

forfeited the right to be deferred to as a young lady. She had told Will to address her as Luke, for safety if they got into company, but the name made her feel much more like a servant than a master. Still, best put a good face on it, after the brave things she had said to her father.

'I pray the farmer doesn't come to count his chickens,' she said to Will's back, 'for if he does . . .' Before she could say more she felt herself seized and held in a strong grasp, a large filthy hand gripping her neck and a pistol pressed against her temple. Her scream brought Will whipping round to see her in the grip of a burly man in unkempt uniform (not Roundhead at least, Will saw with relief), dirty-faced, unshaven, and wild-eyed. He yelled at Will in a voice as rough as his appearance.

'Your pistols on the ground, sir — on the instant, or I'll blow this cherub's head to the rafters. Aye, your sword, too.' Still with pistol pointed at Lucinda, he collected up Will's discarded weapons.

Lucinda glared at Will. 'An excellent scout who can't raise his eyes above his nose,' she said.

'Aye,' agreed the intruder, 'he might have taken a closer look round the hayloft. Now, no brangling, boys and girls — for such I detect beneath that tunic. What mischief's disguised, I wonder? Well, I'll have your story and share your bread.' Without waiting for permission he snatched a piece from Lucinda, then grabbed the wine-flagon and took a long gulp from it.

'Excellent breakfast. Now — what's your business in my barn?'

'*Your* barn?'

'Aye, mistress. Sequestered, you might say, possession being nine parts of the game.'

Lucinda decided to change her tactics. This rough customer was not going to yield to high-handedness; a little guile and charm would go much further with him. She summoned a smile.

'We mean no harm — to a brave Cavalier, as your tunic proclaims you. Oh — you're wounded! You need tending.'

'But a scratch, a graze and a bump. Parted from my horse and company a few miles up the road. We'll have *you* made safe, master, by your leave.' With a length of dirty rope he

71

was tying the furious Will to a post, still addressing Lucinda. 'Foot-slogged it here — spent a fitful night — that's all. Thus, my story is open and honest. I fancy yours takes more explaining.' His eyes were fixed on the sacks of silver. 'What cargo's this?'

Without hesitating, Will answered, 'All my lady's wardrobe — all that she could gather in the speed of her departure.' Lucinda took her cue from him.

'Aye, a Roundhead troop stormed my home, and my gallant servant here helped me escape — saved my life.' The man looked sceptical.

'H'm. From where I stand, your story has a different tone. Why should I believe you?'

'Why should we believe *you*?' Will retorted. 'I read desertion in your face.'

The man's laugh was quick and unconvincing. 'Ha! Deserter, am I, when I still display the King's colours? Sergeant Mellhuish is no deserter, man! You impugn my honour and my valour.'

'I see no valour here — I see a cowardly snivelling pox-ridden rogue, a shabby thieving coxcomb that will see a hanging — a bullying white-livered turncoat cursed Roundhead spy!'

Provoked to fury, Mellhuish slashed a hand across Will's face, cutting his lip open, then, as Lucinda moved, waved his pistol at her. 'Move not, mistress, or I'll slice this loudmouth's head clean off his shoulders!'

Will sighed heavily, blood dripping from his gashed mouth on to his tunic. 'It's all up,' he said, to Lucinda's horror. 'If there's a choice between your father and this rattlenape, I'll take my chance that this one's got a heart.' He gave her a look that told her to keep quiet, and went on, 'Man to man, Sergeant, our story is one of love and lust. Before you stands the noble daughter of a Royalist house. I am steward to her father, Walter Cropwood by name. Cursed is the double misery of harbouring Parliamentary sympathies and a passion for this most excellent young lady — who, torn between loyalty and love, has done me the great honour of following her heart. We are runaways, bag and baggage, with a foot, you might say, in both camps.'

Lucinda, silently applauding his quick wit, hoped that he

would not let his dramatic sense carry him too far, and spoil the effect he was having on his listener. Will continued, dangerously, 'Even within the hour we expect her father and his troop to storm this barn. Whereupon you — our captor — will most surely be rewarded by her grateful parent, and hasten our certain doom.'

Lucinda backed up his rhetoric by kneeling beside him, her head submissively bowed, her ringlets tumbling over her face; a charming picture of pleading womanhood. The sergeant whistled.

'A Roundhead stealing off with a Royalist petticoat — by Heaven, there's wit in it.'

'At your mercy,' Lucinda murmured, 'to set us free or collect the bounty on our heads. At your mercy.'

Mellhuish helped himself liberally to the wine, looking from one to the other. Greed was in his eyes, and calculation. To Lucinda's alarm, he approached the bags and felt them. Silver moved and clinked. His expression altered. Hastily she said, 'What little coin we have for our journey — you may take as your fee.' He looked hopefully at the sacks, but she indicated her saddlebag. 'In there.'

Lulled into belief in her sincerity, the sergeant rootled in the saddlebag and found her purse, which was gratifyingly full of coins. To do so, he had to turn his back on her, as she had calculated. She made a dash for Will's pistol on the ground, and clapped it to the back of the man's head, demanding his own weapon. With a cry of disgust he dropped it. Within a very few minutes, Will was free, Mellhuish bound with the same rope, his sword removed and snapped. Will asked of him the name of his troop-commander, which he refused to give, thereby strengthening Will's conviction that he was a deserter. He began to rave, giving a very good imitation of the kind of fit at which beggars were expert. Lucinda was alarmed, and approached him, but Will thrust her back.

'It's a trick. Up the ladder with you, and sleep — we'll need your watchfulness tonight. I'll guard the rogue. You did well with your pistol,' he added magnanimously.

When he heard her stop rustling in the hayloft, he silently approached the prone sergeant, whose eyes were still shut in feigned unconsciousness. Very quietly and skilfully he cut through the bonds, and just as quietly stole out of sight. The trap was laid.

Mellhuish opened his eyes. Unbelievingly, he found that he was free and alone, the barn-door open, nobody in sight. But beside him, open, unprotected, lay one of the sacks. His dirty face spread into a beam; the fools had fled, too afraid to take their loot with them. Cautiously he peered inside, and drew out the most substantial object: Sir Martin's prized silver dish, chased, inscribed, magnificent. With a mutter of pleasure he tucked it inside his tunic and went towards the door, tiptoeing, clutching the hilt of his broken sword.

As he reached the door, one hand on it, Will's knife came down, swift and sure, between his shoulder-blades.

One peril was past, others lay in wait. Will's sharp wits rescued them from three Roundhead guards, idly lounging on a bridge. While he played the rolling drunkard, distracting them from her, she, quaking with fear and indecision, made her escape with the horses and treasure. Thankfully she saw him return, slipping nimbly under tree-cover to rejoin her. Leaping into his saddle, he grasped the pack-horse's rein, and was off, calling back to her to follow. But her foot slipped in the stirrup, and as she struggled awkwardly she was aware of two horsemen approaching along the path on the high bank which had sheltered her. Their tall hats and plain collars proclaimed them Puritans. Lucinda somehow heaved herself into her saddle, her heart sinking into Hugh's over-large boots. They could not miss her, and they did not. A shout of 'Halt, knave!' was followed by their swift arrival at her side. One snatched at her horse's bridle.

'What's your business?' he asked, in a rustic accent; she was glad to notice that neither man looked particularly bright.

'Be you for King or Parliament?' asked the other, to which she replied pertly 'Does England have a King?'

They laughed, and the second one capped what he took to be her witticism. 'The King of Oxford?' he suggested.

Lucinda laughed too, saying 'An academic kingdom,'

which was altogether beyond them, then enquired, 'And what's *your* business?'

The first man swelled out his chest importantly. 'Is it your business, boy, to ask *our* business?'

'It may be. You know not who I am.'

'A saucy young sprat —'

'Who may be son to your commander, Lord Essex,' Lucinda interrupted. It was worth a gamble.

They looked at each other. 'Didn't know he had a boy,' said one. The other snorted. 'He's no more son to Essex than I am. See how he's dressed. And out alone where any swaggering spawn of Satan could pick on him. He's one of *theirs* — grab him!'

Her bridle-rein was free now — she urged her horse a few steps away from them. 'Touch me and I'll have you both hanged, you uncouth blackguards! I am on my way to see my sister's husband, Master John Fletcher, the Member of Parliament for Swinford, and I'll thank you to escort me through this forest of brigands.'

Boldness paid off. Nervous, uncertain, anxious to err on the side of safety, they told her to follow them.

———————————

Anne, sedate and matronly in her own handsome, severely-furnished parlour, was not only surprised but displeased to see her sister swagger in, immodestly dressed in man's clothing. John Fletcher was mildly amused at her appearance, and less inclined than his wife to press for an explanation. Anne persisted.

'Did Father send you alone to visit Tom?'

'I was accompanied part of the way by Will Saltmarsh, but I lost him — the woods are full of Puritans. I don't know what has happened to him.'

Anne set her lips. 'I find it incredible that you should have attempted such folly. Your mission must indeed be pressing.'

'Can't you guess at it?' Lucinda half-taunted.

'I have my suspicions. But — no, Father would never entrust his silver to you — pranked out like that.'

'But Master Saltmarsh might have it,' John suggested.

Lucinda turned on him. 'Shall you send a troop to hunt him down, then? Your brother's servant, who may often have saved his life? I cannot fathom what you have become, sister, to turn against us. And Tom, would you have him killed too?'

'Tom takes his chance in the field —' said John.

'While you stay closeted in the study, Master Lawyer, waging an academic war. Have you been out and seen the bodies?'

Spots of angry colour were in Anne's cheeks. 'Lucinda, you will leave my house at once, and the Devil take you, if you have merely come to rail at us. No one wants this war, but the King provoked it, and what else could we do but defend ourselves?'

'Defend yourselves!' Lucinda flared back. 'When any moment your army may attack Arnescote, and lay it waste and blot out all our happy days? I invite you to guess at my mission, my *folly*, and all you speak of is silver. I am going to plead with our busy forgetful brother to bring a troop to Father. Now will you let me go?'

The argument that followed between the sisters might well have led to slaps and scratches, had John not intervened. He himself would like to see Tom, he said, and by chance he was going to visit relatives of the late John Hampden. He was prepared to escort Lucinda to an inn on the outskirts of Oxford, and send word to Tom to collect her. That was the best he could do, and the most she could expect. With a last taunt thrown at Anne, she gladly left the room she felt to be filled with enmity.

The inn was quiet when they arrived, after barely an hour's journey. John dispatched a messenger to Tom, and prepared to read until he arrived, in the room he and Lucinda had been given. But the clatter of boots and the sound of loud confident voices heralded another arrival. The tapster, a Puritan friend of John's, put his terrified face round the door. 'A party of King's men on a search. Best make yourself scarce.'

He was barely gone when the door was flung open to reveal a tall, finely dressed young Cavalier officer. Captain Bracewell thoroughly enjoyed everything about his war, and his enthusiasm for Roundhead-catching was boundless. At sight of John's plain clothing his eyes lit up and he strode forward.

'What hornet's nest is this, eh? Your name and business, sir.'

John answered calmly. 'My name is John Fletcher. I am a lawyer by profession, and the Member of Parliament for Swinford.' Lucinda tried not to show her alarm at his dangerous frankness, and the Captain laughed, beckoning in his lieutenant and sergeant.

'Member of *Parliament*? This day grows more triumphant by the minute. Parliament, sir, the King's Parliament, resides at Oxford. I don't recollect your presence there, and by your dress and manner I take you for a foul canting scum of a rebel. Seize him,' he barked to the sergeant who obeyed smartly. Lucinda sprang up.

'Manhandle him, and you'll smart for it, you bully!'

Bracewell's smile was incredulous, as he viewed the small figure and pink indignant face of his challenger. Advancing, he raised his sword and pointed it at her. She managed not to flinch as it came nearer her face, touched her chin and quite gently tickled it.

'Well, well, what are these words,' he asked indulgently, 'from a bumptious young puppy, without a wisp of fluff on its chin? Would you have me shave you, younker?'

John put in quickly 'The younker you address is your own Captain Lacey's brother. Is he downstairs? I wish to speak with him at once — I am married to his sister. The boy here is on your side.'

'Tom Lacey's brother?' the Captain repeated, his tone implying 'With a Puritan for company?'

Lucinda flashed 'What's your name, that I may remind my brother and Prince Rupert of your conduct here today?'

Now Bracewell had exhausted the humour of the situation, his smile faded. 'I am an officer of Lord Digby's troop. Captain Lacey is not here — I am in charge, and I will answer for my conduct without threat from a young whipper-snapper whom I find in strange company.' He swooped on Lucinda and pulled her, resisting, towards the door, calling back to his sergeant to make polite enquiry of the lawyer's knowledge of rebel movements. The man grinned: enquiry, seldom polite, was a speciality of his. 'My pleasure, sir,' he said.

Bracewell was openly delighted. 'We have made a catch the King and Prince Rupert will rightly praise us for,' he declared, and with a firm grip on Lucinda's collar pushed her out of the door.

Tom arrived at what at first sight looked like a madhouse: his sister in disguise, being taunted by Bracewell's men, his brother-in-law undergoing questioning with torture thrown in. Sweeping the surprised Bracewell aside, he commanded the sergeant to stop. Lucinda, behind him, saw with horror that John had been badly beaten. Shaken and trembling, he sat on the edge of the bed, staring at Tom as at a stranger.

'I have seen the ugly face of war,' he said. 'Who were those savages? Were they Englishmen? God forbid.'

'The fox caught in the trap — on whichever side — is fair game,' Tom answered.

'John risked everything to bring me to you, Tom, and this was his reward!' Lucinda said.

John shook his head. 'No, no. I misjudged the war — the tide has turned against us. The tapster told me — Devizes? We've lost Devizes, Tom?'

'Aye. Hopton stormed the chalky Downs, supported by Prince Maurice with a troop ridden hard from Oxford. Together they routed your commander.'

'Then truly the hand of our God has turned against us.' John drained the brandy Lucinda held to his lips, but the colour did not flow back into his cheeks.

When they left him on the road, with a letter of safe-conduct from Tom in his pocket, he turned to ask John, 'What message to your sister?'

'One of good cheer, good health — unforgotten love, and — apologies for your mistreatment.'

John nodded. 'She thinks of you daily in her prayers.'

'And I her. The love of twins endures through all life's contradictions. Farewell.'

Lucinda watched him go, tears in her eyes for his bravery and the cruelty that had been used on him. What had it been worth, this adventure of hers? Tom had told her that the silver had safely reached the Royal Mint, whatever might have happened to Will; so the King's coffers were richer. That was a comfort, but of the glory she had expected to feel there was nothing.

Yet there was a reward waiting in Oxford. Between ranks of courtiers, in a hall that had seen scholars, poets, divines and martyrs, Lucinda moved on Tom's arm to where, in an inner chamber, a small man sat enthroned on a crimson-draped chair. Beside him towered the handsome height of Prince Rupert, who gracefully introduced her.

'Mistress Lucinda Lacey, sir. A gallant soldier for the Cause.'

Lucinda sank into her deepest curtsey, murmuring something, she knew not what. When she arose, the delicate, melancholy face of the King was warmed by a rare smile. He reached out a white hand to her.

'My nephew has told me something of your perilous journey,' he said, his voice light and sweet, matching his childlike stature. 'If we had more of your spirit and devotion, this conflict would soon be over.' He descended the steps of the dais and put round her neck a gold chain, with a medal depending from it.

'In gratitude for special service in the field, I give you this.'

She glanced down at the medal; it bore the unmistakable features of Rupert.

CHAPTER NINE

It seemed as though the war might pass by Arnescote.

But ever since Lucinda's successful adventure, the sharp eyes of Parliament had been upon the castle. It was rumoured, on good authority, that since the removal of the family silver, other silver, from noble houses around, had been stealthily conveyed there and hidden in a secret place. Because it was thought that inner knowledge of the building would help to find it, John Fletcher was given a commission in the Parliamentary army, with a special mission to go to Arnescote armed with the power of the sword, and lay hands on the hoard.

Anne protested that her husband was no soldier; but John himself had entertained self-doubts about his passive role as a civilian, and seized this apparently Heaven-sent chance to become a man of action.

In the event, he was a very poor one. His attempts to enforce military discipline were laughable to his more experienced comrades and, though he gained entry to Arnescote easily enough, and had the suspiciously friendly cooperation of the staff in searching, no trace of silver came to light. Cropper and Will, who alone of the servants knew the secret of the hidden room, kept silence, even when Cropper was savagely tortured. The others jeered at the invading soldiers, Mistress Dumfry offering them pigswill to eat and risking hanging by pertness and insults. At last all were locked up, including Sir Martin and Lucinda, while soldiers turned the place upside down.

All but one. Sue Protheroe sought an interview with the troop's Commander, the worldly Captain Hannibal Marsh, and, by wily flattery, got the pantry keys and her freedom, as well as that of Captain Marsh's bed. Mercifully for Sir Martin, the secret room was unknown to her, since in her mock humility and inward jealousy she was only too ready to betray the Lacey family, and to lie smoothly about it afterwards, crying that she had been raped.

'Bitch,' said Tom. 'Roundhead's whore. Turn her out, flog her through the village.'

But Sir Martin, chivalrous, would have no worse done to her than to be put to work in the castle laundry, thus establishing the permanent presence of a spy in his ranks. Lucinda, from that moment, refused to speak to Sue Protheroe.

Captain Marsh's troop found no silver, and his parting words to Sir Martin were said with grim intent. 'When we come back, we shall go through it again. This time we shall try your panels with axes and your floors with iron bars.'

Before they left, they ensured that their memory would not fade at Arnescote. 'A sacrifice to the Lord to sanctify our work,' ordered Marsh. 'Cleanse the church. Cleanse it to the bare walls.'

They 'cleansed' it with a vigour that had everything to do with anarchy and nothing to do with piety. Joking obscenely, they crashed through altar, pulpit, font and pew with axes and crowbars, tore down crucifixes and flung them on the bonfire which was soon burning merrily in the churchyard. Turning their attention to the stained-glass windows, they demolished the 'wicked images' of Christ and His mother, saints and angels, miracles of beauty and colour wrought by mediaeval craftsmen. Gleefully they destroyed the symbols of everything they had been brought up to revere, which could never be restored or replaced. And for this they, and others like them throughout England, would be cursed down the centuries.

The Lacey flag fluttered from its tower as the Roundheads rode away from the smoking shell that had been the church; and below it flew a scarlet pennant, Sir Martin's flag of defiance, proclaiming that Arnescote was ready to withstand all its enemies. It flew for a year, unchallenged.

The hot sun of a summer day beat down on Sir Martin and Tom, as they surveyed, from the castle wall, the trench which Bates the dairyman was digging, comparing it with the rough plan in Tom's hand. He pointed out to his father the firing step from which the men in the trench might stand to fire their muskets, safely behind cover.

'Those spiked pallisade posts are well done,' commented Sir Martin on the formidable sharpened wooden stakes, studded with iron spikes, which Will Saltmarsh and another man were knocking into the deepest part of the trench, to await the arrival of any enemy soldiers who might be unlucky enough to fall into it.

'Aye. Will and his father made them here in our smithy. "Swedish feathers", they're called, for it was old King Gustavus Adolphus who first used them in the Low Countries.' He looked up at a shout from Walter Jackman, the foreman of the digging operation.

'Sir Martin! Horseman approaching.'

They were reassured to see that the rider wore the burgonet and uniform of Lacey's Troop, and a Royalist sash. His packhorse moved slowly, for it was carrying a double weight. 'He has some baggage,' said Sir Martin.

Tom laughed. 'A baggage it is indeed. Has he taken a wench prisoner? God in Heaven! It's Dick Skinner.' The gamekeeper had been reported missing, probably killed, at the battle of Cropredy Bridge, and as time had passed all hope for him had been given up. Now here he was, alive, a welcome sight. Tom shouted the news down to Jackman, who gladly climbed out of the trench and went to meet Dick.

'Dick Skinner,' said Tom again, 'by all that's wonderful.'

'A good gamekeeper, like his father before him.'

'Aye, and a fine marksman — that's more to the point in the present case.'

'Well, we have our defences — but there are not men enough here to hold them in, if an attack was pressed home hard by the rebels.'

'This war will not be won defending castles,' Tom answered, 'but on the battlefield, between armies. Arnescote, and many houses like it, are made defended as the outer shield of Oxford. That is but prudence.'

'And you will stay with us now, Tom?' Sir Martin hoped greatly for an affirmative. He was feeling his age and his growing infirmity; to have this strong son by his side would be a wonderful comfort. But Tom shook his head.

'No, Father. Once the work is done I must join Prince Rupert and the army near Leicester. Never look so disappointed — in two days you'll have Charles Pike and Peter Crane back from their leave of furlough.'

'I'd soonest have you.' Sir Martin's tone was wistful.

In The Street, the alley of domestic buildings behind the main gate, Dick Skinner was getting a violently affectionate welcome from Rachel Pryke, who had rushed out to embrace him and rain kisses on his face.

'Dick, my poor Dick come back from the dead! But you look as if the devil's had you for breakfast — all skin and bone.' Stepping back to see him better, she caught sight of the girl he had carried before him in the saddle. Ragged, barefoot, dirty, her long dark hair in tangles, she slumped against the wall, her eyes closed in utter exhaustion. Rachel's own eyes flashed jealous fire.

'Who's this? You haven't brought a woman back with you, Dick Skinner?'

'I found her on the way, not far from here, more dead than alive.'

Margaret Goodwife, who had joined them, took in the scene. She directed Jackman to take his comrade into the kitchen for medical help and banished the glowering Rachel to the laundry. At her authoritative voice the ragged girl opened her eyes, cowering away from the terrifying grand lady. But Margaret spoke to her civilly enough.

'Well, what's your name, girl?'

The answer was barely audible. ''Tis Moll, mam, Mollie O'Flanagan.'

'So you're Irish. Did you come over with the soldiers?'

'No, mam — me father was a tinker — there was a lot of us — and the army came an' burnt our carts an' killed me father and me mam also, the murdering beasts. 'Twas on account we were Papists, so they said — and I stole away down the ditch.' She was suddenly terrified again, afraid she had admitted her religion to someone who might also be in favour of her execution. But Margaret said kindly enough,

'We don't kill Papists in this place, Mollie. You're one of God's creatures, and you're weary and hungry. You shall have bread and a place to lay your head — and then I'll see what work I can find for you, for you look strong enough. Come with me.'

Thankful, scarcely believing her good fortune, the Irish girl obeyed.

Sir Martin and Tom listened to Dick Skinner's account of his almost miraculous escape at Cropredy Bridge, where two witnesses had seen him take a musket ball full in the chest, fall from his horse, and disappear from sight. By a happy accident the thick cloth of his coat had kept the bullet from piercing him, but while he lay on the ground, dazed, a pikeman had knocked him on the head. After that he remembered nothing, but when he came to his senses, long after, he was in a peasant's cottage, being nursed by a kindly woman, who told him that he had been left for dead on the battlefield, and that her man had found him and brought him to her. They had kept him until he was strong enough to return to Arnescote, and he had given them what little money he had, to their delight.

'Lucky you Skinners have got thick skulls,' said Tom.

'Aye. And our troop these good burgonet caps — reckon it saved my life.' Tenderly he touched his head.

'Which way did you come back here?' enquired Sir Martin.

'By Swinford town, sir.'

'You were lucky not to be recognized, in that uniform. Swinford is held by the rebels.'

'No, sir. Not at this present — 'tis full of rioting officers and men, Royalist deserters. Many of 'em are drunken, and setting fire to Puritan houses by the score. They were whipping women in the streets when I rode through.' Sir Martin and Tom exchanged glances of alarm.

'My daughter, Mistress Fletcher, lives in Swinford, Skinner.'

'I remember that, Sir Martin. I know not the house, but Master Fletcher being on the side of the Parliament, she should have a care.'

When Skinner had gone Tom said, 'If things in Swinford are as bad as Skinner says they are, I'd best go over to make sure Anne has come to no harm, with John away in London.'

'I think indeed you had.' They shared the same vision: Anne alone, attacked, ravished, beaten perhaps, like the unfortunate women Skinner had seen. Tom was about to leave the Great Hall when Cropper approached with a request from Margaret that she might have a word.

The word concerned the situation of Susan Protheroe. 'She is not well. She does not whine or whimper at her lot, but such a delicate well-born lady is not suited to such work.'

Sir Martin was unsympathetic. 'I can't help that. Delicate well-born ladies should not go a-whoring with the enemy — to put it bluntly. She was lucky to have no worse punishment than the laundry.'

Margaret persisted. 'She pines, and many times has fits of fainting. I fear she will have a flux of the lungs. If I might suggest . . . she is marvellously skilled at stitching and all embroidering. If I could employ her in the sewing room, that might answer. And this Irish woman who's come with Skinner seems strong and willing for such as laundry work.'

Sir Martin turned an impatient shoulder on her. 'Do as you wish. These petticoat matters are no concern of mine.'

Tom went to see the exchange made in the laundry partly by the request of his father (it was, after all, a family matter), partly out of sheer curiosity, partly from an interest in Mistress Protheroe. The place was a-fog with steam and the smell of soap made from household fat and full of red-faced, red-armed girls and women pounding at the linen in wooden tubs or scrubbing it on ridged boards. Among them he recognized his cousin. Sweat streamed down her face, her hair was damp and straight, and she wore a threadbare shabby shift, the only garment bearable in that temperature. She glimpsed him the moment before he saw her, and with a deft movement tossed back her hair into a more becoming fall and pulled her bodice aside to reveal one shoulder and a generous view of her bosom. When he greeted her, somewhat hesitantly, she gave him a tragic look, drawing her hand across her wet brow.

'Cousin Tom. You are a stranger to this steamy place. What brings you here? To see that your cousin does her penance?' She reeled slightly, throwing out one hand as if to save herself from falling. Tom caught it, supporting her, and was rewarded by a pathetic smile.

'I come from my father,' he said. 'You have done your penance — your punishment is over. You may work with Goodwife Margaret in the sewing room, and sit again with us at dinner.'

Now there was no need for her to pretend, for she was truly surprised and pleased. Prettily she stammered thanks, and Tom left, uneasy with her for all her powerful attraction, and anxious to get on his way to Swinford. He missed the violent fight which broke out when Margaret introduced Mollie O'Flanagan to her future colleagues, to the intense resentment of Rachel. With cries of 'Papist whore!' and 'Poxy little Irish impostor!' she taunted Mollie until the Irish girl twisted her hands in Rachel's hair and dragged her down to the floor where they rolled, shrieking and clawing, until the brawl was stopped by the arrival of Cropper. Rachel was sentenced to a sound thrashing and a supperless bed, and Mollie found a warm defender in her rescuer, Skinner. Rachel had a dangerous rival.

Sir Martin heard of the affair; more unsavoury petticoat business. 'Women!' he growled at Lucinda. 'I am accursed by women in this place — quarrelsome, brawling, chattering women, always needing something, wanting something.'

She glanced up from the backgammon board that was their nightly pastime. 'You are too soft with them, you and Tom.'

'How so?'

'Well. At the first breath of rumour Tom runs off to Swinford to succour sister Anne. If sister Anne is beleaguered in Swinford by Cavalier deserters, is it not the price she should pay for being on the side of Parliament?'

'That is uncharitable. She is your sister, and she is with child. It is natural that Tom should be concerned for her safety.'

'She'll not be concerned for his,' Lucinda snapped back. 'If we are troubled or in danger Anne will not lift her little finger to help us — not one finger. You'll see.' She ignored her father's shrug. 'And as for Sue Protheroe with her feinting faints, Goodwife Margaret is easily duped by one like that.

Susan's faints can be put on and off like a courtier's smile, and, like any yard-cat, the lady claws her way back in, first into the sewing-room, and now she will be back at our table — first below and then above the salt. And from there 'tis but a flash of eyes, a sidelong glance, and a small jump into brother Tom's bed.'

'Tom knows the world — he'd not be so deceived,' her father answered, but without much conviction.

'That woman is a wanton, and a traitor. She knows no morals but her own.'

At times Sir Martin felt as though his daughter, not he, should be Governor of Arnescote. This was one of them. 'What would your punishment have been?' he asked.

Triumphantly Lucinda made the last successful move in the game of backgammon, and swept the pieces aside. 'For bedding with our enemy in this house? Her chained bones would be white by now, clattering on the gibbet on the hill, as an example to other ladies so inclined.'

He watched her face in the firelight, grim and set for all its prettiness, looking older than her years. This was the baby of the family, the loving, playful Lucinda, everyone's pet once upon a time. She had not been the same girl since her adventure to Oxford with Will Saltmarsh. She knew her power now, and the need for her to use it. As though reading his thoughts, she turned to him and said, 'I've had a hard upbringing in three years of war. I've seen some hard things done, and likely to see more. I fear weakness above all things.'

'When the time comes you will not find us weak.'

She sighed deeply. 'And when will that time come? Surely we need some great battle to end this war.'

———————

The streets of Swinford had been quiet as Tom and Will Saltmarsh rode to the Fletchers' house. The house itself was quiet, too, though lights burned in some front windows. The two men tethered their horses and approached the front door of the handsome house which had stood since before the time of the old Queen. In the portal a soldier was slouching, seemingly asleep, for he took no notice of their footsteps.

They had almost reached it when he woke with a start, a bottle falling from his hand to smash on the ground.

'Come, fellow, let me in,' Tom commanded. The sentry's answer made it plain that there would have been little left in the bottle.

'No, sir, I have my orders,' he said thickly, groping for his pistol. Will got to it first, grabbed it, and sent the man flying. He groaned as his head hit the corner of the doorpost, and lay immobile. With a word to Will, Tom took the pistol and cautiously tried the door-handle; it turned, and he went into the hall.

Clearly it had been a scene of riot, judging by the overturned furniture, the number of bottles and tankards which littered the table and court-cupboard, and the reek of tobacco smoke and wine hanging in the air. The handsome carved armchair in which the master of the house would preside over the meal was occupied by a dishevelled, very senior Cavalier officer, nursing a half-dressed sluttish young woman as they mutually toyed with one another, while his comrade snored on the floor. At the sight of Tom and Will he cheerfully waved his pipe.

'Welcome, fellow — come and drink.' He had obviously drunk down a fair number of tankards himself. 'More drink here, for m'friends!' he shouted, clapping his hands. At the signal a young woman entered bearing a bottle of wine. She was clearly respectable, though now very upset and frightened, her cap awry and wine-stains on her crumpled apron. The new arrivals were too much for her over-strained nerves. She broke into a wail, backing away against the wall.

'Have no fear,' Tom reassured her. 'Who are you?'

Her voice was very Welsh. 'I'm Emma, sir, Mistress Fletcher's maid — the lady of the house, that is . . .'

'Well, I am Mistress Fletcher's brother, Emma — Tom Lacey of Arnescote.' The drunken officer seemed to be trying to pull himself together enough to follow the conversation, without success. The girl Emma clasped her hands.

'Oh, dear God! Save me, sir — I thought you were another of these wild animals. They've all run away from the King's army, and these last two days they've been in this house, wenching and drinking and all. The place is like a pig-sty, indeed. There's others down now in the cellar, drunk as aldermen, and all the master's wine gone — and one of them tried to . . .'

Tom interrupted the flow sharply. 'Emma, where is your mistress?'

'Upstairs, sir, She's locked herself in her room.'

With a command to Will to get the invaders out of the house, by force if need be, Tom was off up the staircase. The landing was in darkness, but for the flicker of a lantern, an officer's hat and sword-belt flung down beside it on a coffer. Tom felt a sharp pang of fear — was he, then, too late to save Anne? A man's voice was audible from her bedchamber, of which the lock had been smashed. Pistol at the ready, Tom walked in. A young Cavalier officer stood there, very much at ease, jacket off, shirt unbuttoned, a glass of wine in his hand. Behind him, cowering in a corner of her wide bed, was Anne, her face as white as the nightgown which hid her five-months pregnancy. Her eyes met Tom's, hardly believing what they saw. For three years brother and sister had not met: and now theirs was the strangest of encounters.

He gave her an almost imperceptible nod of reassurance. Instinct told him to play this scene quietly and cunningly, with so much at stake. His opponent was older than himself, but still young enough to be dangerous, and of arrogant bearing, surveying Tom as calmly as though the situation were quite commonplace, even taking a sip of his wine.

Tom asked him, very levelly, 'And who may you be, sir?'

'I, sir? My name is Captain Geoffrey Black, an officer in the King's service. And you, sir?'

'I am Captain Thomas Lacey, also in his Majesty's service, and Staff Captain to His Highness Prince Rupert.'

'Indeed.' Black appeared impressed. Anne, who had been dumb with fright, took her hand from her lips. Tom knew that she was about to reveal that he was her brother. It was not his plan that she should, which he conveyed to her by a quick shake of the head. To Black he said, 'I order you to leave this house at once.'

Black took another swig of John's French wine. 'You are plainly unaware, sir,' he said loftily, 'that this house is for Parliament, and its occupants our enemies, yours and mine. My officers and I fought long and hard in the field for the

King's cause, to which you yourself are loyally subscribed. Are we not all of us entitled to the spoils of war?'

Tom bit back an enquiry as to why Captain Black had ceased to fight long and hard. To anger the man now might mean disaster for Anne and himself. He said, reasonably enough, 'This house is private, and you have no right to be here, in a woman's bedchamber.'

'We both have every right to be here, but I have the greater right, being here first. So go downstairs, good fellow — the rebel who owns this place has some good wine — and wait your turn.'

'This lady . . .' Tom began, driven to the need for revealing Anne's pregnancy. But the other had been tried far enough.

'Lady or not, she's mine — so away with you,' he snapped. To Anne's horror, Tom appeared to obey, going out of the room. Captain Black turned to her, smiling lazily. 'Now, my pretty rebel . . .'

But Tom returned, Black's sword-belt over his arm. He flung it at its owner. 'If there is no other way to save this lady from your unwelcome presence, then let us settle the matter honourably.'

Black looked astonished. 'A foolish young blade indeed. I was rightly known as the best sword in Lord Cleveland's brigade.' He drew the sword.

''Tis a pity you should bring shame on such a fine commander,' Tom remarked, taking off his coat and bowing formally. Black went out on the landing and Tom, with a backward smile at Anne, followed him.

The fight began at once, outside her door, a duel fought in a narrow, limited space. Soon they were on the stairs, moving step by step down towards the hall. A picture fell, dislodged by a sword-point, and crashed at the duellists' feet. As they reached the hall Tom backed into a chair, which fell over, causing him to lose his balance for a moment. Anne, watching from the landing, gasped, but he righted himself and lunged again at Black, who now had his back to the wall of the staircase. His riposte narrowly glanced off Tom's side, a mortal thrust if it had gone home. He retreated up the stairs, Tom edging up after him, both men fighting fiercely, stroke for stroke, until Tom was at last in a position to drive his point under the Captain's upraised arm. He gave a single bubbling cry as it pierced his lung, then dropped like a stone, and rolled down the stairs to lie at Tom's feet, motionless.

Tom bent down to make sure of what he knew already: the man was dead. A wholly unexpected pang of regret pierced him. He had killed a fellow-officer, even though a renegade one, a man in the prime of his youth; it was a feeling very different from inflicting death on the enemy in battle. Yet it had been in fair fight, and his sister's honour had depended on it — perhaps her life, and the life of her unborn child. What was done, was done. He threw a napkin from the table over the lifeless face, bloody froth on its lips.

Will and Emma had been watching the fight breathlessly. 'The place is clear, sir, the house and the cellar.' said Will. 'What now?'

'Go quickly to the coachhouse in the yard. Rouse old Jeffreys and bid him prepare the carriage. And you, Emma, pack what you need for your mistress and yourself.'

Anne was waiting for him at the top of the stairs, calm now. He kissed her, a kiss she returned.

'I should thank you for the demise of Captain Black,' she said. 'I had prepared for his end in a less gallant manner.' In her hand was a small pistol, a pretty toy. He wondered how far she would have got with it against the dead Captain, but nodded approvingly, saying, 'You were ever cool. So, I am to be an uncle. Well done, the Fletchers.'

'You have all the news?'

'Yes, we have all the news at Arnescote. That is why I am here. Now get dressed.'

Her eyes widened. 'Whatever for?'

'We leave here at once. I am taking you back to Arnescote with me.'

'To *Arnescote*? For what purpose? All I seek for Emma and myself is protection from your loutish friends, who in a proper army should be stripped of their rank and thrashed. I hope you're proud of the drunken rabble who call themselves officers of the King, yet were no better than a ranting, raping mob of cut-throats.' As she paused for breath she caught sight of Emma in the bedchamber, packing a cloak-bag. 'What are you doing, Emma?'

'Packing, madam, as your brother commanded me.'

'Well, stop!'

'Continue, Emma,' Tom told the maid. 'I cannot give protection from my loutish friends, Anne. That is why you are coming with me.'

'Arnescote is no longer my home,' Anne flashed at him. 'It is a Royalist house, held by my enemies.'

'Where is your husband? Why is John not here?'

'Because he is at the Parliament in London. I would not go with him because I prefer to stay here. This is my house.'

At last Tom let his temper slip. 'So you prefer to remain here in Swinford at the mercy of these cut-throats, and be delivered of your baby in the streets? For they'll have you out of this house, be sure of that.'

Emma was pleading, backing him up, terrified that after all she might be thrown to the wolves who had just been banished. 'Oh, madam, be wise and let us go to Arnescote, for the sake of your unborn babe. Let your brother take care of you!'

Anne's eyes shone mutiny, her chin was thrust out. '*No*, Emma. I will not leave this house. My mind is made up.'

Tom smiled dangerously. 'And so is mine. I'm taking you home — now.' With one swoop he gathered her up into his arms, heavy as she was, ignoring her struggles, kicks and protests. Shouting her down, he said, 'As Goodwife Margaret used to tell us when we were little, you were the one with brains and I with brawn. Well, tonight brawn wins. Now get dressed, or I'll dress you myself.'

Anne saw that there was nothing for it but to yield. Furious tears starting in her eyes, she said between her teeth 'I'll never forgive you for this, Tom — never, never.'

Or for saving your life and your child's at the risk of my own? he thought. What a sweet thing is gratitude. But he only said, 'You will.'

In the hall he paused, looking down at the still form of the man he had killed, and murmured to himself 'Here lies Captain Black, a dubious Cavalier, who fell whilst attempting to reduce a Parliamentary stronghold. Swinford. June 1645.'

CHAPTER TEN

Lucinda was restless, impatient, waiting for she knew not what to happen. Nothing violent and terrible, of course, but something to fan the smouldering fire of excitement in her. Arnescote, too, was waiting, she felt, armed and prepared, the old walls sensing the coming battle as a warhorse senses it according to the Book of Job: 'He smelleth the battle afar off, the thunder of the captains, and the shouting.'

Anne was waiting, too. Since the night Tom had brought her home she had kept markedly aloof from the rest of the household. Her presence at meals was an uncomfortable one, Sir Martin longing for their relationship to be as tender as it had been once, yet always repulsed by her cold disapproval. Lucinda flatly refused to speak to her. Tom knew himself unforgiven for having virtually abducted her from Swinford; all his efforts to lighten the situation were ignored. Margaret Goodwife was also unforgiven for having boldly repeated to Anne her father's words on being told that she wished not to give birth at Arnescote. 'The stupid graceless bitch will come to her senses, when the pains of her labour force her to cry out for Margaret Goodwife in her agony, as a frightened child will call for her mother.' What Anne most resented about this was that it would probably be proved true. Her only attendant was her maid, timid Emma from the Welsh mountains, a virgin with no experience of childbirth even as a witness.

One person alone was admitted to Anne's confidence. One might have known, Lucinda thought bitterly, that Sue Protheroe would worm and wriggle herself into friendship with someone who might be of use to her. Lucinda knew as well as if she had been hiding behind Anne's bed-curtains what had been said by that slimy trollop to soften up her cousin. Of course she had never been Captain Marsh's whore, only his victim, but then, enforced to keep his company, she had in spite of herself been impressed by his wise talk about matters of politics, and had come to feel that there might be right and justice on the side of Parliament. Then she would have glanced sideways at Anne, half-appealing, half-seductive, and Anne, in her self-imposed loneliness, would have turned willingly to this unexpected ally, prepared to give her the affection she much needed, in that house she felt to be so hostile.

Lucinda had a strong suspicion, too, that Sue would pick up information from Anne that could be passed on to the enemy, if opportunity offered. Filthy little spy; it would be a pleasure to see her kicking on the gallows.

Sewing listlessly, hardly seeing the stitches, she started suddenly at the rare sound, like a giant wheel slowly turning, of the great gate opening. She ran to the window in time to see a horseman riding into the courtyard. Who? A royal messenger — Rupert himself? Light-footed as a young deer, she was out of the room and down the stairs into the Great Hall, to hear her father's voice greeting the new arrival. It was Edward Ferrar, as impressively handsome as the last time she had seen him, on the night when he brought her father home wounded. A little older, a little leaner and browner, but still so charming to the eye that she felt a new stab of anger at herself for having been such a fool as to reject him in her silly girlhood.

Slowing her steps, she descended the staircase gracefully, though conscious of her hot cheeks, and wishing she had spent five minutes in front of a mirror. Edward came forward and kissed her hand as she curtseyed. Though he smiled, his face was immediately grave again as he turned back to Sir Martin.

'It is bad news, sir. There was a bloody battle fought this very afternoon at the village of Naseby, over the Northamptonshire border, and our forces are in disarray.'

His tone said more than his words. Sir Martin, sighing, bade him speak freely. 'My daughter is more than loyal to the King's cause, and has proved herself in the field.'

Lucinda listened to the tale Edward had to tell, the charm of his voice almost winning her attention from the dreadful import of his words. The King, against Rupert's advice, had been persuaded to march south and challenge Generals Fairfax and Cromwell in all their combined strength. The battle had been a disaster from the first trumpet call, ending in a general rout. The King had lost all his artillery, his carriages, his colours, and five thousand of his men, with many more taken prisoner. Almost as bad, the King's private papers, wholly confidential, had fallen into enemy hands.

Lucinda asked fearfully, 'Prince Rupert?'

'Safe. But in one sense he lost the battle for us, by going off to loot the enemy's baggage waggons. When he rejoined the King the tide had turned.'

On top of such news, Sir Martin dreaded to ask how Tom had fared. But Edward's answer was reassuring. 'Safe. I saw him riding for Ashby with the Prince.'

Lucinda asked 'Are the Roundheads close to here?'

'Who knows? They will reduce Leicester now, and after that ... they must ride south, towards Banbury, perhaps.'

'Well, we are ready for them,' said Sir Martin heavily.

———————

Through that summer and autumn of increasingly bad news, Arnescote waited. The Royalist cause in Scotland had gone disastrously wrong, in spite of the brilliant leadership of the Marquis of Montrose. Bristol had fallen, yielded up by Rupert, to the King's despairing fury. The royal correspondence seized at Naseby field had been gleefully published by Parliament, the King's private letters read aloud to the people of London, so that all knew of certain treaties he had tried to make with foreign powers to put down Parliament. He had promised on paper to grant Catholics full liberty of conscience, he who had protested often and publicly that he would never repeal the laws against Popery. His letters to the Queen, full of State secrets, were now known to all. The contents of one coach had done more harm, despondent Royalists said, than the battle of Naseby.

Yet Cromwell and Fairfax had busied themselves

elsewhere than Warwickshire. Perhaps they would not attack Arnescote, after all. Tom, riding home weary from a humiliating defeat of the King's cavalry at Rowton Heath near Chester, was infuriated to see, as he and Will Saltmarsh approached the castle, that it appeared to be no more defended than the humblest cottage. On the green by the church a few men he recognized as belonging to the Lacey garrison were playing football in the sun. The main gate of the castle, once so jealously guarded, stood open; no pennant fluttered from the flagstaff. He touched his tired horse's side, urging it to take him speedily into the courtyard.

'No patrol, no lookout, even!' he stormed at his father. 'The gate gaping wide, and the Captain himself absent — within doors, I see. What sort of defence is that?'

Sir Martin looked helplessly at Charles Pike, the troop's Captain, who had been conferring with him when Tom entered. Pike frowned, resentful at Tom's questioning of his authority.

'I gave Charles furlough to spend the day at Boyton,' Sir Martin said. 'He has an estate and a family to care for.'

'At a time like this? This is not holiday time. We are come to the moment when this castle must play its part in history. From every direction this place is threatened.'

'We see and hear no threat,' Pike said sullenly.

'Because you don't look for it!' Tom faced him across the table. 'There are two companies of Roundheads in Stow, and troops of horsemen on all the roads between Campden and Stratford. I myself had to creep round the side-roads by Swinford to get here unscathed. And they're good troops, too — Cromwell's men of the New Model Army, ready to fight.' He turned to Cornet Crane, who had been listening unobtrusively at a distance. 'Cornet, get the trumpeter, if he's not asleep — call the troop to their duty.'

As Crane hastily left, Pike glared at Tom, an angry flush rising in his face. 'By what right does Captain Lacey give orders here?' he demanded. Before either man could answer, Margaret Goodwife appeared on the stairs. Sir Martin waved her impatiently away, but she persisted.

'I think you should know, Sir Martin — Mistress Anne — Mistress Fletcher's waters have broken.'

The news was coldly received. 'Well, what of it?'

'Her labour has begun,' Margaret explained.

'That's as well,' said Tom. 'The sooner we get her and her child out of the castle the better.' His father nodded, dismissing Margaret curtly. Men! her reproachful look said. Men, caring nothing for the all-important, world-shaking things that happened to women . . .

Far off, in the grounds, a trumpet sounded its challenge. Tom's eyes brightened. 'What is the password?' he asked. Neither his father nor Pike answered. No password had been agreed upon, and their faces showed it.

'So,' Tom said, 'no password. There must be one, changed daily.'

Pike seethed with resentment. 'Sir Martin, who commands this troop?' he demanded. Tom thought his father appeared old, and driven beyond his strength, as he answered, 'The King has placed Major Lacey under myself, as Governor, to command all the troops at Arnescote.'

'*Major* Lacey. I see.' Pike was wooden-faced. With a token nod to Tom, he said, 'Then, sir, I await your orders.'

'The first and most immediate thing is to bring the outlying people in behind the walls. Every living soul — and their corn and hens and pigs, whatever they can bring. Then close the gate and place a lookout by day and night to watch every approach. We'll talk about skirmishers and patrols tomorrow. Well, be about it, Charles. We have not so many hours till dark.'

Pike left. He was prepared to take orders, providing he knew they came from an authorised person.

'So Bristol has fallen, or so we heard,' Sir Martin said.

'Yes. We lost half our men on the first day of the attack. Rupert was right to give in, and Lord Fairfax was gracious with his terms — we marched out with sword, pike and drums. Rupert was right to quit, but the King was mightily displeased. He ordered Rupert out of the kingdom, but the Prince came to Newark where the King now lies, and protested that he had been wronged. There was a right royal battle between them, I can tell you.'

Sir Martin sighed. 'So now we fight among ourselves. Is the war finished, then? Be straight with me, Tom — what do you think in your heart?'

'I think it is not. The King holds many great cities yet —

Newark, Chester, Oxford, York ... There are many houses like Arnescote not yet reduced, and there is a split in the enemy ranks between Presbyterians and Independents. The King hopes to raise a new army from Wales and the soldiers back from Ireland. He's not beat yet, father.'

'No, nor are we.' Sir Martin rose stiffly, lamer than he had been, Tom noted, leaning heavily on his stick. As he passed Tom he clapped him on the shoulder. 'Fine to have a brisk young spark about the place again,' he said. Tom smiled. It was good to be home, good to be doing something to defend it.

They had been watched and listened to. When Sir Martin was safely out of sight Sue Protheroe glided in, graceful and silent, her arms full of flowers bright with the glowing colours of autumn. Over them, she smiled at Tom. Gallantly he approached to take them from her; she startled him by rising on tip-toe to kiss him full on the lips, looking into his eyes searchingly, intimately.

'Oh Tom, dear Tom,' she breathed in that soft husky voice she knew well how to use. 'Welcome home. How much we've missed you. You're like a shield and buckler to this castle.'

Half-flattered, half-embarrassed, he answered 'This castle will need more than a shield and buckler before very long, I fear.'

'Whatever a poor weak woman can do for the defence, I will do it. You have but to command me, Major Lacey.' In anything, said her tone. Curtseying, she left him; yet another string to her bow.

One by one, the folk around Arnescote had taken refuge in the castle. From farms and cottages they came, bearing with them what they could: children in arms, a few treasured valuables in bundles, dogs, pigs, poultry, cheeses and hams. It was as though a new Ark opened to take in its cargo of refugees.

There were many who wept, some for fear of the coming terrors of war, some because they were leaving behind their homes. Humble shacks or comely small houses proudly cared for, all must be abandoned to the mercies of the soldiery. Fearful tales had reached them from places where there had been battles, tales of fires and destruction and land laid waste. At the castle gate, waiting their turn to enter, old Matthew Saltmarsh the smith and his wife Lilian looked back to their home, the smithy on the green. Neither spoke, but both knew the other's fear. Will, who had helped them with the cart full of possessions, watched them compassionately.

The last of the refugees was within the castle walls; the great gate creaked and rasped home, and was made fast. The light of the September day faded into sunset. Massive, steadfast, a fortified city, the castle loomed dark against the many-coloured sky, the two round bastion towers of its great gateway as firm as when they had been built four centuries earlier, their arrow-slits ancient ever-open eyes, keeping watch for the enemy. Above, on the battlements, two flags stirred in the light breeze, the Lacey standard and the red pennant of defiance.

Night fell. Outside, no sound could be heard from within the walls. But in Anne's bedchamber a loud and lusty wailing came from the cradle where her new-born son lay.

In the grey of early morning two men crept low, like snakes, to a sheltered spot where they could see without being seen. The telescope, invented almost half a century before, was still too unwieldy an instrument to have come into military use, but the eyes of the two men were very sharp and far-seeing, taking in every detail of the castle, across the valley between. Hannibal Marsh had been promoted to Colonel since his last attempt on Arnescote; his companion, Captain Leckie, was a hard-bitten soldier who had seen service abroad in the Thirty Years' War and at home in Scotland, fighting Montrose's troops, as well as in what he considered the soft, gutless realm of England. He was completely ruthless, cynical and unscrupulous.

'Aye,' he said with relish, 'that'll be a hard nut to crack, Colonel Marsh. That's a real solid castle for you. I'll need some of the big guns to knock down yon wall — demi-cannon or culverin at least, and a mortar wouldn't come amiss. All I've got with me now are a couple of wee pop-guns, four-pounders. The cannon balls will bounce off like peas.'

Marsh eased himself out of his uncomfortable position.

'I'm no artillery expert like you, Leckie, but I've seen musket-shot encased do some rare peppering.'

'Aye, that's so. If you can tease them out into the open you can have some good sport with case-shot. Iron nails are fine for that game.'

They talked of Cromwell's plans for other fortified houses. The siege guns would be brought to Arnescote, but not yet; for the time being the attackers would need patience. Marsh reminded Leckie that the castle held a Roundhead sympathiser, Anne Fletcher, presumably being held hostage — 'and she a daughter of the house turned to a godly woman'.

Leckie snorted. 'A turncoat, eh? I'd blow her out. It's the best way with that ilk.'

Marsh shook his head. 'John Fletcher's a Member of Parliament — we must needs be politic.'

'Politic! I've no time for the Parliament. All hot air and blabber.'

'They are there in London by God's will — and they are our paymasters still, remember.'

'General Cromwell'll soon change that, I'll warrant.'

'Well, I have sent for Fletcher to come and take out his wife. For the moment you'll keep the place sealed up — those are your orders.'

Leckie had no choice but to accede — reluctantly, for he liked nothing better than a good, noisy siege with plenty of smashing of stones and bodies and fine looting to follow.

Tom was unhappy. His scanning of Cropper's books had revealed to him an alarming lack of defence supplies. The castle was filled with people, but there was not enough food to keep them for long. Powder stocks were low, nor was there anything like enough artillery. The place was as ill-prepared as it could be, and his father's protests that there had been no help with such things only confirmed him in his belief that in his absence nothing substantial had been done to defend Arnescote. Sir Martin, for all his bravery, was living in another age, not this new brutal one. Arnescote was at the mercy of at least one company of Roundheads; not the earnest Puritans of early days, but tough trained soldiers of Cromwell's New Model Army, with plenty of resources and few scruples.

There was only one thing for it: someone must be sent to Oxford for help, to the Governor, Colonel Legge. But who was it to be? Cropper volunteered; Tom thanked him, but refused. Serious, conscientious, a man of figures, not of action, the steward would be quite incapable of such a hazardous errand. There remained Will Saltmarsh, too good a soldier to be spared from the pitiable garrison, and Lucinda, heroine of an earlier adventure, both in the secret priest's room and the underground passage. Tom would not hear of Lucinda's going, and Sir Martin pointed out that if the castle were reduced to rubble there would be very little need for a hidden exit.

'I say we send Hugh Brandon. He'll do it. I trust that boy with my life — and since the war began he's for ever pestering me for some valiant commission.'

Cropper was not enthusiastic. 'He's very green in such matters, Sir Martin, and frail of constitution.'

But Tom mused, remembering the boy's slight build and musical voice. 'He speaks well, and could pass as a maid, which would double his chance of success. It seems to me we have no great choice. And besides, he has a good memory, and will need to carry no written word.'

That afternoon, disguised in an old plain gown of Lucinda's, with a shawl over his head, Hugh entered the secret passage and made his way into the bleak, despoiled church. Fortunately it was empty of soldiers. Those who had begun to surround the castle were some way off, cooking a meal in the open air, accompanied by singing and shouts. Hugh gave them a swift glance as he emerged from the church, then hurried down the path, holding the basket he carried close to his side and trying to keep himself in as small a compass as possible. But, when he was almost past the soldiers, one spotted him, hailing him with a shout.

'Here, girl, come here.'

Hugh ducked, pulling his shawl further over his face and quickening his steps.

'Be not bashful!' encouraged the man. 'Come sup with us, and you shall have good company, the company of the saints.'

Untempted by this alluring invitation, Hugh broke into a run and was soon beyond catching. The soldier looked after him with disgust. 'These country whores,' he told his comrades, 'lack instruction, but by God's will they shall soon get it.'

Tom, from a high window, watched the escape, and smiled approval. Such lady-faced lads often had as brave a spirit as old campaigners. Hugh was on his way, fleet-footed, to Oxford. Help might not be long in coming — if Hugh got through safely, and if Legge could spare men. Now there was no more to be done for the present.

Restless, anxious to pass the time, he went to Anne's bed-chamber. She was asleep, the baby quiet. In a chair by the window Susan Protheroe sat sewing. He went to the cradle and inspected the small red crumpled face on the pillows.

'So you're the guardian of our little Roundhead,' he said. She put her finger to her lips.

'I am here while Anne's serving-woman is at her meal. Don't wake your sister, Tom, she is quite exhausted.'

'I'll not wake her. I came to see my nephew — who looks to be a very ordinary small piece of humanity. They say that bearing babies is harder work than spawning them.'

She kept her eyes on her work. 'As to that, how should I say?' Then, after a pause, 'You still love your sister? The war has made no difference?'

'Of course I love her. War and politics are pishwash. I tell you this, cousin, I not only love Anne but I admire her for her strong belief, for she is loyal to her husband, and that I count a great virtue in a wife, or any woman, come to that.'

'Loyal! I see, now you seek to turn the blame on me again. I thought I was forgiven.'

Tom laughed softly. 'For what? For coupling with a Roundhead a century ago — or so it seems? I'd forgotten it.' He had not, but needs must be civil when the wench was behaving herself so meekly.

Sue sighed. 'Lucinda has not forgotten, or forgiven. She has not spoken a word to me since. She still condemns me, yet I had no fair trial. What was near forced on me, I consented to for the general easement of the whole family.'

Tom raised an eyebrow. 'Certainly it gave the gallant Captain Marsh some easement. You went a-whoring for your own gain, and were discovered. That was your fault. Now, I've known as many women's beds as the tassels on that fringe.' He was looking up at the valance surrounding Anne's four-poster. 'Yet I was never caught. You turn your head away, cousin? You think I corrupt the child?'

Tom saw the process of thought behind her still, quiet face as clearly as through a pane of glass. He waited, amused, for the outcome.

Very softly she said, 'Would you blame me if I confessed a secret of my heart? I love my cousin.'

Tom affected ignorance. 'What blame is that? I love her, and I am her brother.'

'I speak of that brother,' Sue almost whispered. Tom could not help a smile creeping over his face. What a strategist; yet she had met her match. He took her gently by the shoulders, turning her towards him.

'Cousin Susan, I do not blame you. As a soldier in battle must use his weapons to his best advantage, so a luckless lady, such as you, must use the weapons God has given her, as best she can. A good body, a pretty face, and a cunning brain.'

She was twisting in his hold, protesting that she meant no guile, that she had only spoken truth. He silenced her with a finger touched to her mouth.

'Hush. A cunning brain, I said. When it comes to battle, those two bright eyes are worth two cannon any day. I'll warrant they've won you many a bedroom siege ere now. Oh, I've seen them flash and fire, and read the invitation in them many times, dear cousin Sue. But this siege you lose. I am impregnable in this castle.' He dropped a light, affectionate kiss on her cheek, a kiss she understood perfectly, and knew that her siege of this particular fortress was indeed hopeless.

Very well, then. If the other and greater siege were successful, the siege of Arnescote, she had plenty of ammunition left.

CHAPTER ELEVEN

Anne was leaving the castle. The women of the household were shocked that she should be up from her bed so soon, for in normal times she would have lain in for a month, after which she would emerge to be churched, with all due ceremony. Now, as though she were only a peasant, the poor lady must be on her feet and jolted about in the carriage that would take her to Swinford. John had hurried to her as soon as he heard the news, and a special request from Sir Martin to Captain Leckie had secured permission for her to leave.

Pale, and tottery on her feet, she descended the stairs into the Great Hall, John solicitously beside her. The family waited, surrounding Sir Martin in his chair. Anne went to him and kissed him.

'Thank you, father, for the trouble and sweetness you have shown me. I had not expected such treatment in this house. Would you see your grandson?' She took the baby from Margaret and uncovered its head. Sir Martin, on the verge of tears, laid a trembling hand on it.

'Bless you, child,' he said, 'and I pray you are untouched by the sad distempers of these times, and that one day you will come to live in peace and happiness in this sweet island, a loyal subject of your lawful King.'

Anne and John looked their displeasure. But Anne bent again to kiss her father before she left the room, pausing to embrace Tom and Sue on her way. Lucinda stared coldly at her, and received a cold stare back. John hesitated.

'Sir Martin — Tom — I would have a word in private . . .'

Sir Martin turned his head away. 'I have no wish to speak to you, Captain Fletcher.'

'But I am no longer a soldier,' John pleaded. 'I am back in the Parliament — I could speak for you, help you . . .'

'We don't need your help, and we have no words for you,' Tom said. 'Go with your wife.'

Unhappy, John followed Anne. The dividing sword had carved out a chasm between the two who had been boyhood friends which would never again be crossed.

Colonel Marsh was happy to welcome the Fletchers back to their own house, admire the infant, and enquire into the state of things at the castle, particularly its defences. Indignantly Anne refused to answer anything that might mean trouble for her family. Marsh instantly switched his questioning to Emma, who, nervous and inarticulate, yet managed to give him a very fair idea of the numbers of the garrison, the quantity of the food stores, and, to his great interest, the position of the barrels of gunpowder, in the cellars, and the store of grain, by the clock-house. Anne heard her babblings with horror, and Marsh's parting words.

'If we can starve Arnescote into surrender, that will be the best end for all. But if I am forced to take the place by storm and battery against a stubborn resistance, then by the orders of Lieutenant-General Cromwell no quarter may be given, and the malignant defenders pistolled and put to the sword, their land sequestered and the castle brought to utter ruin.'

It was no more than Anne had known in her heart, yet the ruthless speaking of it shocked her more than anything had done since the struggle had begun. She had taken John's side so completely that she had never paused to imagine her father and brother dead, cut to pieces, perhaps, or savagely mutilated by cannon-shot, the servants murdered, the women raped, the treasures of the house seized on and greedily carried away. For Anne, though still idealistic about the Cause (because John was), had no illusions about the kind of men who fought for it: Hannibal Marsh among them. His words were pious, but something far from piety lurked in his eyes, and she was afraid of it.

'Oh, how I hate this cursed war,' she said to John, when

Marsh had left them. 'And I hate that man. Who knows what mischief he will make out of the tale he got from Emma?'

That night, while all in the castle slept except for the pacing sentries, the darkness was ripped by a bright flash followed by three brief explosions and then one loud enough to shatter the ear-drums, while a blinding glare lit up the garden of the back courtyard. Three forms that had been crouching scuttled away like shadows.

In the grey early morning the scene Sir Martin surveyed was a dismal one. What had been a good store of grain was now reduced to a scatter of corn, burnt beyond saving, sodden with the dousing of the fire, and mingled with brick rubble from the damaged walls. Something lay, very still, under a sack. The small boy who had been employed to scare away the rats from the corn had been killed outright by one of the hand grenades flung with deadly accuracy into the powder store; Arnescote's first war victim. Utterly downcast, Sir Martin turned away.

The three Laceys met together to talk out the cause of the disaster. There had been treachery, for someone knew exactly where to place the grenades. But who? Nobody had left the castle since the arrival of the enemy at its gate but Hugh Brandon. Not Hugh, said Sir Martin; he would not have spoken even under torture.

'Susan Protheroe — that two-faced whore bitch at her old tricks?' suggested Lucinda.

'No,' Tom said. 'She has not had the opportunity.'

'Then it was Anne, of course,' Lucinda said triumphantly, wanting it to be Anne. '*She* has left since they came. It must be Anne.' She stared out her father and brother, both startled and alarmed. 'Anne is a sly, cunning woman, and she's hard as you are soft with her. She would sell us in the name of God without a thought. She is utterly corrupted.'

Tom shook his head. 'She was close confined. She could not have known . . .'

'All those chattering women were always in her room, fawning on her and petting her. She could have learnt from them.'

Tom was beginning to agree. 'Aye, she was ever change-able and obstinate. Their evil preaching may have turned her sweetness into poison.'

Sir Martin was deeply grieved and troubled. That their betrayer might have been Anne, sweet Anne, his favourite child, ready to sacrifice her family and her old home for the Roundhead beliefs she had married; he could scarcely believe it, yet the possibility was there . . .

'She must be killed,' Lucinda said vindictively. 'Although she is my own sister, I will kill her myself.'

Into the shocked silence came Cropper, long-faced, bearing an account-book. Solemnly he read out to them the details of devastation. Only three parts of a barrow of powder left; all the corn gone, no bread but what was in the ovens — half a pound per man, less for the women and children. The cook had suggested she might make pease pudding bread, enough for two more days, and two barrels of puddle ale remained. The prospect was not cheerful.

'We should discuss with Charles Pike what terms we should accept of the enemy,' said Tom, despondently.

Sir Martin rounded on him. 'Surrender this place? What a dishonour to the name of Lacey!'

Lucinda snapped. 'Dishonour to be betrayed by a vile turncoat, and then starved? I see no dishonour, only shame — shame to my sister. We are not Romans, to commit some bloody family suicide.'

'No,' her father echoed sadly, 'we are not Romans. No; it seems our time is nearly come.'

The sharp blast of a trumpet-call pierced the morning air: the alarm. Men scuttled to the battlements, Tom and Charles Pike to the fore of them. Tom scanned the valley, shocked to see a party of cavalry trotting towards the castle, not two hundred yards from the green. So the Roundheads had reinforcements — the attack was coming even sooner than had been thought. If they only had a cannon, Tom thought — just one. At his command, Pike gave the order for those manning the battlements to prepare to fire their muskets.

The cavalry were dispersing now, cantering up towards

the enemy bivouacs, and Roundheads were emerging from cover, coming to meet them, waving their hats and cheering. Tom cursed silently and then aloud. With this extra force, what chance had the Arnescote defences?

Suddenly, to his incredulous delight, the riders flung off the orange sashes which proclaimed their allegiance, and with sword and pistol fell on the Roundhead besiegers. Shocked, taken by surprise, they turned and ran, impervious to Leckie's furious rallying-cry, scattering like chickens before a fox. Tom laughed aloud, the men on the battlements joining him. Then came a new welcome appearance; down the road, coming towards the village, there advanced a body of foot-soldiers, armed with pike and musket, among them women, flanking and guarding three big farm-carts.

'A feint! A feint!' Tom shouted to Pike. 'The cavalry came to clear the way for these, and I warrant they carry shot and provisions!' The cavalry officer had turned away from the fleeing Roundheads and was riding towards the new arrival, saluting its officer. Pike stared, uncomprehending, at Tom, who shouted 'Hold your fire! hold your fire! open the gate.'

'What, sir?' Pike was sure his commander had gone suddenly mad. But he gave the order, and as the gate creaked open the relief party, horse and foot, converged on it in a body, the cavalry turning as they reached it and galloping off, their mission accomplished, pursued by enemy musket shots, none of which reached their targets.

All but the Cavalier leader, who galloped into the courtyard, his second-in-command at his side. Dismounting, he shook hands with Tom, who had recognized him afar off: Edward Ferrar, glowing with exultation.

'Well, Tom! This was well done, was it not. Get those carts unloaded — they carry good store of powder, match and shot, and food besides.'

'Had you heard, then —?' Tom began, but the flying figure of Lucinda had reached them, cheeks pink with haste, and smudged like a kitchen-maid's, alight with excitement to match Edward's and Tom's. Edward bowed over her begrimed hand as though she had been the Queen, and held it for a moment afterwards.

'I'm come to stay, if you'll have me,' he said. Her eyes told him the answer. 'I do believe,' she said, 'God has sent you to us.'

Edward smiled. 'God, and this brave fellow.' He drew forward one of the foot soldiers and turned him face on to Lucinda. It was Hugh Brandon.

'Hugh!' Impulsively Lucinda flung her arms round him. Danger and campaigning had not driven the blushes from his face; he turned a girlish red and hung his head as praises rained on him from Lucinda and Tom. It was easier to risk his life dodging the enemy than to listen to compliments, for shy Hugh.

Edward Ferrar, too, had a streak of shyness. Lucinda's welcome had been warm enough to encourage any admirer, but when he found her alone, writing, he hesitated to disturb her, much as he wanted her company. But her smile and the alacrity with which she put down her pen reassured him. She had washed her face and changed her gown in his honour, and there was a radiance about her that had been extinguished in the recent dark days. He thought she outshone all the beautiful women in the Lacey family portraits that looked down from the panelled walls.

'Are your men safely settled?' she asked, and when he replied that they were, and all the food and ammunition safely stowed away, said, 'Are they your men — your own troop?'

'No. After Naseby many regiments were broken up — these are part raised in Ireland, and part in Yorkshire. They're far away from home.'

'Yes. But I think they should be happy not to have the war clawing at their own walls.' She hesitated, then braced herself to say what she could not voice to her own family. 'It sounds faint-hearted, I know; but how can this house and all of us escape destruction?'

'Only by fighting — and winning.'

'Yes . . . Oh, we are in such a sea of dangers and distractions — sometimes I have such strange and dreadful dreams.'

He glanced at the paper before her. 'Is that what you write down?'

'No. I have begun a history of the siege of Arnescote, so that, whatever becomes of us, people may read it in the future and know how brave you were today. Listen: Chapter the First. "Love, Honour — Aimez, Honneur." '

'But that is our family motto. Did you know?'

'Indeed I knew. Your forebears carried it on their banner, at Hastings and Creçy and Agincourt, and now you yourself at Arnescote. I know all your family history, you see — our steward instructed me in it, and schooled me in it most diligently before . . .' She stopped, embarrassed. Edward helped her out.

'Before we did not become betrothed. That's five long years ago, long forgotten.'

'Truly forgotten, Edward?' He could not tell from her tone whether she hoped that it was.

'No. But let it be buried. My father never did understand Sir Martin's withdrawal with no plain reason, when all was so far in train. But we never pushed the matter further; we wished no quarrel with the Laceys. Yet it seemed strange.'

Lucinda took a deep breath. 'What was told your family was a sham — a false tale. It was a most wicked and shameful thing to do —'

'And most unlike your father.'

'But it was not my father — he was most grievously vexed and distressed. It was *my* doing — all mine.' Having made up her mind to confession, she launched into every detail of that five-year old story: her flight, Tom's finding of her in the church, her punishment by whipping. Edward, at first astonished, now looked deeply hurt.

'Was the thought of marriage to me so fearsome and hateful to you, then?'

'No! It was not you, Edward, as God is my witness. I didn't know you — a few hours at the masque at Hampton Court, surrounded by all that rout, that was all I knew of you. I was an unruly churlish creature, still half-boy, half-girl, lacking a mother and rather spoiled. I loved no man, I had no feelings of that sort, I was not yet made a woman . . . can you understand me, Edward?'

Edward tried his best to understand. Perhaps it was not possible for a man fully to take in the strange whims and humours of girlhood. And he was not quite sure where this was leading. Cautiously he answered, 'Now we are all changed by time and war, so let's bury and forget the past.'

But she was not ready to do that. 'It can't have been a deep hurt to you. I was no great beauty at sixteen, and you the son of an earl and handsome, surely much pursued by beauties and their mothers.'

Edward admitted that it was so. They were playing a game now, and he understood the rules. Her next question would be, 'And yet you are not yet married?' It was.

'Don't press me,' he said, happy to see the disappointment in her face. Then she was in his arms, his lips against her ribboned curls, saying 'Yet do — do press me.'

She answered, softly, 'Then I do,' and stayed where she was, very satisfied to be there.

'You have made full confession to me, so you shall have my truth. That day at Hampton Court, amid all that rout and noise, I lost my heart to a girl of sixteen of no great beauty. It was pierced as never before, and never since.'

Held close to that heart, she whispered, 'Oh, Edward, will you ever forgive me?'

'Yes, on one condition — that you marry me. For my love for you has grown tenfold — no, more, much more.'

It was quite ridiculous that she should burst into tears at this happiest moment of her life, but she did, as though she had still been that foolish girl of sixteen. Through them she said, 'Yes, Edward, of course I'll marry you — I will, I will, I will. I love you.' It was their first embrace, all the sweeter for five years of waiting. Now Lucinda knew that she was a woman indeed, and rich in happiness beyond measure.

The word spread through the castle with amazing speed, for in a time of so much fear one piece of good news was an event to be shared and celebrated. In the kitchens they chuckled and speculated and made bawdy jests; Edward's troop, manning the defences, drank good health and long life to the betrothed pair. And Sir Martin's delight was hard to conceal, but he managed to conceal it long enough to keep Edward and Lucinda in suspense, just for a little. Long-faced, he said 'Children, you put a new burden on a poor Governor already overburdened. Had you not thought of that? As if there were not enough...'

They exchanged anxious looks, and Edward said (prepared to go on his knees if necessary), 'I beg you, sir, for your permission and your blessing.'

Sir Martin let his true feelings come out in a warm smile. 'You had them before — now you have them again, most willingly. God give you all the happiness He is able to give, in these desolate times.' He took the right hand of each and held them in his own. That moment made up to him for countless hours of trouble; in his happiness he was too charitable to say to Lucinda, 'I told you so. If only you had listened to me ...'

Tom, entering, took in the scene. 'I hear news of another war — and a victory — and woundings!' he cried, dramatically.

They all looked at him, startled. He explained. 'Cupid's arrows deep bedded in two hearts. Dear sister, and dear friend, soon to be dear brother — what a lightening in such a dark sky! When are you to wed — when all this is over?'

Lucinda had not thought about it, but suddenly she knew the answer. 'Tomorrow.' Edward, lost in her eyes, did not quarrel with such haste. 'Tomorrow, if you wish it.'

Cropper and the Reverend Butterworth appeared, in answer to a summons neither understood. Their faces were a study in astonishment when Sir Martin announced 'Lord Ferrar and Mistress Lucinda are getting wed tomorrow.'

Butterworth faltered, 'Happy news indeed — but the banns must be read on three successive Sundays.'

'Pish-wash, Butterworth,' pronounced Sir Martin.

'But the law —'

'I am the law here. The King has graciously given me full powers as Governor of this place. The wedding will be tomorrow, and that is good Arnescote law.'

Cropper had been making mental lists. 'Then must I get the spousal papers, the dowry agreements, and — but then Lord Walmer is not at hand ...'

Sir Martin thumped the table. 'Stop fussing and bleating, Cropper. When this war is over there may be no gold for dowry or estates, or even stewards. Forget the papers. We'll make the marriage here, in the Great Hall.'

Lucinda touched his arm. 'No, Father. You should respect the wishes of the bride. I would be wed in our own church, where all the Laceys have been brides for many centuries.'

Whatever the others had thought of, it was not this. 'It is under the guns of the enemy,' protested Tom. Lucinda laughed.

'Do you think they'd shoot a bride and bridegroom? Those men out there are Englishmen, not Turks. They have the same God as we have.'

Butterworth was by now thoroughly frightened. If he should be seen by the enemy to be conducting a service in that church whose 'profane ornaments' he had denounced to please them . . . 'Foolhardy, most foolhardy, Mistress Lucinda,' he stammered. 'There is no proper furniture now in the church, no altar cloth — '

'I think the good Lord who looks down on all of us will forgive us that small omission. If you do not have faith that He will protect us from harm, Master Butterworth, doubtless my father, who has special powers from the King, will marry us.'

'How will the enemy know that you are a bride?' Tom enquired.

'First we shall ring the bell. Then, I shall be wearing my bridal gown — I have it in my closet from . . . from before. I have not changed in shape so much, except in certain places. Margaret and Hannah can fit it for me tonight.'

Sir Martin smiled wryly at Edward. 'I warn you, this lady will need a strong bridle. Now — there will have to be a ring — had you thought of that?' He produced from his pocket a small leather purse, took from it something that shone in the palm of his hand. 'This was your mother's, Lucinda. It has been on my person since the day she died.'

Lucinda held out her hand, tears starting to her eyes, and her father put the ring on her wedding finger. For a moment nobody spoke. Then Sir Martin removed it and handed it to Tom in its case.

'Take it, if you're to be groom's man. This would please your mother greatly.'

Her portrait gazed down on them, young and bright and pretty, with a look of all three children. She had not been smiling when it was painted, but in the flickering candle-light it seemed that she smiled now.

The Roundhead sentry on look-out could hardly believe the evidence of his own eyes as he saw the great gate of the castle open, and a most unwarlike small company appear. Lucinda, shining like a star in white and silver, smiling and composed on the arm of her father. Butterworth, black-suited because his cassock was gone, trembling like a jelly. Tom and Edward, dressed in their best, a couple of fine swaggering young blades. After a long stare, to make quite sure that he was not seeing visions, he shouted to the gunner to fetch Captain Leckie.

When Leckie arrived the party had been in the church for some little time. He waited by the gun, expressionless, until the gunner gave notice that they were coming out.

'Is the gun loaded?' he asked.

'Aye, sir. With case-shot.'

'Unload it with some care. Leave in the powder and the wads.' Astonished, the gunner obeyed, looking questioningly.

'We don't shoot brides on their wedding day — even Royalist ones,' Leckie informed him. The bridal party were on their way towards the castle gate. 'The piece is gauged, sir,' the gunner told Leckie.

'Then you may fire it.'

At the harmless explosion, followed by a cloud of dense black smoke, Butterworth flung himself on to the ground. But Lucinda looked to where Leckie stood and he swept off his hat and bowed to her.

Smiling, she dipped him a curtsey. From the battlement, even from the enemy bivouacs, a cheer went up, as the bride disappeared through the gate of her home.

'Now,' Leckie said, 'put back your piece and load with case-shot.'

As Sir Martin raised his glass to the newly-wed Viscount and Viscountess Ferrar, a great bang which this time was not harmless was followed by a whistling scream and the shattering of glass, as the case-shot demolished one of the windows of the Great Hall. From outside came a terrible cry of a man mortally wounded. The floor by the table spread with its simple wedding-feast was scattered with deadly rusty nails.

There had been the briefest of armistices; from this moment, there was to be no quarter.

CHAPTER TWELVE

Warning having been served, the celebrations were curtailed. Lucinda went away to her rooms to replace the bridal gown in her closet in exchange for more practical garb, better suited to what promised to be a hectic time in the September heat.

There had been no opportunity for music and hymn-singing at her ceremony. The only hymn which sounded in those parts on that day came from without the castle, and the voices which upraised themselves were the rough ones of the men who sat at a distance on the warm grass amongst their tents and cooking fires, cleaning and examining muskets, filling powder flasks, honing sword blades, eating or talking easily together.

Their leather coats were uncomfortable wear for this weather, but no order had come allowing them to divest themselves of them. As if to remind them that bodily inconveniences were but small concern in this life, an under-officer whose boast it was that his voice was as melodious in song as penetrating in the bellowing of orders struck up the well-known hymn:

> Now, Israel may say, and that truly;
> If that the Lord had not our cause maintained,
> If that the Lord had not our right sustained,
> When all the world against us furiously,
> Made their uproar, and said we all should die.

Continuing their tasks, or their idling, the men joined in, some sparked by religious fervour, others merely because soldiers the world over have always enjoyed a rousing chorus:

> The raging stream's most proud and roaring noise,
> Had long ago o'erwhelmed us in the deep;
> But lov'd be God, which doth us safely keep
> From bloody teeth, and their most cruel voice,
> Which, as a prey, to eat us would rejoice . . .

'Hear the damned hypocrites!' snorted Sir Martin, driving the ferrule of his stick hard against the ground. 'If there's any appetite for eating, it is they who would wish to make a meal of us. By God, they'll find no dishes tamely served if they come seeking 'em here.'

Tom, Lucinda and Charles Pike, who stood with him above the main gate of Arnescote, between the twin towers, could not but exchange a smile at the old man's choice of metaphor. But the smile was fleeting, and Tom's voice was grim as he said, 'All the same, their task would be the harder had we but at least one cannon for use against them.'

Sir Martin made no immediate answer, scanning the landscape with his glass. Presently he handed it to Tom and pointed with his stick towards a bank between two big trees. Tom obediently trained the glass, and saw what he had so far missed: a pair of five-pounder sakers, almost hidden from view by the drooping, leafy boughs. Their Roundhead crews lay about them, inert in the cool shade.

'Those fellows do not seem much to treasure what they have and we have not,' Sir Martin said. 'Had I the best use of my limbs, I know that I should be making a move to relieve them of 'em, before the time comes for them to rise from their swinish slumber and put 'em to use.'

Tom and Charles exchanged an open grin.

'A hint may serve as a command,' said Tom, and the two dashed off to muster others into speedy action.

Not much later, a party of men was concealed among trees and bushes beyond the church. They were some ten in number, with Edward Ferrar in command. Corporal Jackman and Dick Skinner were close behind him. All were lightly dressed for swift movement, carrying only pistols and daggers.

116

At a little distance further, Will Saltmarsh, a canvas bag in his hand, peered from behind a separate bush towards the place where the two cannon stood, their crews still recumbent. He turned and waved to the others, bringing them creeping softly but purposefully from their cover.

Hymn-singing still charged the air. The afternoon hung warm and drowsy. The Arnescote men crept forward, closer and closer to the guns.

With a last brief dash, they were upon the four idling soldiers, who heard them coming, but without time to do more than widen their eyes in terror at the drawn daggers and the resolute eyes of the men wielding them.

'Hold hard, friends!' the sergeant-gunner cried urgently to Jackman. 'We are King's men.'

'King's men?' Jackman turned enquiringly to Edward.

'How so?' Edward demanded, glancing about to make sure that this was no time-saving ruse.

The sergeant's anxiety was genuine, though. He swallowed hard. 'Captured with our guns at Naseby, sir. Forced to throw in our lot with them or die.'

'Then it's simple,' Edward told him. 'Join us, or die.'

'Join you, Milord Ferrar,' came the ready assent. 'I know you, sir, and your cause is ours.' His men growled approval.

'Then keep your voices down and help swiftly. We need these guns.'

'Pardon, sir, but there's only the one of 'em worth the taking. The other's got a wheel off, as you see, and no pin to replace it.'

'Then we'll make do with one, but make sure no one uses the one we leave. Will!'

Will stepped forward and withdrew from the bag he carried a long, thick nail and heavy headed hammer. He slipped the nail into the vent of the defective saker and prepared to hammer it home. Edward stopped him.

'Wait till we're on the move with this other before you make a clatter. As soon as you've driven it hard home, come fast after us.'

'Aye, sir.'

The others were already attaching drag-ropes to the second gun and the little waggons of match and shot, helped willingly by the gunners. They heaved them round and over the bank, and set off with them in a brisk trot towards the castle. Edward nodded to Will, who raised his hammer and lost no time spiking the stationary gun before hurrying after the rest.

No shots or commotion followed them. They seemed to have got cleanly away with the raid, which was as well, for the uphill haul to the castle was long and gruelling. And there remained one more task to be performed before they were back behind the walls. It was one that Will Saltmarsh had volunteered to do, to the surprise of Edward who had hesitated even to tell him it was intended.

'If any man has to burn our smithy down, sir, let it be me. I'll make it blaze in the cause of depriving the cropheads of cover to come creeping upon us from. That, my old father and mother will manage to comprehend, but they would weep sorely for to see it go for any other reason. What with our daft Sam over there alongside the cropheads ...'

He broke off and shook his head. Edward clapped his arm. 'Good fellow. Go to it, then. The blaze will be a further diversion for us to get that cannon the rest of the way.'

Within minutes the last of the hymn-singing from the Puritan camp had died away, replaced by drumbeats and shouts as the smithy was seen to erupt in flames. Will had made sure of his work and had caught up with the gun party as they heaved their burden the last of its way. They had been observed by now. Out-of-range musket and pistol shots were directed harmlessly at them, while a party of running men, led by a sword-waving Captain Leckie, chased after them.

The great gate of the castle opened at their approach.

'On to the battlements?' asked Edward of Tom, who was waiting to congratulate them.

'Give 'em a first taste from here,' grinned Tom, and the men wheeled the gun right round to point back the way they had come. The captured gunners needed no urging to load it with case-shot. Lucinda, who had come out to watch, ignored Tom's order to go inside, but stuffed fingers into her ears as the fuse glowed near the touch hole. Muskets on the battlements above rattled as the pursuing Roundheads closed on the castle.

'Fire!' Tom ordered.

The gun went off with a roar which was all the louder for being within the stony gateway. Although only a small cannon, its spread of shot — a mixture of musket balls, nails, small scraps of iron and even stones — was enough to bring down several men and make Leckie curse aloud and clutch his slightly-wounded arm. A spattering of musket fire from above forced them to run back the way they had come and behind the smithy, now thoroughly ablaze. The castle gates clashed to and its occupants cheered, as the raiding party and gunners began manhandling the weapon up to the battlements.

'The first rule of a siege,' rasped Colonel Marsh, 'is to out-number the besieged. That we do — about six to one — not to mention that our cause is in the name of God.'

He glared round the officers assembled in the hut which had been appropriated by the Parliamentary officers for the headquarters and mess. 'Lieutenant Truscott, you will lead the assault on the trench they have dug round the castle.'

'Yes, sir.'

'You will take it by the pike and lay faggots for other men to cross. Instruct your people that they shall be neither tame nor sparing with the malignants. This place has been a thorn in our side too long.' He gave a dismissive gesture. 'You all have your orders. Go and prepare.'

They rose to troop out. It was next morning, the weather promising another hot day. Marsh and several others had come up in the early hours with more musketeers and pike-men and a heavy culverin, able to fire fifteen-pound shot more than a mile. It was at present being set up on a timber foundation, alongside another of its kind. Further forward, a mortar was being secured on even stouter foundations, its wide mouth, angled skyward at forty-five degrees, waiting to swallow the huge powder-filled ball which it would lob high through the air above any wall, to burst beyond.

Leckie was the only officer who had lingered behind in his colonel's presence.

'Sir,' he responded to the raised eyebrow of enquiry, 'have I no rôle to play in the assault?'

'A sorry rôle you have played so far — the place reinforced without loss, a gun snatched from under your nose. I think if your part were reported to the Lord General I should lose my command and you your head.'

'I request the chance to redeem myself.'

Marsh half-smiled, half-grimaced. 'Very well. You may lead the Forlorn Hope. You will place a petard on the main gate while we attack from the other side.'

If he had thought the other would blench at hearing his suicidal task, Colonel Marsh was disappointed.

'Most willingly, sir — with God's help.'

'You'll need more than a psalm to get Him to carry you through this time.'

As Leckie left the hut he recognised the truth of this. His task was to lead a small party of men up to the very door of the castle, carrying with them a gunmetal canister, containing pounds of gunpowder and mounted on a stout board which had to be hooked or nailed into position before its fuse was lit, to cause it to blow a great hole through the entrance. Forlorn hope, indeed, of achieving the objective, let alone getting away again alive.

Leckie's scarred face contorted into a kind of smile. It was not even as though he believed in the God who might carry him through. Soldier's fortune, or lack of it, would be what told for him. He was determined of one thing: that petard would be placed and exploded, even if he himself fell in the doing of it, so that Arnescote could be invaded and its cursed folk put to the sword.

Both God and the King were being invoked in the hall at Arnescote, where Tom had been giving his lieutenants orders for the defence. Sir Martin closed the proceedings with a little speech, at which all uncovered and lowered their heads.

'Let us pray to our just God for victory, and though we perish in the work, we shall rest satisfied that we have preserved our faith and honour untainted. Should all others desert us in this resolution, we will not fail ourselves nor our duty to our King and Country. God save the King!'

'God save the King!' from them all.

The only person present who did not echo the sentiment was out of their sight, in the shadow of the gallery. It was night now, and she had listened from there to the discussion of tactics and dispositions for next dawn, by when it was unanimously agreed the attack would be ready to commence. Sue slipped quietly away, and slid down shadowed passages to tap at the door of the small room in which, as he heard her, the Reverend Butterworth thrust out of sight the bottle from which he had been swigging and picked up his book from the table before going to the door.

'Who is it?'

'Mistress Protheroe,' she hissed low. 'I need your help.'

He turned the key and she came in quickly. He began mumbling something about proffering spiritual assistance, but she cut him short.

'I am sore afraid. The Roundhead army has brought great guns up against the house, 'tis said, and by this time tomorrow all will be rubble and a charnel house for our dead bodies.'

Butterworth's blubbery lips trembled, as he asked, 'Are you ... sure of this?'

'I heard Tom Lacey say so in as many words not five minutes past. Sir Martin and the others are speaking of surrender. I am thinking that may be all very well for gentlemen, but not for womenfolk, nor for priests ...'

'Dear Lord! I fear you may be right.'

'You a preacher to a malignant family, and I only a poor female relation, both of us treated by these proud Laceys like servants. Yet to be found here by the Roundheads and thought to be sympathisers with that weakling king ...'

'You are right, Mistress Protheroe. I am a man of God, yet handled like any servant.'

'... They and their arrogant disdain. What loyalty I have tried to give them has been spat back in my face. Why should you and I be slaughtered like innocent lambs for being thought part of them and their conceit?'

'Why indeed? But what is to be done?'

'I ... have a friend or two amongst the Parliamentarians, as so have you, I think. When they were here before we treated them with respect, and they will recall it.'

'I fear the first to enter will settle for us without giving us chance to make any such reminders.'

'Exactly so. But have you not still the key to the little

121

wicket gate by the laundry — the way you used to pass through to the church?'

'I have it still,' he said, taking it out of a drawer and showing it.

'Thank God for it!' She took it from him swiftly. 'It will be our salvation. In the small hours of the night, when it is full dark, we will go out by that gate.'

'But the reb ... the Roundheads will kill us.'

'Dress not in holy garb, but in some plain, dark fashion. They will not kill a brother and sister ...'

'Brother and sister!'

'... As we shall represent ourselves, who are known to their commander, and come with information about the defences of the castle.'

His watery eyes glittered with understanding, and he nodded. She turned to leave.

'Be ready after midnight strikes, Master Butterworth ... And no more liquor meanwhile. Temptation is a sin, and best removed.'

She went quickly, leaving him dumbfounded. She hurried away — but not too quickly for Master Cropper, who chanced to see her come out, to follow curiously after, and see her satisfy herself that the key did fit the wicket gate. Cropper limped away, to seek out Jackman, and they talked for some time before parting, nodding agreement.

When midnight at length struck, Sue went again to the gate, where Butterworth immediately joined her. The key was inserted again and turned, but no sooner had the gate swung open than figures loomed out of the blackness. Susan was seized and a hand clapped across her mouth before she could make a sound. Butterworth's only utterance was a low, gurgling cry as blood swamped his lungs from the knife wound in his back.

Jackman wrenched the blade free and wiped it roughly on the priest's cloak.

'That's the way to deal with traitorous rats,' he told Dick Skinner, the companion who had lain in wait with him since nightfall. 'As for this whore, take her to the cellar and put her in chains.'

Mumbling and crying, Susan Protheroe was dragged

122

away. Jackman paused only to kick the priest's body before following after.

The early morning brought, first, a single culverin shot, which hit the parapet of the defensive trench before the north battlement, as a sample of what was to come; and second, an emissary from Colonel Marsh, demanding surrender. He was sent packing with a defiant reply; and then the battle was on.

From the battlement, Edward watched the advance of musketeers and swordsmen into the park, where they went to ground behind a bank, halfway up the slope towards the castle, in order to load their weapons. Edward saw Marsh, the only one on horseback, wave a signal to them, at which they rose again and came on, some of them clearly still struggling with the laborious loading process. He shouted to the Irish greencoats and Yorkshiremen lining the parapet of the trench below, 'You may fire your muskets.' It was an advantageous blow to strike first, and several Roundheads fell before their own muskets were even fully charged.

Dick Skinner, the marksman, began firing selectively from his chosen post on the battlements. Beside him crouched Lucinda, loading one musket for him while he aimed and fired the other. His shots began to take steady toll. The attackers visibly wavered, until forcefully urged on by their commander, Lieutenant Truscott, and Colonel Marsh.

Their morale was shortly lifted by the discharge of the ugly mortar. Its huge explosion sounded behind them, followed by a banshee screaming as the great projectile arced high in the air, aimed to strike the castle. It fell short, but the damage it did in consequence was more serious than intended, for it hit the trench, close to where the saker gun had been repositioned on a mound. The violent explosion shattered the gun and hurled its crew in several directions, leaving one of them impaled, screaming, on one of the spikes forming the pallisade.

Colonel Marsh needed no glass to see the lucky effect of the shot. He jumped down from his horse, calling to his trumpeter to blow the charge, and ran uphill to take place behind a line of pikemen, under Ensign Salisbury, who were moving up the rest of the slope at a panting trot. Skinner, aiming at Salisbury, who bore the flag, missed, but one of the pikemen fell.

The musketeers reached the trench first and leaped in, to grapple hand to hand, clubbing with the butts of their weapons in the confined space. The pikemen arrived soon behind, their fourteen-foot, steel-headed pikes striking terror in the defenders. It needed only a few to be seen to be skewered for most of the rest to throw down their arms and run.

After the pikemen came the bearers of faggots, to bridge the trench for the main body of invaders to swarm across, whooping triumphantly. The closer they came to the castle walls, the harder it became for Skinner and the others to fire at them, having to lean far over to take aim, exposing themselves dangerously to counter-fire.

In her haste to keep Dick supplied, Lucinda's fingers fumbled her task, making him wait impatiently for her. Down in the kitchens, meanwhile, all was bustle and urgency as Mrs Dunphy and Minty, instructed by old Matthew Saltmarsh, melted lead in cooking pots over the hottest fire, to pour it into moulds and then hissing into cold water, to be scooped out with a ladle as rounds of shot, and poured into a bag for the kitchen boy to run with to the battlements.

Seeing a fresh danger, Dick Skinner sent the lad scurrying back with new orders, which set Rachel and Hannah tipping boiling water into a wooden bucket to carry between them across the lawn.

A group of pikemen had cast their weapons aside and were heaving at a ladder, which they were endeavouring to hook on to the wall. It caught, and a man swarmed up. Lucinda raised the musket she had just been handed to load and clubbed him hard with its butt. He fell away, but others took his place. She called Rachel and Hannah to hurry, and they were in time to empty the boiling water over the climbing men, sending them tumbling away, screaming. Dick and Lucinda seized the chance to thrust the ladder from the wall; but another was being set up not far along, urged by Ensign Salisbury. Dick levelled his freshly-charged musket, and shot him dead.

Thick though the fighting for the northern battlements was, the eastern side's defence had not been neglected. Charles Pike was in command there, and when he saw a group of men with Leckie at their head, carrying a heavy burden as they stumbled towards the shelter of the walls, he knew what their business was. Although two of the party fell, the rest came on unscathed and were soon out of view from above.

'They're fixing a petard to the gates,' Pike yelled to Moresby and Bates. 'Quick — with me!'

They ran together towards the gates, intending to throw them open and tackle the raiders before they could complete their work. But they were too late — the fuse was already sizzling. As Pike and his companions raced forward the explosion sounded hugely, sending splinters of wood and metal hurtling in. Pike and Bates were killed instantly, Moresby pierced agonisingly in the stomach.

Tom Lacey, who had just then run from his father's side after reporting the overall situation, saw what had happened. He saw through the acrid smoke cloud that a great hole was gaping in the gate, and knew that it wanted only moments before attackers would come clambering in.

He turned to the surviving defenders at that side of the wall.

'Back! Back to the house!' he yelled.

They obeyed, their numbers reduced by now to little over a score. As they ran, the petard party, shaken and deafened by the explosion of their own making, scrambled through, swords in hand, followed by other men with pistols or swinging muskets by their barrels for use as clubs. Colonel Marsh joined them as they stood peering about.

'What is it, boy? What the devil's happening?' demanded the astonished Sir Martin, to see Tom and his men come running into the house.

'They've blown the gate,' Tom gasped. 'They're through.'

'Are they, by God!' Sir Martin exclaimed. He threw his stick aside. 'Hand me my sword.'

Grimly, Tom took the big weapon down from where it hung on the wall. He placed it in his father's grasp, and all there turned to face the doorway.

Marsh's shout came to them over the din of fighting. 'I

call you to surrender, Sir Martin Lacey.'

Sir Martin smiled grimly, and shouted back 'Come on! Let's see your mettle, Colonel Marsh.' Fighting men, attackers and defenders burst through the open door like a tide. Tom shouted to his own men to retreat into the house, then to his father to come in from the steps, where he stood, alone, a terrifying figure, slashing and flailing with his great sword, limping from side to side, cutting down two Roundheads before he and Marsh came face to face. A slashing blow from his sword laid Marsh's cheek open from eye to chin. Sir Martin laughed, and in that moment a Roundhead sword pierced his side, running clean through his body.

He fell without a cry. Tom dared not waste time trying to help — he knew a mortal wound when he saw one. In one move he was inside the house, slamming and locking the door against the attackers.

'Back, back, all of you, to the stairs!' he shouted to the men in the Great Hall, and beckoned to Edward and Lucinda to join him. Lucinda, white-faced and blood-spattered, asked, 'What of Father?'

'Don't speak . . . listen.' Tom raised his voice over the thundering of sword-hilts and musket-butts on the door. 'Lucinda, take Edward down to the cellars — show him the secret way. Edward, you are to go to the King and tell him Arnescote died for him.' Lucinda gave a great gasp, clutching Edward's arm. Edward held her tightly.

'Tom — no — I cannot,' he said.

Tom snapped, 'It's an order,' and Edward, pulling Lucinda with him, ran off, leaving Tom to face the triumphant invaders who now crashed in through the beaten-down door, Marsh, his face pouring blood, at their head. As they rushed towards Tom he held up his hand. Marsh stopped, holding his hand up in turn. Tom reversed his sword, offering the hilt to Marsh.

'As Governor of this place, I hereby offer you the surrender of Arnescote Castle. I pray you show compassion to the survivors.'

'On behalf of God, King and Parliament I accept your surrender. But on my own terms.' Tom shrugged, in no position to dictate *his* own terms. Everything was lost; all that was left to him was to maintain his dignity.

In the cellar, Edward was moving away the last of the wine-barrels, revealing the secret door. Lucinda rapped on the lever-stone, and they watched a dark hole slowly gape open.

'There,' she said. 'The air is fresh enough — your candle will not go out. The passage leads into the church, and from there you may go along the trees and down the hill. Her voice broke. 'Safe passage — God keep you . . .'

'My dear beloved wife.' They clung together, kissing, murmuring, unable to let go their hold on each other in what might be their last embrace.

'I could come with you,' she whispered, hoping that even now he might agree. There was nothing for her at Arnescote, and it would be better to die with Edward than to face whatever might be her fate if she stayed behind. But he gently detached himself from her arms.

'No, you must stay. Be valiant — strong, as you were today. I will come back — you have my promise. *I will come back to you.*'

He was gone, leaving her only darkness to stare into. A verse came into her mind — that she could remember such things, at such a time!

> We shall grow old apace, and die
> Before we know our liberty.
> Our life is short, and our days run
> As fast away as does the sun . . .
> All love, all liking, all delight
> Lies drowned with us in endless night.

Farewell, Edward, my love and my husband; the jewel I flung away when I knew not its value, now lost to me again. For the first time that terrible day Lucinda sank down and gave herself over to a flood of tears.

The conquerors must not see her thus. When the worst of her grief was spent, she began to push the casks back into position, hiding the door. It was a relief to have something to do, anything. Then, slowly, willing herself to appear calm, she went upstairs, through the cellar exit that led into the courtyard. A horrid sight met her eyes. Dead men lying in distorted attitudes, men with dreadful wounds being tended by their comrades; fallen rubble littered the ground, from holes knocked in the walls — and among it, a square of cloth shot through and through, but still recognizable as the Lacey flag, fallen from the battlements. She picked it up and cradled it in her arms as though it had been a hurt child. The motto had survived intact: *Virtus et Veritas*. But what had been a chevron argent, charged with five mullets gules, was gone, shot through and through; and of the three silver crosses paty only one remained whole on a tattered fragment of purple ground. Brave emblems, brave colours, savagely destroyed by men who bore no arms. *Virtus et Veritas* — what had they done for Arnescote, in the end?

Lucinda thought of old Lord Verney cut to pieces at Edgehill, his severed hand still clasping the King's standard, emblem of what he had died for. Virtue and Truth: they had not saved Arnescote.

Still nursing the flag, she entered the hall. Roundhead soldiers were everywhere, seeking what they could find in the way of loot, pulling open cupboards, rooting in chests. One was chopping away with a knife at a long oak table of Tudor date, richly carved, standing on legs each in the shape of a Chimaera, half-woman, half-monster. He had already hacked off the breasts of the figures and was busy mutilating their noses. Another, wavering on his feet and clutching a bottle, was reeling from one family portrait to another, addressing them facetiously.

He paused in front of one of the earliest portraits, a crudely-painted stiff figure in ancient armour, glassy-eyed and heavy-bearded.

'Don't give me such a sullen look, insolent fellow. Would you insult a soldier of Cromwell's New Model Army — would you, sir? Have at you.' He thrust at it with his sword, ripping it across, a savage new tear across the dark old paint. The gesture raised a laugh from his comrades. Lucinda ran forward.

'Please, please do not damage the paintings! That is Sir Robert Lacey, who fought for England at Creçy.'

A drunken laugh answered her. 'Did he, now? Sir Robert Lacey who fought at Creçy? Well, he's a brave enough fellow, never squawked when I cut him. And *I* fought at

Edgehill and Marston Moor and Newbury and now at Arnescote, so who'll limn a picture of me, Mistress?'

Lucinda stood her ground, staring him down. Suddenly he lunged forward, grabbing at her skirt, then advanced on her and tugged at her bodice. As she fought and screamed, another soldier pinned her arms behind her back. Brutally they dragged her dress off, tearing buttonholes and gussets and seams (only the value of the fabric mattered). 'Let's have these sparklers too', the second man said, and yanked at one of her long pearl earrings. She shrieked as its hook tore at her ear. There was nothing for it but to detach the jewels herself, before her ear-lobes went with them. Furious with pain and outrage, she cried 'I'll tell your officer and have you shot.'

The drunken one made her an ironic bow. 'You can tell old Noll Cromwell for all I care. Clothes and trinkets are ours, but not the ladies' virtue, for we are godly men. That's Noll's rule.'

Stripped to her shift and petticoats, the Lacey flag still held to her breast, she ran for the staircase, to the mocking laughs of her despoilers. On the way she met a man bearing an armful of her dresses.

Colonel Marsh was highly pleased with his conquest of Arnescote. his slashed face bandaged, he sat writing his report to Parliament, which made the most of his own powers of leadership. An interruption arrived: Leckie with reports. There had been some looting in the house, he said.

'And why not? Let the men take what they will. They fought well and deserve the fruits of the victory God has given them.'

'The prisoners, sir — what are your orders?'

'Lacey and my Lord Ferrar are to be close confined.'

Leckie coughed. 'Ferrar is missing.'

'Doubtless slain. Never mind him. All Papists and Irish, men and their whores, to be shot or put to the sword forthwith. The others, disarm and let them begone where they will. There's no more war for them, and we have enough mouths to feed already. I am writing my report on this day's work, Leckie. I have mentioned your action, and I hope you may expect promotion.'

Leckie looked modest, not an easy feat. 'It was little compared with your own exploits,' he said. 'And there is a woman without who seeks a word with you. Ragged, but with a genteel voice, and claiming an old friendship with you.'

Marsh frowned, but agreed to the woman's admission. She was Susan Protheroe, in rags and tatters, filthy-faced, her hair hanging like string, and on her wrists and ankles the red abrasions of chains. Yet with this desreputable figure came in a waft of seduction; Marsh, in spite of himself, looked on her with attention.

She gushed, clasping her hands prettily. 'Oh, my dear Hannibal, what a blessing to see you again!'

'Who treated you thus roughly — my men?'

'No, my own family. When I knew you were here I tried to escape last night, but they caught me and threw me in the dungeon, and put me in chains.' Pathetically she held out her raw wrists.

'I would have shot you in their place,' Marsh said dryly.

'Oh, I pray you, Colonel, see that these malignant Laceys have their faces ground into the dirt!'

'Sir Martin is dead.'

She smiled. 'Good news indeed. A pity his spawn aren't in the same way. When you bring down this place I will dance on the rubble.'

Marsh could well believe it; even he was slightly shocked at the woman's whole-hearted malice. He did not quite believe anything she said, he certainly did not trust her; and yet she had an appeal, an undeniable appeal, and she had been useful in the past, in more ways than one. He turned to Leckie. 'Escort this lady to my room. Bid one of the women attend her, and see that all her wishes are cared for.'

He returned to his report, smiling.

———————————

At last, as though in obedience to some decree of Fate, the brothers Saltmarsh, Will and Sam, came face to face. It was in the kitchen, where Sam and two other Roundheads came strolling, with a leather bottle passing between them and looking for food. Will and his father, with Minty, Mollie and the other kitchen women, were doing their inexpert best to treat the gaping stomach wound suffered by John Moresby, huntsman-turned-trumpeter.

130

Mollie raised her head, in time to see one of the soldiers swing his sword and cut down one of the hams hanging from its hook.

'Drunken beast!' she spat, to her companions' horror. 'Haven't you made enough trouble for one day?'

'Another Irish whore,' remarked the third soldier. 'Take her away.'

The other man seized her and bustled her struggling out of the kitchen.

Sam Saltmarsh, whitefaced and tensed from the fighting, was emboldened to deliver a kick at his brother, sneering, 'How are the mighty fallen now, my precious brother, who kicked me, knocked me down, called me coward?'

'And so you were,' returned Will. 'And a turncoat rogue into the bargain — a crop-eared Puritan.'

Sam whipped out his sword. 'Try me now, then, brave brother — now that the power of the Lord is in my arm to avenge evil.'

He made a wild lunge. Will skipped aside and grabbed a cleaver from the kitchen table.

'Sons! Sons!' old Matthew cried, but they took no notice, beginning to circle one another, looking for an opening. Sam's longer blade gave him the advantage, and, clumsy though he was, he spiked Will through the arm, causing him to fall. Sam would have lunged down at him to finish the work, had not his Roundhead companion seized him, shouting that there had been enough blood spilt for one day.

'Let me go!' Sam ground. 'Leave me finish off this poxy malignant brother of mine.'

His father stepped forward to thrust his face at his, saying, in a tone which caused Sam to turn even whiter: 'As Adam cursed Cain, so do I curse you. I curse you from the earth which hath opened her mouth to receive thy brother's blood from thy hand. From this day on, Sam Saltmarsh, you are no longer son to me.'

Recovering, Sam spat. 'Nor are you any more my father, nor he my brother. For sure, you both have rotten, stinking hearts within you. If you are for the King, then you are for the Papists, and you must perish in hell-fire.'

His companion, still holding him, jerked him away out of the kitchen. After some moments' shocked silence, Matthew

131

turned to help his other son to his feet.

''Tis their preachers, with their strange words,' Will told his father. 'They have driven him mad. He's not our Sam any more.'

Matthew shook his head sadly. 'He was a good lad when he was young . . .' He sighed. 'Come, let us look at that wound.'

All Papists and Irish, men and their whores, to be shot or put to the sword forthwith. That was what the Colonel had said, and Leckie was quite happy to comply with the order. Nine of them were rounded up, in varied states of misery, dirty, hungry, weary, some wounded. Among them four of their poor doxies were taken, including Mollie O'Flanagan, who had done no wrong but to raise her voice in the kitchen. Firmly they were lashed to stakes driven into the ground and lined up against the castle wall, to be targets for thirteen musketeers. Some wept, some prayed, some struggled in their bonds, others could only tremble with eyes tight-shut: a more wretched bunch of victims could scarcely have been gathered.

Leckie, not even glancing at them, gave the nod to his sergeant, who raised and dropped a red handkerchief, the signal to fire. A volley rang out, and seven corpses hung limply on the stakes. But two had escaped being hit, and in their desperation broken free. A man and a woman, Mollie, were scurrying away. Leckie and the sergeant were after them like terriers after rats. A couple of blows, and they were felled to the ground. Then colonel and sergeant systematically cut them to pieces where they lay. The girl screamed before she died, so long and agonisingly that it seemed the noise would penetrate the old stones of the castle wall, and linger there for centuries.

Death, in its calmer form, was within the castle. In the great chamber, on what had been his marriage bed, Sir Martin lay, covered by a canopy of velvet, all but his face. Pale, stern and peaceful, it resembled more closely than ever in life the stone effigies in Arnescote Church, Sir Thomas of the last century, Sir Martin from King Harry's time, his grandfather who had fought at Barnet field for the Kingmaker. Lucinda remembered how she had crouched among their tombs the night she ran away from marriage with Edward. Now they were defaced, those noble effigies, their praying clasped hands knocked off, noses flattened, the small animals couchant at their feet destroyed as being the images of devils. Sir Martin would have no such effigy, perhaps none at all.

Around the bed stood Lucinda, Tom and Hugh Brandon, the singing-boy lost in tears, the others dry-eyed. Their grief was not allowed privacy; two Roundhead soldiers guarded the door, Leckie hovering behind them. Tom knew what it imported. He bent to kiss his father's ice-cold cheek, as did Lucinda.

'No Lacey ever died better,' Tom said. 'I think he would not have wished to live beyond this day.'

Leckie approached. 'Sir Thomas, I pray you come with me.'

Tom nodded. Turning Lucinda's face up to his, he smiled and kissed her. She watched him go then, between the two guards. First father, then husband, then brother had been taken from her. Was there any more to lose?

CHAPTER THIRTEEN

Colonel Marsh was a strict enforcer of the letter of the law. Whatever sympathies he might have had with the bereaved Laceys were not to be allowed rein. In any case, he had few. To him they had become objects, losers, to be treated as the rules of war dictated. When the coffin of Sir Martin was laid in the Great Hall for the household to pay their last respects on the day following his death, Marsh watched impassively as the weeping, bewildered servants filed round it. The Hall was a sorry sight, all its glory gone. Where rich tapestries had hung, only the poles that had held them remained, crooked and broken; the family portraits were gone, the panelling slashed, the floor bare of furniture. Cropper was glad his poor master could not see it.

Old Minty, half-crazed, raved out, and was instantly grabbed by a guard and dragged towards the entrance. Will Saltmarsh stepped out of the line with a protest; the guard struck him across the face, making him reel and almost fall. Several women, including Margaret, screamed, at which Marsh looked up sharply.

'Silence! or I'll have you all whipped. Take them out, corporal.'

Tom and Lucinda had entered in time to see, and Tom came hastily forward.

'They merely wish to pay their respects, Colonel Marsh — this house and my father was their world. You must allow us all to shed our tears.'

'I am not unmindful of that, Sir Thomas. But unruliness —'

'Unruliness is the order of the day, Colonel, if what I see of your soldiers is the measure of it.'

134

Marsh would cheerfully have had them all turned out and whipped, but against Tom's authoritative voice there was little he could say. He gave the sign for the servants to be left alone, then asked, 'Are we ready to proceed to the church?'

At Tom's nod of agreement, four troopers stepped forward to raise the coffin. Tom cried 'Stop! Walter, Stephen, Will!'

The three left their places and went to stand at each corner of the coffin. 'Family honour, Colonel,' Tom said pleasantly enough. Marsh made no answer, merely nodding impatiently for the cortège to move off. As it left, Corporal Turner, at the door, turned his musket on the servants who were beginning to follow. 'Not you people,' he snarled.

As the bearers of the coffin moved slowly towards the church, Tom saw an unfamiliar carriage halted in the courtyard. There were no occupants, but two of Marsh's men were loading one of the family portraits into it from a handcart. Others could be seen inside. Leckie, beside the cart, was taking money from a strange man in city clothing. Fury boiled in Tom, who halted the procession, shouting, 'Colonel Marsh, what are those vultures doing?'

Marsh suppressed his annoyance that the transaction had been seen. 'It is the natural course of war, Sir Thomas, as you are well acquainted.'

'God in Heaven! Not at this moment, with my father not yet laid to rest? Have you no common decency?'

'I have my soldiers to feed . . .'

'Damn you, get them out of my sight!' At Marsh's signal, Leckie sped away with the money he had been given for the portrait of Sir Martin's grandmother, a maid of honour to Queen Elizabeth.

In the shell that had been Arnescote Church a few soldiers lay about the floor, passing a flagon of wine from one to another. At the entry of the coffin they scrambled up and came to attention. Marsh ordered them out, seeing the look in Tom's eye. Another person was present, a middle-aged man darkly habited and grave of face, whom Marsh introduced as Master Skerritt, the army chaplain, a man of God. In his hand he bore something which the Laceys had never seen before: the New Directory of Worship, concocted to replace the Book of Common Prayer, not yet legalised but soon to be so. Seeing it in his hand, Lucinda and Tom

135

guessed what was going to be said. Both held their own prayer books, the Liturgy as approved in the reign of King James the First, familiar and beloved. Brother and sister exchanged a look of agreement. When Skerritt began to read, in a flat matter-of-fact tone, 'We are gathered here in the sight of God . . .' Tom interrupted.

'Colonel Marsh, I object to this man whom I do not know speaking from a book I do not acknowledge.'

'I object also,' put in Lucinda. Marsh pointedly looked past her, addressing Tom. 'Sir Thomas, the words of the Directory of Worship will soon become familiar to all when they replace the common Prayer Book by *law*. As for Mr Skerritt, he is a man of the cloth . . .'

'A man of the Presbyterian faith, whom we do not recognize,' said Lucinda. Walter Jackman, behind her, spoke up.

'Aye, a rebel churchman, in our spiritual home. Let him preach in his own place — he's not wanted here.'

'Your name?' Marsh snapped.

'Walter Jackman.'

Marsh ordered his corporal to remove Walter, and in spite of Tom's violent protest, he was taken out. Tom, now furious, stepped forward and addressed those present, Roundheads included.

'As my father's heir, and briefly master of this estate, does anyone question my prerogative to conduct this service in my own way, since it only has meaning for some of us present? Is there anything in the law of this land that denies a man the right to bury his own father?' Nobody spoke. Tom turned to Marsh. 'This was my father's church, sir. I would thank you kindly if you and your men were to leave.'

Marsh hesitated. He was in no position to enforce his wishes. As a compromise, he asked, 'May I not pay my respects also, to a gallant loser?'

'The first mark of respect, Colonel, is that you allow this service to be conducted in the manner your gallant adversary would have wished. Surely that is a courtesy you will not deny me.'

Marsh answered stiffly 'The nature of war, sir, is that the rules are laid down by the victor. I have already made concessions.'

'May I respectfully remind you that you have not won a war but a minor skirmish? The King still sits on the throne of England. He has not surrendered — we are still his subjects in the sight of God!'

'A matter of debate sir. This is not the proper time or place — and may I respectfully remind *you* that you are my prisoner?'

Tom took a deep breath. Slowly, patiently, in the silence, he said, 'Allow me this simple wish, Colonel — that I read this service, in my father's honour, in words he would have understood.' He raised his prayer book. 'Then do what you will with me.'

Skerritt scowled. 'You cannot allow this, Colonel.'

Susan spoke up priggishly. 'Mr Skerritt is right.' Marsh rounded on her. 'What, you have an opinion?'

'Aye, do you, Mistress Protheroe?' Tom asked, sarcastically. Attacked from both sides, she had no answer. The interruption had given Marsh time to think, what to say to put himself in the best light.

'I am not an unreasonable man, Sir Thomas, though you may judge me so. I am merely a soldier doing my duty. Were it my own father, I would feel as you do. Conduct the service how you wish.'

Skerritt slammed shut the Directory of Worship, and marched out of the church, making as much noise as he could to register his sense of outrage. When he had gone, Tom opened the prayer book and began to read, in a voice uncertain with emotion.

'I am the Resurrection and the Life, saith the Lord: he that believeth in me, though he were dead, yet shall he live. And whosoever liveth and believeth in me shall never die . . .'

The simple service proceeded, Tom's voice recovering strength as he went on, the three who stood at his side joining in softly at moments. Lucinda fought to restrain her tears. The last time she had stood at a graveside was at her grandmother's funeral service, which, though she had been young at the time, came back to her in all its poignancy, so different from this scene: the church in all its ancient beauty, undespoiled, a full congregation of mourners, flowers and hymns and the playing of the organ, now ripped out and chopped up for the soldiers' firewood. Now all that was left from that time was the wall monument which had escaped the bludgeoning which had destroyed others — a simple marble rondel containing a bas-relief bust of her mother.

Lucinda tried hard not to disgrace herself and interrupt Tom by noisy weeping, biting her lips and twisting her hands together painfully. Sudden help came with a noise at the church door; looking up, she saw Anne and John Fletcher enter, black-clad. The sight dried up her tears instantly, as a hot wave of anger went through her. She watched Anne open a prayer book (so she still possessed one!) and join almost inaudibly in the service, under the disapproving eye of John. Some very un-Christian thoughts went through Lucinda's mind, including the words 'canting bitch' and 'stiff-necked crop-eared strumpet', which, if inaccurate, served to relieve Lucinda's feelings and allow her to keep her dignity.

Tom pronounced the Blessing, then sank to his knees beside the coffin. His whispered words were unheard by any: a sacred vow to avenge his father's wrongs, to bring his enemies to justice, and to restore the fortunes of Arnescote. He had never experienced such an intensity of feeling as in making this, his promise to a dead man.

Marsh's patience was worn out. Even as Tom knelt, a heavy hand grasped his shoulder. He rose, knowing his last moment of freedom was over. 'Am I not permitted to see him placed in the tomb of his ancestors?' he asked, already knowing the answer.

'It will be done according to your wishes, Sir Thomas. You will come with me now.' Marsh signalled to four troopers, who lifted the coffin and moved with it towards the door. A hole had been dug in the churchyard, where Sir Martin would lie apart from his forebears, the grave unmarked by any memorial. But one day, Tom vowed inwardly, he should be restored to them, laid with all due honours in his rightful place.

For the first time he noticed the Fletchers, and greeted them sarcastically. 'Sister — brother John — I am pleased you could spare the time to attend our father's funeral.'

Anne's face convulsed with tears. Tom continued lightly, 'I believe I'm to be your new neighbour at Swinford, in my prison cell. Is that not so, Colonel Marsh?'

John touched his brother-in-law's arm. 'Tom, my friend,

understand it was not our design. Look on your sister, and forgive us. Take the Covenant and the Negative Oath, and start your life anew, I beg you.'

Tom met his pleading look with a steely one. 'And forfeit my soul, John? You know me better than that. And Anne knows me best of all. I had rather incarcerate this feeble body than my immortal soul. Look after Lucinda, Anne. She is more in need than I.' Marsh was urging him towards the door. John made a last attempt at reconciliation, calling after him, 'Tom!'

Tom called back over his shoulder, 'Sir Thomas now — squire of Arnescote.'

Lucinda followed him out of the church. About to pass Anne she stopped, looked her full in the face, and said, 'You are not welcome here, Anne.' Her tone was icy.

'You silly girl,' she returned. 'He was my father too!' But Lucinda did not turn. If anybody was going to look after her, as Tom wished, it would not be her sister.

Tom was taken, under heavy escort, to a waggon which would bear him to Swinford. Cropper managed to have a word with him, assuring him that he had made an inventory of all items pillaged, and that the family papers and a few valuables were well concealed. Commending him, Tom asked that the deeds of the castle might be brought to him for safe keeping. That was important, he said; not knowing, at that moment, how important.

As the waggon began to jolt away Tom watched another vehicle on the move: a cart, with a cage inside it, carrying away the family dogs, driven by a rough fellow. Money had changed hands for them, too. For years the spaniels and gazehounds had hunted and run free in the lands about Arnescote, friends of all in the castle and Sir Martin's dear companions. By night they had shared his hearth, quiet at his knee; since his death they had searched and howled for him. Now they had been sold, to what fates Tom did not let himself imagine. Brown eyes implored him through the bars, but he could do nothing for them.

———

In the ravaged Great Hall a few of Marsh's soldiers were

sweeping and clearing, supervised by Susan Protheroe, briskly playing at lady of the house, bustling and authoritative. It was sweet to give orders where one had been used to taking them. Besides, Colonel Marsh was watching, and she wished to impress him with her housewifery.

Anne was not so impressed; she could feel nothing but shock. To hear of a siege and a surrender was one thing, to see the results of it was another. That the heart of the old house, the grandest room in her old home, should have come to this! Everything she remembered, but for the bare stones, gone or shattered, leaving the place unrecognizable. She had seen her father dead; his corpse kept more of himself than this wreck did of her old home. She listened to what John and Marsh were saying, John asking if any orders had been received about the fate of Arnescote.

'The news has scarce reached London,' Marsh answered. 'But as the stronghold of a known malignant, which gave us so much aggravation, I shall be much surprised if my orders are not to raze it to the ground.'

John heard Anne's cry. 'That,' he said, 'we must do our utmost to avoid. As you know, Colonel, it is my wife's home — it has many happy associations.'

Marsh made a token bow. 'I regret you see it so reduced, madam. It was gallantly defended, beyond all rational hope.'

'As I would expect of my father. Did you see him fall? Did he suffer?'

'I was a witness to the fatal moment. His death was sudden.' Marsh hated all this chat, with the opportunities it gave for sentiment and weeping. He wished heartily that the Fletchers would return to Swinford and let him get on with whatever remained to be done. But Anne said, 'I wish to see Goodwife Margaret, before we leave.'

Another tiresome request. 'I felt it expedient to confine the household staff to their quarters,' Marsh answered.

'I should like to see her, nonetheless.'

'As you wish, madam.' A typical Lacey, stubborn and difficult.

Anne clung to John, sobbing out her memories and her grief. He held her, helpless, troubled, patting her shoulder mechanically. 'Even though I came late to this house,' he told her, 'I share the pain of it.'

'But what can we *do*? If Cromwell gives the order to burn it to the ground?'

'It would be an order from the army, which can be rescinded by Parliament and law.'

'You would defy Cromwell?'

'It would be Cromwell who defied the law. I must talk with Master Cropper, as soon as may be. Here is Margaret.'

Goodwife Margaret stood with her hands folded before her, stony-faced. Anne smiled. 'Please sit beside me, Margaret, and take that scolding look off your face. I remember it too well as a child.'

Margaret stared with disapprobation at the rough bench which had been dragged into the Great Hall instead of the furniture which was gone. 'Mistress Fletcher,' she said.

'My name is Anne, Goodwife. I understand your feelings, but I hope and trust, for the sake of everyone we love in this house, that time will heal the breach. *I* was not responsible for Father's death — it was his own decision to fight it through.'

This feeble apologia made no more impression on Margaret than it deserved to. 'Did he have a choice, madam, when the enemy came storming over the walls and took what was rightfully his?'

Anne's familiar temper was roused. 'I do not wish to talk politics with you, Margaret — it is quite fruitless. My concern, at this time, is for the household — how it may survive, until such time as I and my husband and baby — who is after all Sir Martin's grandchild — may return in peace.'

Margaret seared her with a look. '*You* — return here?'

Anne started to speak, but Margaret cut in. 'Forgive me if I'm misguided, madam, but this house belongs to Sir Thomas Lacey, your brother.'

'Margaret! He has forfeited his right to it!'

Margaret ignored her. 'And if not he, then Mistress Lucinda and her husband, Lord Ferrar, who fought so bravely in its defence.'

'Did not Lord Ferrar run away in the heat of battle?'

Margaret bridled. 'That is not true! It's a slander — ask your brother.'

'So be it — if I am misinformed. Let it not stand between

us. As for my sister, pray you give her this. It is a letter of safe transit should she find it in her heart to visit me.'

Margaret took the letter and put it in her apron pocket, her expression so cold that Anne began to plead with her. 'Margaret, I ask only that you maintain order and good spirits among the servants, as you were wont to do. Report any instances of ill-treatment by the soldiers. Will you do that for me?'

Susan had edged herself nearer, and was trying to listen to their conversation. Margaret made sure that she had something to listen to. Loudly she said, 'The Colonel's whore is housekeeper here now — you'd best make that request to her, Mistress Fletcher.' She turned on her heel and left before Anne could reply. Susan seized the opportunity to sidle up to Anne.

'Colonel Marsh asks if you'll take refreshment with him, cousin.' It was her hope that the relationship which had grown between them in the time before Anne's child was born would stand her in good stead now, giving her some status in the castle besides the one Margaret had thrown at her. But Anne could see through her now; it had been lies, her tale of being ravished by Marsh for the sake of the family welfare. She was his willing whore, a creeper into beds, a creeper into power, if chance offered. It was not her friendship Anne wanted, but Margaret's, Lucinda's, the friendship of people whose love and respect she had forfeited and might never get back. Coldly she told Susan to thank the Colonel, but explain that she and her husband must return to Swinford.

Susan listened at the door of the steward's room, where John and Cropper were talking, and not talking amicably, by the sound of it. But however closely she eavesdropped, the stout door kept her from making out the words. John had spent almost an hour of argument and pleading, attempting to persuade Cropper to yield to him the deeds of the castle. Without them, he himself would have no hope of saving it, titular owner though he was. He had met with nothing but stubborn refusal, the same answer over and over.

'I am steward to the Laceys, sir. The deeds are the property of Sir Thomas Lacey, and to him I shall hand them in the proper manner.'

John heaved an exasperated sigh. 'This house belongs to Parliament, Cropper. Come, man, will you have the Colonel's men bring more ruin, in the search for them? Where have you hidden them? Where is the family chest that once stood here? It is far better the deeds should be in my safe-keeping than that of others I know, who have no feeling for the place.'

Cropper looked down at his deformed wrists, the legacy of the torture inflicted on him by Roundhead soldiers in search of the horde of silver, two years before. He was not a young man, and they would never be whole and strong again. 'I can scarce lift a quill,' he said, 'my legs are run with gout. They can break my body in small pieces and scatter them in the great park before I betray my trust to this house.'

John exploded. 'You — withering old fool, Cropper!'

Susan entered, hoping to hear more inside the room. 'Forgive me, Master Fletcher. Your wife is in the hall and bids you attend her.' Without another word to Cropper, John strode out, seething with anger.

Susan might consider herself the new housekeeper of Arnescote, but nobody in the kitchens was prepared to take orders from her. They were gathered in conference, Margaret and Walter Jackman, Mrs Dumfry the cook, Will Saltmarsh, pretty Hannah and fat Rachel, and, cackling in a corner, old Minty, who was if anything madder than she had been before the siege.

Jackman said, 'No use crying over spilt milk. We got to stay together, work together as best we can.'

Minty looked up from the amulet she was making of sticks and cloth. 'Poison — I can do it. Make 'em retch up and drown in their own vomit.'

'Mistress Protheroe along with them,' said Margaret sourly. Jackman threw her a reproving look.

'That's old woman's talk, now. That won't help us.'

'What do you suggest, then, Walter?' Will asked. 'Murder 'em all in their beds?'

Everybody began to make suggestions at once, until Hannah said 'Why don't you listen to Master Jackman? He's the only one talking sense.'

Walter thanked her with a look. 'Now the soldiers are here,' he said, 'under our roof, and that bears no arguin' about. Best we ignore 'em, go about our business, puttin' our home back in order in any little way we can. As for *them*, we can make difficulties.'

'Don't answer when spoken to,' Hannah suggested.

'That's it, girl.'

Margaret folded her arms. 'They won't get a word out of me. No, nor shall that Protheroe woman.'

'That's the spirit!' exclaimed Walter. 'Dumbfound 'em! and remember who we serve.'

Hannah's charming face was full of admiration for his brave words; and something rather warmer than admiration. Feeling a small rough hand slipped into his, he looked down at her. A long look passed between them which was not unnoticed by the others. Will smiled to himself. In all the misery and distress and hatred that surrounded them, it was good to see two people falling in love. He had always been much inclined towards Hannah himself, but this was no time for fighting over her; he wished them both luck.

It was his task to carry to Tom, in his prison in the basement of the Guildhall at Swinford, the documents Cropper had so stubbornly withheld from John Fletcher. The deeds of the castle were in the hands of their rightful owner, but the fate of both hung in the balance, with the scales listing towards total disaster. Marsh, about to eat his supper with Susan at his side, told her 'A week or two should decide it. I have sent my report, and recommended that Arnescote shall be laid flat as a pancake.'

'And the fate of Sir Thomas Lacey?'

'I have no power over that. But I'll hazard he'll be removed to the Tower, tried and executed.'

CHAPTER FOURTEEN

Tom's place of imprisonment was not the narrow cell he might have had to endure. The room under the Guildhall which sometimes served as a prison was spacious, sparsely furnished, and cold, but not actually uncomfortable. It was lit by a high window, securely barred, through which Tom could hear voices, hooves and wheels passing, but see nothing. At first he had paced up and down, half-maddened with frustration, he who had never known a day without liberty; but then good sense prevailed and he concentrated his mind on the future, the possibility of escape and what, in that case, he should do.

More comforts had been provided by his jailer, a rough but kindly man. Syms too had been a soldier, and like others in army employ was finding Parliament a bad paymaster. The New Model Army was grumbling that Cromwell had not kept his promises; for the past fourteen weeks not a penny had come into their pockets, and what they had got by plunder was soon gone. Syms was grateful for every coin Tom slipped to him for the purchase of wine, cushions, candles, a chessboard, and ready to give his company when required. He was neither a sparkling conversationalist nor a good chessplayer, but Tom was glad of human presence to relieve his isolation.

He had no illusions that Arnescote would be spared, or that anything would be left of the home he had known. Syms had brought him an account which one of the officers had received by carrier of the fall of Basing, the beautiful and noble house which had been one of the wonders of England. At long last, after years of siege, Cromwell had taken it.

'The plunder of the soldiers,' said the writer, 'continued till Tuesday night; one soldier had one hundred and twenty pieces in gold to his share, others plate, others jewels . . . the soldiers sold the wheat to country people, which they held up at good rates awhile. After that, they sold the household stuff, whereof there was good store, and they continued a great while fetching out all manner of household stuff, till they fetched out all the stools, chairs and other lumber, all which they sold to the country by piecemeal. When the house was near emptied fire broke out and consumed all but the walls. Before this three hundred prisoners were taken and penned in the vaults, where after the fire they could for days be heard crying, but none might come at them for the rubble piled above. What stones were left standing of the house, General Cromwell gave out might be carried away by any that would come to fetch them.'

So there could be no hope for Arnescote. It came as a surprise to Tom to hear that anything else was even possible. John Fletcher, visiting him to warn him solemnly of his own danger, had another purpose — to obtain the deeds of the castle. But first the warning. Tom's face darkened with anger.

'You may call me malignant, delinquent or any one of your insulting titles, but I am a prisoner of war, John — the King's loyal subject and a prisoner of war! Prince Rupert will speak for me. He will write to the courts in my favour.'

'I have heard by good account he means to leave the King's service and return to Holland. The war is over, Tom.'

Tom stared at him, shocked. 'Over? Impossible. You believe that?'

'It is not what I believe that counts.'

Tom slumped back in his chair. 'Then I am truly finished,' he said quietly.

'Not so. Tomorrow the Committee sits for the sequestration of Arnescote. You may be present to speak your case. There is still hope, Tom.'

'If I agree to compound, and take the Negative Oath?' At John's nod, he slammed his fist against the table. 'If that is the choice, then let Cromwell do his worst and burn the place down. I am wholly with his decision.'

John, embarrassed, said 'There are others to consider . . .'

146

He needed to go no farther. It was there, written in his face. Tom laughed harshly.

'My sister — and you, John? You wish to become squire of Arnescote in my place? Do what you will. I have made a vow to my father.'

John, nervous and awkward, could not meet his brother-in-law's eyes. Tom was a difficult man to reason with. He wished he had not had to find himself in this position; Anne would have done it better.

'Can you afford Arnescote?' Tom asked him bluntly.

'My father, Sir Austin . . . he has found his fortune in the Americas, in Pennsylvania. He has fond memories of Sir Martin, of all the Laceys. He wishes me to save Arnescote.'

'For the Fletchers.'

John was roused. 'My son is Sir Martin's grandson, and named Martin after him! Through him, the Laceys will live on at Arnescote.'

Tom was silent. The old friendship was shattered. There was only cold talk possible between him and this changed John. 'What is it you require of me?' he asked.

'I need certain papers — the deeds of the castle. But I found Master Cropper in unyielding mood.'

'I have them here.' Tom unlocked a box on the table. 'If you take them does this mean I yield possession, in law?'

'Not until the Committee reaches its verdict.'

Tom took out the documents, old and yellowed and frail, bound up in a bundle. 'This Committee for compounding: you have a place on it? Of course you have. Is it a Court of Criminal Law — does it decide my fate?'

'That is quite beyond its powers,' John pronounced.

'Good. Then I can misbehave.'

He was amused at John's alarmed expression. 'I pray you, don't! If you conduct yourself with a show of penitence, we may still help secure your exile. You could go to France, taking Lucinda with you — find Edward Ferrar, and wait for more favourable times.'

Tom made a wry mouth. 'Thereby removing two pimples from your back. You always were a pragmatist, John.'

The door opened; Syms was showing in a cloaked lady. Tom went to greet her. 'Lucinda! Are you alone? How came you to escape their clutches?' As they embraced, John explained, 'I arranged a letter of transit for her to visit us any time she wished — I imagine she made use of that. You are our welcome guest tonight, my dear. And tomorrow we shall all return to Arnescote to resolve this wretched business.' Gathering up the papers, which he bestowed in a bag he had thoughtfully brought with him, he bowed curtly. Neither spoke to him as he left, Syms accompanying him and locking the door. Lucinda looked round. 'This room is not so bad as I feared. You have a bed — blankets — a chessboard, and brandy.'

Tom poured some into two of the glasses with which the useful Syms had supplied him. 'Take one. A gift from Mr Fletcher. Is it a condition of your visit that you are in their custody?'

She drank. 'A condition for my leaving the castle gates. What I do now is my own business. I may live here with you. What is one prison compared with another?' Impulsively she hugged him. 'Oh, Tom, I am so glad to see you! You are my only hope with Edward gone, and no word from him. I have stayed for a letter so long, yet none comes.'

Tom shrugged. 'It seems I am a forlorn hope — the victim of circumstances, manipulated at will; utterly forsaken.'

'What? Have you settled for martyrdom? That's vanity, Tom — there is too much left to fight for, as I heard on the road. The King is yet free . . .'

'And Rupert disgraced — that is what I heard. Disgraced, and about to leave for Holland. And you, my angel sister — what am I to do with you?'

Lucinda set her mouth. 'I shall not go to the Fletchers. I should rather live on bread and water than take sanctuary with them.'

'That too is martyr-talk,' said Tom. 'One of us must live. Go to Anne — she is wretched with remorse. Live for both of us.'

Anne did not appear either wretched or remorseful as she showed off her baby, under the admiring gaze of John and Emma. He was six months old now, a well-grown child though still deformed in swaddling bands, as he would be until he was weaned. Lucinda viewed him with no great affection. He was Anne's and John's, his name was Fletcher and not Lacey, and she was not yet attracted to babies for their own sake. On Anne's invitation to cuddle her nephew she took him gingerly and held him awkwardly. He began to whimper, then to cry. When the cries turned to a roar Lucinda hastily handed him back to the waiting Emma, saying 'He does not know me.' Emma, with Welsh endearments, carried him out. John, with a murmured excuse, followed, feeling himself useless.

The sisters confronted each other, separated only by a few yards of flooring in fact, by an abyss in feeling. The fragrant smoke of a log fire curled out into the room, and autumn flowers in a copper jug caught the late afternoon sun. The scene was peaceful, comfortable, domestic: Lucinda should have been charmed by it, contrasting it with the ruin of Arnescote. Now was the moment for her to return to her old affectionate self; naughty Lucinda, over her temper and forgiven. Anne asked pleasantly, 'How did you find Tom?'

Lucinda returned a stare for her smiling look. 'In a cell.'

'A room,' corrected Anne quickly.

'The door was bolted and the window barred.'

'John has made sure he's comfortable and wants for nothing.'

'But his freedom.' Lucinda spoke as though words were taxed.

'That he denies himself.' Anne leaned forward, all appeal. 'Lucinda, do not despise me. My house is yours for as long as you wish. Open your heart to us.'

Lucinda looked very far from opening her heart to anybody. 'You know I cannot,' she said, 'what would my husband think?'

'That you are safe from Roundhead troops and cared for by those that love you. You will be near to Tom, who needs you. And our house is surely more agreeable than Arnescote at the present time. What other choice is there?' She moved across to lay her hand lightly on Lucinda's shoulder. It shrank away, as from the touch of a murderer.

'I acknowledge your kindness,' Lucinda said stiffly, 'but it suffocates me. I remember it all, you see — your certainty, your righteousness, just as you used to treat me when we

149

were children. Tom indulged my wildness, but you were a Puritan even then. You did well to marry one.'

'I was obliged to play mother to you, since our own was dead,' Anne said helplessly. Lucinda swung round on her.

'And still? Would you have me still a little child? I am a married woman now, you may recall, and I cannot any longer endure your censuring looks and slaps.'

Anne sought for a defence. 'Your memory is clouded. *I* remember happy times and mischief — for which Margaret and Father slapped us both. Oh, Lucinda! if we pledge not to speak our differences, this house can resound with laughter. How I wish it so!'

'Is there laughter in your solemn husband? I have yet to see it,' Lucinda said coldly.

'Stay, and you will see there is! Watch him play with our son. It is only duty and the mournful state of England that makes him wear a frown. Lucinda, there is but one difference between us — we fell in love with different men. It was our father told us to be loyal to husbands, above all else, and so we are. I should feel the same as you, were our rôles reversed. As long as you remain with us, I shall respect and honour your loyalty, my dearest.' She dropped a kiss on Lucinda's cold cheek, and left the room, with her placatory words hanging in the air of it.

Lucinda looked after her, not kindly. 'By such means,' she said under her breath, 'the Devil does his work.'

On a bleak morning the brother and sisters met among strangers, in what had been their home. The Great Hall, stripped of its splendours, battered and defaced, had been cleaned up enough for decency, like a corpse taken from the battlefield. The Committee for the sequestration of Arnescote sat in a row behind the great table at which kings and queens had been entertained, its six support pillars now kicked and damaged, the elmwood surface proudly polished by many generations of servants dull, scratched, marred by the white rings where glasses had stood and wine been spilled. Their chairman was Sir Henry Parkin, dry, dispassionate, familiar with the routine of such cases and not likely to be moved by sentimental considerations. Nor were the burghers who sat with him, or their clerk. Their indifferent faces were eyed apprehensively by the tenant farmers huddled together like a bunch of their own sheep, waiting to hear their fate, nervous of the soldiers who guarded both doors. Among them was Walter Jackman.

Beside the fireplace, now stripped of its flanking caryatids, Tom sat with Cropper and Hugh, who nursed the household books. Tom looked up as the Fletchers entered, soberly dressed and solemn-faced. As John took his place at the table Anne passed by Tom, her skirts brushing his knees, trying not to look at him. But he said, loudly enough for others to hear, 'Welcome to Judgement Day, sister. Who would have imagined it would come to this?'

She made no reply, hurrying on to take her seat at the other side of the fireplace. Lucinda, following her, stopped and sat down beside Tom. She was saddened to see him, in the full light of day, look far more pulled down by imprisonment than he had seemed in the Guildhall cellar. Close confinement had driven the colour from his face, and his chin was stubbly from bad light for shaving. There seemed even to be a droop to his shoulders. Impulsively she took his hand and squeezed it. Cropper, on the other side of her, frowned and twitched. The muscles wrenched beyond bearing when they had hung him up by his wrists to extract a confession ached more than ever, partly from anxiety, partly from the cold of the Hall. The wood burning in the grate was miscellaneous debris, some of it panelling and furniture: it gave out a sullen heat, as cheering as the embers of a martyr's fire.

At the usher's bidding, the company rose. Parkin opened the proceedings. 'The duty of this Committee is to assess the value of the Estate of Arnescote Castle and all its tenancies as it was before the war, in addition to all outstanding debts and liabilities, and to determine its future ownership. The estate being the residence of the known malignant and rebel, the late Sir Martin Lacey, and his heir, Sir Thomas Lacey.'

Tom raised his head and stared defiantly at the chairman. Lucinda hissed in his ear 'How dare he call our father malignant and rebel? Puritan scum.'

'Hush. Leave him to me.'

'Is the steward for the property in the Hall?' asked Parkin.

Cropper rose stiffly and hobbled to the witness chair facing the Committee.

Parkin informed him of what he already knew, that he was compelled by order of Parliament to produce all the books relating to estate business, dating back to 1640, for examination. At Cropper's signal, Hugh came forward with them; four thick volumes bound in calfskin. Mears, the Receiver, elderly and short-sighted, viewed them with some horror.

Hours passed, as the books were examined in detail, long hours of boredom and discomfort. At times Tom fell into an uneasy doze, waking to hear yet another column of figures being read out. Lucinda yawned and let her thoughts wander; John and Anne looked profoundly unhappy. Lucinda wondered if Anne thought of the times gone for ever in this Hall, the feasts and merrymakings, the joys of Christmas, the Twelfth Night wassail-songs, bobbing lights in the winter orchards as farmers wassailed their trees for a good crop, last of all coming to sing their song in the Great Hall, with flowing mugs of cider and carraway-seed cakes in their hands.

> Here's to thee, old apple-tree,
> Whence thou mayst bud, and whence thou mayst blow,
> And whence thou mayst bear apples enow.
> Hats full — caps full,
> Bushel, bushel sacks full ...

Great fires had burnt then, of sweet-smelling logs, warming the merry company and the large amiable dogs who had always been about Arnescote, lying at Father's feet, sometimes raising their heads gratefully for the touch of his hand. And in the gold days of autumn, when the fire was let to burn low, the Hall would be full of the good scents of fruit and new-baked bread, the tributes brought to the family by its tenants after Harvest Home. Lucinda and Anne had worn garlands of flowers and corn-ears and been given a bright red apple apiece ...

Tears gathered in Lucinda's eyes and began to trickle down her cheeks. Tom glanced at her. The pressure of his hand on hers was comforting, yet warned her not to let her emotion be seen. Obediently she scrubbed her eyes and managed a smile for him.

At last the audit was over, Cropper allowed to go back to his seat. It was Tom's turn to take the witness chair. He took it, confidently, no trace now of a stoop to his shoulders, glancing from one face to another, then fixing his eyes on Parkin. He had noticed, with amusement, John's apprehension that he would say or do something outrageous.

'You are Sir Thomas Lacey?' came the unnecessary question.

'You well know I am.'

The chairman was displeased. 'Confine yourself to a straight answer, sir. You do not deny you were an officer in the King's service, quartered at Oxford, and as such you have been named a delinquent and traitor to your country?'

'Sir, I abhor the thought of treason to my country. I believe, as you do, that I fought a just quarrel.'

Parkin frowned. 'This Committee is not here to argue that point, sir. But I must remind you that you are under oath, and your demeanour will be reported to the Committee of Both Kingdoms, whose task it will be to decide your ultimate fate.' He sat back, waiting for this insolent young man to blench. Instead, he laughed.

'You think to frighten me, Sir Henry? I am happy to let God and my conscience decide my fate, not you, or the toads who are gathered beside you.' A gasp went up from his listeners. John Fletcher put a hand over his face, and Lucinda stifled a giggle. Tom added, '*Or* their cousins in London.' The atmosphere at the table was cold, as became the element of toads. John, appalled, began to stutter an apology, but Parkin waved him down. 'Nay, Mr Fletcher, let Sir Thomas hurl his insults. They are all recorded.' He glanced at the clerk to make sure this was the case before returning to Tom.

'Your estate, sir, is estimated at one thousand pounds a year. Though we have not yet accounted for all debts and the residue of land rents. They must needs be further investigated, by your steward Mr Cropper, and Mr Mears the auditor. Suffice it to say, you have a right to petition to compound, that is to pay the agreed sum yearly to Parliament and maintain nominal ownership — on one condition, that you hereby take the Covenant and forswear all your past misdeeds.'

Tom said loudly and deliberately, 'I would rather burn in hell-fire.'

There was a heavy silence. Parkin let Tom's defiance register before saying, 'Then, by the powers invested in this Committee, *de facto*, I declare the sequestration of this estate; one half to be possessed by Parliament, and the remainder to be open to purchase by persons other than Sir Thomas Lacey and his dependants.'

John, who had been nervously fidgeting, got to his feet. 'Sir, before we move on to such matters, which as you know are of particular concern to me, I beg this Committee to allow me a few words on behalf of the defendant.'

Tom laughed. 'What, save my bacon, John?'

Without looking at him, John continued, his dry lawyer's voice measured, his emotions controlled. Years of practice in the law could be useful at such a perilous time. 'As we know, sir, feelings can become roused in these matters, and I think it sometimes unnecessary for everything that is said to be recorded. But if they must be, I beg you to indulge me a moment. To set the actions and character of Sir Thomas Lacey in their true perspective.'

Parkin suppressed a yawn. 'Speak, if you must.'

John summoned all his resources for the defence speech which might mean life or death to his brother-in-law. 'I have known Sir Thomas,' he began, 'since we were boys together at Oxford. Indeed, I have always counted him as one of my closest friends, albeit that this sorry war has divided us. He is first and foremost a brave soldier, and I would remind this Committee that he fought valiantly for the Protestant cause — our own cause, gentlemen! — for several years in the Low Countries. There he made acquaintance with Prince Rupert, who, for all his, er, belligerence has won grudging admiration among our own generals. I believe that the personal friendship and loyalty that was forged between Sir Thomas and the Prince in that most deadly struggle was the over-riding reason for Sir Thomas's subsequent actions.'

Out of the corner of his eye he saw Marsh slip in through a small door at the end of the hall. His arrival gave John a new cue.

'Just as Colonel Marsh there carries unswerving loyalty to our Lord General Cromwell, so my friend Sir Thomas felt for the young Prince. As for charges of Papist idolatry that have been laid against him, I can swear to you that in all the years of our acquaintance I have never heard him utter one word...'

Marsh interrupted. 'He buried his father by the Common Prayer Book, sir — refused the services of our chaplain.'

Lucinda leapt to her feet and shouted, 'The Prayer Book was a Protestant answer to Rome!'

'With respect, madam,' Marsh answered coldly, 'it is not considered so now.'

Parkin held up a hand. 'Gentlemen, ladies, let us not become embroiled in religious argument.' He turned to Tom. 'Sir Thomas, you should be grateful to Master Fletcher for so eloquently pleading your case, though it may avail you little, should you continue in your previous vein.'

'I thank my old friend, John Fletcher,' Tom said warmly. 'He has rekindled a hope in me that this country may yet be ruled by reason, love, and a cherished belief in individual liberty.'

Lucinda clapped her hands together audibly, and Anne smiled at the praise of her husband. Then Tom took the smile off her face as he continued, 'A hope that was fast being extinguished by the antics of this Committee. And now, sir, if you have no further use for me...'

Parkin was by now thoroughly incensed. This impertinent puppy had certainly broken the dull familiar pattern of such hearings, but had incidentally broken all the rules. 'You will be conveyed under escort back to confinement in Swinford,' he snapped. Parkin caught John's eye.

'As to the matter of purchase, Master Fletcher; you wish to speak?'

John, uncomfortably eyeing Tom's farewell to Cropper, said, 'Without the full assessment, sir, it is impossible for me to name a price. I merely wish to notify my intent to become the purchaser.'

He was interrupted by the arrival of a messenger with a letter for Marsh, who moved aside to read it. Parkin had been considering.

'There is one small point, Master Fletcher, regarding your

intent to purchase. You are, are you not, married to Sir Thomas Lacey's sister?' John assented. Parkin said, disapprovingly, 'Thus the castle would in some part return to the Lacey family.'

John said hastily 'That part of the family which espoused our cause, sir. Are you suggesting there is something irregular . . . ?'

'I am not suggesting anything, Master Fletcher. Simply that the matter may have to be referred to a higher authority.'

Marsh approached, smiling. 'I must interrupt you, gentlemen. I have just received an order direct from Lord-General Cromwell that Arnescote castle is to be burnt within twenty-four hours, so that "not a trace of it remains for habitation".' He folded the letter up, smiling complacently.

Of all those shocked by the order, John Fletcher possibly felt its impact most. He had wanted so much to take over the castle: for Anne, for his son, for his father who had begged him to save Arnescote, the house that he had always admired and envied his friend Lacey. And he had wanted to save it for the sake of Tom, his old friend.

The only hope now was to find legal means of hurrying up the purchase. Once the house was in his name, and not Lacey property, then Cromwell's order would be rescinded. All night he worked, and at first light he was out, bound to the nearest notary's, haggard and exhausted, but sustained by feverish anxiety, the hope against hope that he could succeed against such heavy odds.

The last of Arnescote's contents were leaving it. Clothes and bed-linen, such as remained (for Lucinda's dresses and possessions had all been looted, and the contents of garde-robes), and trifles too unimportant to attract the looters' eyes — a well-worn hobby-horse that had been Tom's as a child, a few dolls, a horn-book. Margaret gathered them up bitterly; they at least, poor things, should not perish in the flames.

The kitchen was in a ferment, pans, cooking implements, the roasting-jack wrenched from the wall, candlesticks, box-irons, knives, salt-boxes, colanders, skillets — all heavy cumbrous things to be dragged out by the sweating Rachel, panting and protesting. She was still loaded down with saucepans when Susan Protheroe burst into the kitchen.

'Leave the rest,' she ordered. 'You have but twenty minutes.'

Mistress Dumfry turned on her. 'This'll surely send me to my grave, and you're one of my executioners, you devil's spawn!'

Susan spat back 'Get out, you greasy old hag, and take your pans with you!' Cursing her, the cook hurried out, followed by a shower of pans. Her temper still at boiling-point, Susan seized on another pile of objects and flung them to the stone floor with an ear-shattering noise, if there had been any to hear, before rushing out towards Marsh's waggon, where her personal possessions had been put.

When she had gone, the door of a large store-cupboard opened stealthily. From it emerged old Minty. Nobody had missed her, nobody cared about her. She was free to stay in her life-long home, like an animal refusing to be evicted from its burrow. Her wits were gone too far for her to feel fear or anything but an infantile glee at the prospect of a thrilling holocaust that would release her into her fantasy-world.

'Easy come, easy go,' she muttered to the empty kitchen. 'But not Minty, me dear. *She*'ll know how it'll end. Bang, bang, and up she goes, Robin. Won't know a thing.' She squinted at the ceiling. 'Are you there, John? Minty come to claim her soul back, wicked lad. We'll be wed tonight by Hell's preacher . . . bride'll wear red . . .'

Toadlike she squatted in her place by the grate, waiting.

Around the castle piles of gunpowder were laid at strategic points. It was almost noon, the time set for the combustion. Soldiers were waiting for the order to light the fuses. At a safe distance the household refugees were gathered; Hannah was weeping in Walter Jackman's arms. Anxiously they watched Margaret and Lucinda emerge from the gatehouse, where Marsh stood checking that all had left.

'Are you the last?' he asked Margaret.

'Aye. And you'll take this moment to your grave, Colonel Marsh — I swear it!' He let them go, impassive. Satisfied that he might now give the signal, he moved towards the gate; to be stopped in his tracks by the sight of three horse-men galloping through it, halting, dismounting. They were John Fletcher and two outriders. John hurried up to the puzzled Marsh, waving documents at him.

'Stay your execution, Colonel Marsh. Here is proof of my ownership.'

Marsh stood firm. 'Master Fletcher, with respect, you come too late.' But John strode past him into the Great Hall, bare now but for its table, on which he flung down the documents.

'Too late? I think not. These papers say I am the new owner of Arnescote. And you would not have placed on your record that you destroyed the residence of a Member of Parliament, would you?'

'I am no lawyer, sir. I am merely a soldier obeying orders from our Lord General.'

'But these documents countermand your orders, Colonel. I am prepared to stand here debating the point with you until we are *both* blown to eternity. I think you cannot leave without me.'

Marsh was thinking very rapidly how to save his face and pay his men's wages at the same time. 'I have soldiers, sir, without the gates,' he said, 'their fingers itching to light the fuse, whether you or I stand here or not. Men who have no love for me or you Parliament people. Men who have fought the fight and not been paid for their valour. Men who are disillusioned with you *and* me, sir. Their quickest way to satisfaction is to blow the place to Heaven, and shift off home. So I say, you have come too late.'

John read him rightly. 'If it's money you need...'

'Two or three hundred pounds — by six of the clock this evening?'

'By six of the clock. You will have it.'

The ransom would come out of John's pocket, but it was worth it; Arnescote was saved.

CHAPTER FIFTEEN

The Royalist cause was not dead, but it was rapidly dying.

King Charles's own character was the instrument of his destruction, even his supporters agreed. In the two years following the taking of Arnescote Castle, one negotiation after another between himself and Parliament failed, because of his own intractability. Nothing could drive him from his absolute notions of Church and State but death. He was accused of sheer mulish obstinacy, but the reason for his stubbornness lay deeper, in his early training for kingcraft and his profound attachment to the Anglican church. Serene in his beliefs, he had no doubt but that he would be restored to his throne with honour, even when taken prisoner by the Scots.

Yet the most loyal of his well-wishers held little hope for that restoration. He seemed like a man doomed, unable to fly his fate. The great Italian sculptor Bernini, seeing a youthful portrait of the King, had exlaimed, 'The possessor of that face is born to destruction!' In the paintings of van Dyck the small armoured figure on the powerful war-horse seems to be riding on the path of his tragic destiny. Deep melancholy is in his dark eyes, in his bearing; he rides, not recklessly but with a solemn intent, blind to every sign that might guide him to safety, led on by the beckoning of Death.

Early in 1647 the Scots yielded him up to Parliament, which ordered his removal to Holdenby, one of his own favourite houses in Northamptonshire. There he lived peacefully, enjoying country pleasures and the company of friends, while Parliament struggled with the problem of the money it owed its increasingly fractious army. John

Fletcher's three hundred pounds, paid to Marsh, had been a drop in the ocean of that huge debt of unpaid wages. Driven to desperation, the armies' leaders threatened mutiny. If they refused to obey orders, it might not be possible for the King to be kept in custody. It seemed that the affairs of England might soon be in chaos.

But at Arnescote order had been restored to the war-torn castle. Patient rebuilding, patching, redecoration, under Cropper's direction, had made it whole and habitable. Some of its old glories could never be created again, but John Fletcher, with infinite trouble and at great expense, had sought out and bought back such vanished possessions as could be traced. Now, with their own furnishings from the Swinford house, the time had come for the Fletchers to make the castle their home. Marsh and his soldiers were still in residence, but the Lacey staff, supervised by Cropper and Margaret, were all at their old employment, even Hannah, now married to Walter Jackman.

On a summer day the Fletchers' coach rolled through the great gate and stopped in the courtyard. Cropper, Jackman and Stephen the gate-keeper helped out Anne, Lucinda, Emma and young Martin, now a sturdy two-year old, still skirted like a little girl. Cropper made his stiff, awkward bow.

'Welcome to Arnescote, Mistress Anne, Mistress Lucinda, young master — and Master Fletcher.' Family loyalty would not allow him to be more than polite to John. In the Great Hall the female servants were curtseying, Margaret, Hannah and Rachel, Margaret highly emotional.

'Oh, madam — Mistress Anne, I am so happy to see you back and all these nasty wars ended!' She swooped on young Martin and gathered him to her spare bosom. 'Oh, the little darling! Forgive me, madam, but I brought this handsome boy into the world, aye, and I raised you from a child. Well is he named Martin, after his grandfather — the same eyes and lift of his head . . .' She bestowed kisses on Martin, who wriggled away and ran to Emma. Lucinda opened her arms to Margaret, who wept as they embraced each other, Margaret noticing with pity that the girl had lost her childish looks; two years of the stress of living with Anne had changed her, added to anxiety for Tom, still in prison,

160

and the absence of news about Edward. He had escaped to France, that she knew, but since then hardly a letter had come. Letters from Royalist fugitives were dangerous, addressed to one living in a Puritan household.

Anne was gazing round the Hall, regretting its barrenness. But the long table had been found, and refurbished by a skilful cabinet-maker, and the oaken chairs with their scrolled carving. Two or three portraits had been recovered, including that of Lady Lacey; John had someone in London on the lookout for others. Margaret, seeing Anne's critical look, said, 'You will find all to rights elsewhere, madam, down to the last press of bed-linen.'

John congratulated the impassive Cropper. 'I must thank you before all others who have remained in our service, for it is your work that has made this house fit for our return.'

Cropper answered carefully, 'I have been steward to Arnescote Castle since my youth, sir, and as long as I am permitted to, I shall continue to serve Arnescote Castle.' Not you, said his tone. It was not lost on John, who returned an embarrassed murmur. Then Cropper led forward the man he proposed to take over his post as steward, when he finally retired from it; the one who had assisted him for so long, Hugh Brandon.

Hugh was shy as ever, somewhat grown, his silver voice deepened to mannish tones, but still retaining his slender delicacy. Music and mathematics went together, it was said; in Hugh's case it was true, for he had great skill with the account-books. He was bright, and had some learning, Cropper pointed out — they could not hope for a better future steward.

Anne frowned. 'He fought against Parliament. It was he who brought the relief from Oxford, was it not?'

'Parliament has wisely allowed old scores to be dropped, mistress,' Cropper said.

'Only for the commoner sort!' she flashed back, regardless of Hugh's feelings at being described thus. 'My brother is still imprisoned in Swinford waiting to know his fate.'

'The boy will be as devoted to you as he was to Sir Martin, if you will let him,' Cropper assured her. She surveyed Hugh, as keenly as any magistrate with a hard case before the Bench. Cropper thought how she had changed, and not for the better, from the young mistress he had once known, and how little her father would have liked the change in his Sweet Anne.

'Hugh,' she said, 'Hugh Brandon, will you swear me an oath to give up for ever the misguided and lost cause of the King?'

Hugh looked her in the eyes frankly. 'I will swear no oath, ma'am. But I will give you my word of honour that as long as I am under your roof I will avoid all embroilment, and will render you honest service.'

She would have liked to quibble and dictate, but knew she would get no support in that company, even from John. 'Very well. I will accept that. Train him well, Master Cropper.'

'Indeed, madam.' He turned to John. 'Sir, I have been waiting to ask you — can you explain the news that Walter Jackman has just brought us?'

Hannah interrupted, excited. 'The King, sir! We saw the King pass by. He was in a carriage, with soldiers all about him.'

Hugh added 'And travelling south towards London, sir.'

John looked blank. 'I have heard nothing of such a move. Can it be true, and if so, what is afoot?'

Unnoticed, Marsh had slipped into the Hall, and listened to the conversation. 'Permit me to enlighten you,' he said. 'But first, I must welcome you, Master Fletcher, to your new home. Ladies, Master Fletcher, I wish you all happiness under this roof.'

John thanked him. 'But as to the King. He was at Holdenby House in Northamptonshire. Why has he been brought away from there?'

'The King is being escorted from Holdenby with all honour, and with his own officers and counsellors all about him, to a place of greater security.' His meaning, rather than his words, was clear to all. The net was closing in on the royal captive. Lucinda's heart sank. Anne, at a nod from John, dismissed the servants, before asking Marsh whether the King travelled of his own free will.

'By the will of Parliament, Master Fletcher.'

'This was never decided in Parliament, that I know. The Army has done this.'

'It is the Army,' Marsh answered smoothly, 'which guarantees the safety of all, therefore the Army must decide how best to secure it. The King is under guard for his own good, on the way to Hampton Court, I believe, where he will be able to confer with Parliament.' He would say no more, and they might make what they liked of his words. He addressed Anne. 'Mistress Fletcher, I do not wish to incommode you, but I must maintain my quarters here for the time being. I expect orders to move soon.'

'We are at your service,' Anne said, not warmly. 'But I would like to enjoy privacy in my own home.'

'Indeed, ma'am. For that reason I have withdrawn to the North apartments, which are separate from your residence. There we shall not intrude on you, except to obtain supplies from the kitchen. The rest of the regiment is in the park, and troopers will only come and go hereabouts when on duty.'

A cry reached them. 'Cousins! oh, my dear cousins!' Sue Protheroe was descending the staircase, a bundle of folded sheets over her arm. She was, Lucinda noticed, flashier in appearance than she had been, more buxom, dressed becomingly enough in what looked very like a new pink gown, her hair not as plainly dressed as it had been, but twisted into curls under a quite frivolous coif; far from being the ideal of a Puritan maiden. 'I am sorry I was not on hand to welcome you,' she said, 'but I have been *so* busy overseeing the movements of the officers. But let me greet you now.'

She advanced on the ladies, the linen laid aside, all smiles and open arms. In total agreement for once, they froze and stood motionless, not even acknowledging her. At the rebuff she stopped, curtseying in response to John's stiff bow.

'Dear Cousin John. I . . . I needed a little more bedlinen.'

Lucinda said to Anne, loudly, 'We heard that our cousin was most assiduous in providing *comforts*, did we not?' Sue bridled, throwing a glance of appeal at Marsh, who ignored it.

'After all,' she defended herself to Anne, 'I was the only member of the family here — it was my place to act as hostess. But now you are here the place is yours, Cousin Anne.' Anne acknowledged this undoubted truth with a small cold smile.

'I will look after the officers' quarters — you will have no

163

worries there — although I could happily keep my room here in the house — it is not far to come and go. Would you agree, Colonel?'

She got no support from Marsh. 'I suggest you dwell in the North apartments, Mistress Protheroe. It will facilitate your kind activities.' Was there a barb in the sentence? Certainly no encouragement lay in it. Sue flounced out, with a parting shot.

'I give you good day, cousins, and hope for warmer regard than I received under the Lacey flag.' Nobody answered.

Will Saltmarsh was visiting Tom in prison, the same quarters he had occupied since his capture. The room had a certain lived-in look by now, but the furniture and comforts the Fletchers would have brought Tom had been severely rationed. Syms continued to be his jailer, amiable but ever-vigilant. Tom was thinner, paler, older. The exercise and fresh air his active body needed so badly were denied him; he felt sometimes stirrings in his bones like the onset of rheumatism, that bane of prisoners. For his mind, he was no scholar, and the books brought to him only occupied him until his eyes grew tired of skimming their pages. Oh, for a gallop in open country! Warfare in the Low Countries now seemed to him like a remembered Paradise, and his last days of freedom at Arnescote unimaginable happiness, despite their stresses. He would be an old man, at this rate, long before he was thirty. Yet, as Will pointed out, it was better than the Tower of London, from which few came out with any great prospect of keeping their heads on their shoulders above an hour.

As Will unpacked the clean linen, wine and roasted fowl he had brought, and a purse of money, Tom asked him how matters stood at Arnescote between the Fletchers and Colonel Marsh.

'Too soon to know, sir, them having only just come. Why, sir?'

'There is bad blood between Parliament and the Army. It may mean a chance for me. If my sister and John Fletcher can see that their interest now lies with mine . . .' At the tramp of heavy footsteps in the corridor he rapidly switched subjects, pointing to the door, whose bolts were being undrawn. 'How goes it with your father, Will? Is the smithy built up again?'

The jailer lumbered in, eyeing Will and the wine-bottle on the table. 'Your time's nearly up, sir.' At a nod from Tom Will passed Syms a coin, and the man subsided on a bench.

'Thankee, sir, thankee. I'll just sit quiet. Don't mind me.'

The friends talked, saying nothing that Syms should not have heard. But there were things that Tom must say. Amiably he told the man, 'Good Syms, I have a message to give my fellow for a certain lady of title. Leave us, and there's another crown for you.'

Syms showed black teeth in a grin, and got to his feet. 'A gentleman's a gentleman, sir, and must be treated as such. Thankee. But I've one thing to warn ye — no bribery.'

Tom stared as though bribery were the last thought in his mind. 'Bribery?' he echoed.

'Aye. If you've a notion to get away I'll report you, be it a hundred pound you offered me.'

'Honest man.'

'I'm honest, right enough. Accepting a little consideration, now, to lodge you apart from the common lock-up, and a few favours, is no more than a man's right. But if you escaped I'd be . . .' He mimed the hideous grimace of a man who feels the noose tighten round his neck. 'Master Baynard promised me as much, knowing of your rich and mighty friends. He said, if you made off I'd swing for it and no excuses took. Accessory after the crime. Five more minutes,' he said to Will as he went out, pointedly locking and bolting the door behind him.

'So,' said Will, 'not much of a chance there.'

'I had no great hopes. But Will, I must get away — I won't wait like a lamb for the slaughter. If I can bring my sister to help me more actively . . .'

'Through fear of the Army? Emma — that's the lass I told you about sir,' said Will with something almost like a blush, 'she do tell me she've heard them talking with great alarm about the Army mastering Parliament.'

'Good. Good. Then find out everything you can about how they fall in, or out, with Colonel Marsh. Anything that may help me get out of this place.' He shivered suddenly, looking round the cheerless room. 'Will, do you ever think of how we came home to Arnescote from the wars, five long years ago? How as Lacey lands came into sight you said the valley would make good cavalry ground — and I hushed you, saying that we had left the wars behind us?'

Will nodded. 'Aye. Little we knew. 'Twas to be all peace and good living, and never a cloud in the sky. And now ...'

Tom was remembering how, that day, he had been joyfully reunited with Anne, the twin who was almost a part of himself; how lightly he had questioned her about her forthcoming marriage, thinking there was no import to it but her love for John and her future happiness. Yet in that marriage had lain the seeds of the great division that had split the Laceys asunder and raised a barrier between the twins.

For all that, there was some kind of comfort in another thought; had it not been for John Fletcher, Arnescote might now be a smoke-blackened ruin, scarcely one stone standing upon another, and himself, perhaps, dead, instead of wasting in prison with a hope of life left to him.

Will, helping to serve at table that night, listened keenly for every scrap of conversation between the Fletchers and Marsh that his ears might catch. The tone of it was not cordial. All were polite, but it was not hard to sense that there was no great liking between them. Refilling wine goblets, Will managed to overhear John and Marsh crossing verbal swords.

'Have you, er, had any troubles in your regiment?' John enquired.

'Troubles? What troubles?'

'I hear of nothing but discontents, uprisings and even mutinies all through the Army, not to speak of those who call themselves Levellers, would-be confiscators of well-earned wealth — and there's talk of a thousand addle-pated religious sects —'

Marsh looked affronted. 'We will not talk of religion, but as to the Army's troubles, they have not touched my regiment — which is disciplined and faithful, sir.'

'A pity other commanders cannot boast as much,' John said drily.

'A pity, Master Fletcher, that Parliament does not find money to pay the men.'

'Parliament has its work cut out finding money to restore this ravaged land.'

'Parliament is full of fat merchants with fatter money-bags, made out of the war,' Marsh snapped back.

'I hope,' said John carefully, 'that you are not talking sidelong of my father.'

No love lost there, thought Will. The conversation grew even more contentious, ending in Marsh rising abruptly and bidding his hosts goodnight. Anne followed him to the door, with a very resolute set to her lips, and Will, with a dexterous shift to the end of the table, on the pretext of refilling Margaret's glass, contrived to hear what her clear cold voice was saying.

'Colonel Marsh. Touching upon Mistress Protheroe. I hope you took the sense of my words today. I will not have her in my house.'

'A pity, ma'am. She is loyal to our cause.'

'She will turn with every passing change of breeze — or man. It would be immodest of me to say what I know of her personal connections. But I will not be insulted by the presence of a turncoat trollop. To speak even plainer, if I am not heeded, I shall write to General Cromwell — I shall prevail upon my husband to speak in the House of Commons upon immoralities practised under my roof. And to speak even plainer than that, the matter would then touch you, Colonel.'

Marsh's answer was cold and clipped. 'I thank you for your plain words. I have already declared that no member of my establishment will be denied access to your kitchen and its stores. Otherwise you will not be given any cause for offence. Goodnight, madam.'

No love lost there, either. But Will had grave doubts that Mistress Fletcher's dislike of the Colonel would provoke her to the extreme measure of helping Tom to escape.

Marsh remembered with anger John's dig at him about troubles in the Army when such troubles reached his regiment next morning. There was a show of mutiny, the

men standing sullen, refusing to obey the Parade call —
unless, it was made clear, the Colonel would receive a
deputation presenting grievances. It was headed by a young
man with a yokel's features, but with the eyes of a fanatic:
Sam Saltmarsh, younger brother of Will, and shedder of his
brother's blood in the siege. Now he, like the other men, wore
the green ribbon, badge of the Army revolutionaries calling
themselves Levellers, who demanded, among other things,
equality for all ranks.

Marsh pointed to the ribbon. 'You are a Leveller, Corporal
Saltmarsh. Like the serpent in Eden, you have poured your
venom into the ears of my regiment.'

'Not venom, sir.' Sam flourished his pocket bible. 'I got it
from this same Holy Bible you praised me for having the
night you asked me to join your regiment, sir.'

'Since when did the Holy Bible sanction anarchy and
theft? Now hear me, men. I stand by your rightful demand
for pay. Not a day passes but I demand it for you. But I
cannot coin money. It must be got, and got from Parliament.
We soldiers must march, if need be, and get it from them.
Yes, we must march — but united, and disciplined.'

Cornet Salisbury stepped forward. 'Sir, I think that is
sufficient. Permission to withdraw, sir?'

'Nay,' said Sam, 'it is not sufficient.' Marsh smiled grimly.
'It is not indeed, Cornet. You wear the green badge of the
rabble, the meaner sort who wish to rule and ruin this land.
Off with it. Cast it down. Now, the rest of you. Hear me once
more, and for the last time. The wearing of that political
ribbon goes beyond your legal rights. It is sedition. And
refusal to parade is mutiny. Such conduct earlier would have
lost us the war — it can still lose us all.' He paused, to give
effect to his next words. 'For sedition and mutiny the
punishment is death.'

One man after another took off his green ribbon and threw
it down. Sam retained his. 'Pick 'em up, lads,' he said. 'With
all respect, sir, you talk of anarchy and theft, who are a landowner, but to common folks like us 'tis justice.'

'And God's Paradise in this land, sir,' put in Trooper Hind.
He still wore his ribbon, as did Trooper Wallis, silent and
stubborn-faced. Marsh ordered him to cast it down, without
effect.

168

'You will be hanged if you disobey.' Wallis stared sullenly at him.

'Very well. Cornet Salisbury, you will be brought before an officer's court on the reduced charge of failing to carry out your orders. I will bring forward no other matter, if you redeem yourself by marching those men who have obeyed me to the camp, and bringing the regiment on to parade, where I shall address them and end this disorder. Corporal Saltmarsh, Trooper Hind, Trooper Wallis, one pace forward, march!'

An escort of six armed men, on Marsh's orders, formed round the three. Marsh addressed the prisoners.

'You will be tried for your lives, all three. Tomorrow.'

Unconscious of his brother's perilous situation, Will sat by the kitchen fire opposite Emma. She sewed diligently, not looking at him. He studied her intently, trying to find words which did not come easily to him. Since he had lost Hannah to lanky Walter Jackman his fancy had turned more and more towards this neat, pretty girl whose Welsh accent had ceased to sound strange; indeed, it charmed him by its musical intonation, and difference from the voices of other women. He had known a great many females during his service in the wars, a few since his return home, but this lass had some quality he did not remember in any of them. Unless it was that he was growing old, as he sometimes thought.

He summoned up something to say, with an effort. ' 'Tis a wild country, Wales, they say.'

' 'Tis a sweet country.'

'I never soldiered there.'

'I hope there'll be no more soldiering anywhere . . . it is so peaceful, where I was born.' Her eyes, which seemed to see nothing but her careful small stitches, were covertly taking in Will's form, stocky but strong and manly, and his features, that you could not call handsome, but very pleasing. She had enjoyed living at a real castle and seeing how gentlefolk behaved, and such fine things; but she was not over-fond of her sharp-tongued mistress, and at heart she was a loyal subject of the King, God pity him. It would be a happy change . . .

'Peaceful, is it?' Will was saying. 'A place a man could

settle down in, eh? When the time came, that is. With his . . . with his family.'

It was not the low-burning fire which put such a colour in Emma's cheeks. The other women in the kitchen, at their own work, glanced often at the pair of lovers, for such they clearly were to any feminine eye. Margaret approved, Minty cackled silently to herself, Rachel, scrubbing the floor, hummed a country song whose words were much too improper to sing out loud.

Into the kitchen, with a flaunt of skirts and a lifted chin, came Sue Protheroe, a trooper attending her. She marched up to Margaret, saying imperiously, 'The officers' provisions, if you please.'

Silently Margaret pointed to a bulging sack on the floor, then abruptly turned her back on Sue. Rachel and Hannah followed her example. Emma turned sideways in her chair. Sue addressed Margaret's straight unyielding back.

'Is all provided in my list?'

Rachel giggled to her scrubbing-brush, 'Let her look and find.'

There was nothing for Sue but to point to the sack, with a nod to the trooper, who gathered it up. Minty uncoiled herself, pushing a piece of crust she had stolen into her cheek.

'You wish to be spoke to, madam,' she croaked. 'I tell ye naught will come from your womb but toads. And the dogs shall eat Jezebel by the wall of Jezreel.'

Sue glared round the kitchen, trying to shut out Minty's mad laughter. She noticed Will, staring, no part of this female conspiracy, and rounded on him.

'Trooper! look you, that is the brother of the man who is arrested for mutiny.'

CHAPTER SIXTEEN

If Marsh had not already appointed the trial of the three prisoners for the day after their arrest, he would have been forced to do so by the order which arrived barely an hour later. Within two days the regiment was to move to join the main army. He broke the news to John Fletcher, who politely restrained his pleasure at the information.

'I was about to seek you out, Colonel,' he said. 'News has come to me, too, from the committee in Parliament. The case of Sir Thomas Lacey has been scrutinized — he is to be sent to the Tower of London without delay.'

Marsh nodded gravely. 'Justly. But I cannot rejoice. He is your lady's brother, and a brave enemy.'

'My office does not permit me sentiment. I shall send him to London, and I shall require a cavalry escort from you, Colonel.'

'I regret that I cannot supply one, sir. I must move my regiment complete.'

'But the roads are unsafe,' John protested. 'Parties of obdurate Royalists lurk everywhere. Without a strong escort, the prisoner could be rescued.'

Marsh was completely uninterested. The whole thing was now out of his hands, and the Devil might take Sir Thomas, so far as he cared, though he would have put it more piously.

'You must send for the garrison at Banbury for your escort, sir — you will have it in three days.'

Anne was shocked at the news. For two years she had known that some day it must come, unless Tom saw reason and made his submission to Parliament on parole; yet when it came her heart sank, leaden, knowing how unlikely it was that Tom would yield to her persuasions. She pleaded with him, as she had done often before, but never with such urgency.

'If we can but send it by fast messenger to reach London before you, to appear a voluntary act, Sir Austin may yet use it to save you. He has wealth and power . . .'

Tom patted her hand. 'And rivals, my love. These Parliament men are all in conspiracies to frustrate each other — there are enough who would kill me to spite him. Besides, what if they did spare me? The war is over. My home is lost — oh, you may protest, but it is so. Arnescote belongs to John now. I'd be a penniless loafer in London or Paris. I couldn't even go as a mercenary, for they say the war in Germany is as good as finished.'

Anne was on the verge of tears. 'You'd have your life. And I'd have my brother.'

He drew himself away from her clinging hands. 'Anne, I cannot do it. I am Sir Thomas Lacey. I would sooner kneel at the block than kneel to those who killed my father.'

She was weeping now, and at her most vulnerable. Tom pressed his advantage. 'Anne, I *could* be saved. I could break out. Would you help?' The horror on her tear-stained face answered him, but he persisted. 'Forget our twinship. In cold reason, to whom are you and John closer — men of your own station, like me? Or this Army which rewards your help by moving to put a tyranny upon the land?'

Anne shook her head, wretched, despairing, knowing that if it had been possible she would have agreed to do anything, risk her life, to save her brother, letting principle go hang. 'Oh, Tom. It's not possible. Not because of matters politic, but because only proper efforts of the law can save you. All would be wrecked by a mad escape — you'd be caught and killed, for sure.'

Tom was cruelly disappointed. He had let himself hope for too much from Anne, more than he should have done. But he could not press her further, or try to coerce her. Instead, he took her in his arms and dried her eyes; in vain, for the tears still flowed.

The trial of the three mutineers was soon over; all were condemned to death. But because Marsh prided himself on his talent for combining justice with mercy, two were to be spared by the drawing of lots, for one of them to die. The drawer was Sam Saltmarsh. He looked expressionlessly at the paper in his hand, a black cross drawn on it. Marsh addressed the others.

'Trooper Hind, Trooper Wallis, you are cashiered out of the Army. Corporal, when they are dismissed they are to hand in their arms and accoutrements. They will be brought on parade tomorrow morning for their disgrace. Trooper Saltmarsh, for your past good service you will not be hanged, but in front of the regiment tomorrow you will be shot to death.'

Will was not permitted to see his condemned brother. But old Matthew Saltmarsh was allowed access to the son he had once disowned. Brokenly he pleaded for peace and reconciliation at this, their last meeting. Sam met his pleas inflexibly.

'Make peace? You are a King's man now.'

'I am your father, naught else, Sam.'

'You are my father no more. My own true father is God Almighty, who will put me in my proper place, a seat among the highest in Heaven. Corporal! Take me back.'

———————

Will, listening tensely to what was happening on the parade-ground, heard the continuous roll of drums and its ending. Then a defiant shout — Sam's voice — a rapped order, and a volley of gunfire. A pause, then a single pistol-shot. Will knew, as well as though he had watched, that Sam had not died under the hail of bullets; they had had to finish him off. The little brother, once so mischievous and sweet and simple, whom he had always protected, always stood up for, had died by violence, hating those who loved him, corrupted and fanatic.

He put his head against Emma's shoulder, and wept in her arms. Gently, timidly, she comforted him. At this moment of sorrow, as one family breach was ended by death, another, new family had its beginnings in the betrothal of Will and Emma.

———————

The regiment was going. Their accoutrements were being

piled on to baggage-waggons, their horses were saddled and waiting. Soon Arnescote would be rid of them. Lucinda watched from her window. She should have rejoiced, but there was nothing in her heart but the thought of Tom, soon to be on his way to London and the executioner's block. She had thought before that all she cared for was lost to her; soon it would be, in truth. And there was nothing she could do, no wild sortie she could make — she, that had once fancied herself a dashing heroine. Listlessly she watched the preparations for departure.

Marsh, in his quarters, was writing his last report, surrounded by papers and maps ready for packing. On the wall was a blank square from which the ugly features of Cromwell had looked down until a few moments before. A genteel cough behind him made him turn. At the door stood Sue Protheroe, wearing her most wistful, winning smile. Marsh did not smile back.

'Mistress Protheroe?'

'I must consult you, sir. An urgent matter.'

'I am much occupied, ma'am. May we talk later?'

'I fear the business is too pressing.'

Marsh sighed impatiently. To the man hovering by a pile of saddle-bags, waiting for orders, he gave a dismissive nod. When they were alone, he barked at Sue, 'I told you never to set foot in this place.'

'Where else might I speak openly with you? I have not seen you alone these two days — or nights!'

'What would you?' His tone softened a little. 'Sue, we are leaving.'

'My dear, I wish to speak of that. I leave with you, I take it?'

'Oh, certainly you must leave,' he said with a half-smile. 'Mistress Fletcher has made that quite clear.'

'And how shall I leave?'

'How? With becoming dignity, my good Sue.'

Her fine eyes flashed. 'Oh? As your camp-follower? I have been discreet in our connection, but every officer, aye, and every trooper knows of it. I see their smirks. Colonel — I am a lady, of good family and kin to the Fletchers by marriage.'

'I hope I have always treated you accordingly.'

Sue came up to him, putting out all the powerful

magnetism she knew so well how to radiate, a warm, seductive sexuality which had seldom failed with any she wanted to fascinate. The scent of the orange-flower water she had stolen from Margaret's still-room floated up to his nostrils, and her bodice was invitingly disarranged.

'Then treat me so now,' she said softly. 'Take me as your wife.'

Marsh was sufficiently surprised to break into a hearty laugh. 'My *wife*? My dear, I have a wife.' Her face changed, the smile wiped off it as by a wet cloth, her pale cheeks turning paler. She mouthed, 'A wife?'

'And three delightful children. No, I did not mention it — it was not germane to our situation, now, was it?'

'Deceiver!' she hurled at him. 'Wretch! Betrayer! So you cast me off, after all we have been to each other? You abandon me to starve, to be waylaid upon the road, to perish?' She was looking almost ugly now, transformed by rage and self-pity.

'Never, my dear, never,' he soothed. 'I shall give you an escort to the main London road, which is safely patrolled by our troops, and see you sufficiently in funds to establish yourself in London. Once there, I have no doubt your charms will assure your future.' He opened the door and ushered her out. Her last words to him, with a glare of fury, were 'Seducer! Viper! Monster!'

As she left the courtyard in a horse-litter, looking neither to right nor left, the loud jeer of a soldier followed her. 'There goes the Colonel's whore!'

———————

Anne returned from Swinford in deep distress. She poured it out to John, even telling him rashly of Tom's appeal to her.

'Escape? That's madness. You know that on Marsh's advice I have taken steps to make escape impossible. The turnkey is a strong man, and armed. The doorkeeper is also armed, and at his hand is an alarm bell which in a few minutes will ensure that every way out of Swinford is blocked by the train band.' He touched her hand tenderly. 'My dear, I share your feelings, but I do my duty.'

It was the first time since their marriage that Anne had

turned away from him, with bitterness in her heart and on her lips. 'Oh, you will always do your duty.'

He was duly shocked. 'Why, Anne, what tone is this? You force me to remind you that you are a Fletcher now, not a Lacey.'

'Blood is thicker than I thought,' she returned. She had just now, after so long, discovered that fact, and the discovery made her angry with herself as well as with John. His face was stern, unfamiliar; he had never looked so before, or spoken to her as he did, like a stranger.

'Then I must preserve you from rash and useless thoughts, wife. I must ask you to keep to your room until Sir Thomas is safe away from Swinford.' At her shocked look, he added, 'The husband, Anne, is master.'

The curtsey she made him was dutiful enough. But the long-forgotten Anne Lacey had come back from the shadows, to take possession of Anne Fletcher.

Will Saltmarsh had manfully put sorrow behind him, after the execution of Sam. Life must go on, and his own had a bright future. In the smithy he had rebuilt with his own hands for his old parents he worked every day, happy enough to be peacefully employed again, thinking, as he worked, of the home he would have one day with Emma. As he worked, repairing a damaged sickle, he sang. He broke off as someone entered the forge behind him. No one he had seen about the village before: a tall youngish man in Puritan clothing, hair cropped close in the fashion that had given the Roundheads their nickname, small steel-rimmed spectacles on his nose. Some kind of wandering preacher, perhaps. Will greeted him civilly, and was told, by a pleasant voice, 'My horse needs a shoe, blacksmith.'

Will shook his head. 'We have no horseshoes left, sir, and no iron to make them from. The Roundhead troopers who were here took all — they was like a swarm of starlings — begging your pardon, sir, if you're of the Puritan persuasion.'

The stranger's voice was altered as he answered, 'No, Will Saltmarsh, I am not of that persuasion.' Off came the broad-rimmed hat and the disguising spectacles; Will was looking into the smiling eyes of Edward Ferrar.

He gasped in amazement. 'My cropped hair doesn't deceive you, then?' said Edward. 'It is the greatest sacrifice I have made for the King.'

Will ran to the door and glanced apprehensively about. Nobody was in sight but some children at play, a man driving a farm-cart. Returning, he said, 'But you're outlawed — your head is in danger, my lord. Why come back here? Where do you come from?'

Edward shook his head. 'No matter. Will, you see one Simon Greenworthy, a buyer for the tailors of Cheapside in London, at present making my round of the western counties to get cloth. Can you give me shelter? 'Tis for one night only.'

Will, thinking hard, pointed to a haystall at the back of the forge. 'Travellers in your fix generally bed down there, my lord.'

'It will do very well.' He laid down the pack he carried. 'I saw the Roundheads leaving. Do any remain at the castle?'

'No, sir, not one?'

'And my wife — is she still there?'

'She is, my lord.'

'Glory to God! Is she well?'

'Lovely as ever, sir, but she do have a pining look.'

'Can you bring her to me?' Will was glad to hear the ardour and eagerness in the tone of this man who had been absent from his wife for two years. They said absence changed, and he would have been grieved if Lord Ferrar had changed towards Mistress Lucinda.

'Aye, sir, and safe too — she is often in the smithy with physic and food, bless her. My old dad and man are ever glad to see her. Dad,' explained Will, realizing that Edward could know nothing of Arnescote affairs, 'is out all day buying charcoal. Work's the best remedy for his grief, as it is mine. My brother Sam, that turned Roundhead, was shot for mutiny.'

Edward expressed his sympathy, then turned the conversation to Tom. He had heard, he said, that he was still imprisoned in Swinford.

'Aye. And to go to the Tower of London tomorrow, sir; for the war is over.'

177

'Over? We shall see. Will, Sir Thomas Lacey must not go to the Tower. I need your help. I must get word to him.'

That afternoon, when Will was by arrangement with the jailer to visit Tom, he finished packing the sack he was to take with him. It was full to bursting, and not only with provisions, though on top of it lay two bottles of good French brandy and a mutton pie. The two men had talked, Edward hurriedly and purposefully, Will nodding agreement. He would do what was asked, forgetting nothing he must say. Outside the forge, his horse neighed, expecting its pleasant canter. As he was about to leave, Edward asked, 'Did you get word to my wife?'

Will slapped his thigh, with a rueful grimace. 'Now I forgot. How could I?'

As Edward's face fell in disappointment, he stepped aside. Behind him stood Lucinda. Will mounted and rode away, grinning, not wishing to intrude, but out of the corner of his eye he saw them rush into each other's arms and heard their rapturous greetings as they kissed away two years' separation.

An hour had passed, though it seemed but minutes, before they rose from their bed of hay. Lucinda was rosy and radiant, transformed with happiness. She sat, prettily disarrayed, looking up at her husband. They had found time for some talk; she knew his plans and the part Will played in them.

'May I not help?' she asked. Edward shook his head.

'Your part is to go back to the castle, lest an alarm be raised.'

'Yes. I know that, of course. I've been too long a hoyting girl. I'll be as calm as — my Roundhead sister, though I burn with joy and freeze with fear at what you intend . . . Edward — when must you go again?'

'Tomorrow's dawn.'

'Then let today be longer than any twelve-month.' She pulled him down again into the sweet hay.

In the prison late that night, Tom and Syms were drinking, one of the bottles of brandy on the table between them more than half-empty. Syms was jolly, Tom outwardly so, inwardly fuming. What was this cursed man's head made of — pig-iron? By a sleight of hand Tom had got most of the brandy into Syms's tankard, himself only pretending to drink, and yet there was no sign of serious drunkenness. Perhaps it was the pie, of which Syms had eaten several lavish helpings; eating was said to diminish the effects of drink. Smiling artificially, he sat listening to the jailer's boasts of his own accomplishments, his steady hand and true eye, the valour of his military exploits (which seemed not to have included any active service), and the sincerity of his regret at parting with Tom. The bottle, empty, rolled off the table. Tom produced the other one, and refilled the other's tankard, before relapsing into a despondent attitude.

'Every second brings my extinction nearer,' he said gloomily. 'How goes the hour?'

'Near eleven, sir. You'll hear the town clock any minute.' Tom bowed his head, and dashed the back of his hand across his eyes.

'What, do I see a tear, sir? For shame. Drink, sir, and be brave.'

'I am no match for you, friend; I began to feel queasy,' said Tom, managing to look it. 'The dregs are yours.'

'More than dregs here, sir.' Syms began on the new bottle, making heavy inroads, until it too was finished.

'There goes our second dead man, sir. I wish it were the last, and you to be spared. But since that's not to be, may hell-fire be not too warm for you!'

As he pronounced the toast, a sharp rapping was heard at the door. Syms, startled, cried, 'Who's there?' No answer came, but another knock.

'It's an inspection,' Tom said. 'Else why would the door-keeper let him by?'

Syms, somewhat unsteadily, lumbered his way to the door, drawing his pistol at the same time. Tom rose and stood, poised, tense. Before Syms could reach the door Tom was upon him like a tiger. With the wine-bottle, a heavy thing of glass cased in wicker, he struck the pistol out of Syms' hand, seized him by the shoulders, and banged his head against the stone wall three times, like a human battering-ram. At the third impact the man fell and lay prone, but still feebly stirring. Tom bent over him and deftly finished the job.

Then, taking the key from the ring on Syms's belt, he opened the door and admitted Will.

'Done?'

'Done. Now for the rest.' From the sack that had been stowed under his bed he dragged out a cloak, a hat, sword-belt, pistols, a dagger in its sheath, and hastily put them on. 'The doorkeeper?' he asked Will.

'In his cubbyhole. Knifed him, cut the bell-rope. Hurry.'

The blacksmith's hooded cart jogged through the night along quiet lanes, Will driving, Tom hidden inside. Both prayed that no untimely Roundhead might appear to question them and search the cart. None appeared: they reached Arnescote in safety.

In the dark hours before dawn Tom and Edward talked at the forge, low-voiced. Tom, starved for real news of the country and the Cause, heard it from Edward for the first time.

'I am here because I was sent from France by the Queen and the Prince of Wales with orders to prepare another rising for the King. My task is to go about the country and rally groups of gentlemen to prepare themselves for battle.'

Tom raised his eyebrows. 'After all the battles we have lost?'

'You cannot fail me, Tom! Rupert himself — yes, he's with them — said I must find you and free you if need be. I bring you your orders — I but the messenger, you the soldier who will prepare and concert plans of action. Tom, we count on you.'

'It matters more what forces you can count on for a rising.'

'The whole country is sick of Parliament. The Army is split. There is a sentiment for the King growing fast even among common people. Why, the London 'prentices, Parliament's right arm, even they have rioted and shouted for the King. And, Tom, the Scots are gathering a great army of rescue for him.'

'The very Scots who sold him to Parliament, after he had gone to them for protection?'

'This is a new Scots army, Presbyterians,' Edward said urgently. 'They are afire to prevent the destruction of the church. They've able leaders — Hamilton, Montrose. Oh,

Tom, one dashing swoop and we shall save the King as we saved you tonight.'

Tom did not answer, staring at the glowing embers of the fire. Edward was anxious, pressing. 'In Heaven's name, Tom, are you for us or against us?'

Tom lifted his head, the old smile on his lips.

'Edward, I am Sir Thomas Lacey, who serves the King. I'm with you to the end — and victory, whatever the odds.'

They clasped hands. 'God bless you, Tom,' said Edward. 'And God save the King!'

———————

Their parting from Lucinda next morning was in the shelter of the castle woods. Edward had resumed his merchant's disguise, Tom was dressed as a servant. Lucinda clung to him.

'Oh, Tom, if only I could come with you.'

'You've Arnescote, my lamb. You are the last true Lacey there, and I give it into your charge. All the servants and people about will look to you — keep up their courage, and your own.'

She managed to smile. 'I'll try to be as brave as my two men.'

Tom kissed her, and led the horses away, far enough not to see the parting of husband and wife.

———————

She went home alone, once the two riders had passed out of sight, walking slowly down the hill. Whatever might be waiting at the castle, she was ready for it. Beyond the trees the outer walls loomed up, and behind them the tower, and an empty flagpole. She thought of the battered old flag, hidden now among her possessions: the looters had not troubled to take that. Suddenly she blinked — as the sun came out, gilding the castle stones, she saw the Lacey arms flying from the pole, proud, bright, whole again.

Then it was gone. But the glimpse had been enough; Lucinda had seen a vision of steadfastness and hope. *Virtus et veritas*: Virtue and Truth shall prevail, now and for ever.

Blood Red Wine

Laurence Delaney

Alicia Orsini was beautiful, even as an unripe peasant girl.
Which brought her to the notice of the old *Padrone*, feudal
master of that backward part of Italy. He used her – and
paid. Alicia's brother, Rafael, was forced into a grotesque
act of brutality to save his family honour.

To escape retribution, Rafael fled to California, where he
built up a prosperous wine-producing dynasty, a shining
example of immigrant success. But the simmering feud
pursued the Orsinis even there – over decades, turning
Rafael's dream into a nightmare of savage vendetta that
only one supreme stroke of destruction could bring to its
dramatic end . . .

Moving from poverty-stricken, turbulent Italy of the
1920s to ruthless big-business in contemporary America,
BLOOD RED WINE is an authentic, hugely compelling
story that seizes and grips to its last, power-packed page.

HISTORICAL ROMANCE   0 7221 2994 7   £2.25

FLOODTIDE

Suzanne Goodwin

Stella grew to womanhood in a land torn apart by the
Boer War, but the thunder and flash of guns on the
distant horizon did not trouble her until her sixteenth
year. To the battle-hardened British troops the fire at the
farm was just another brutal act of war: to Stella it was a
blazing beacon burning her past to ashes and lighting the
way to a strange new life in distant lands.

Who would not pity a wounded soldier dying in the
parched veldt far from his English home? How could
Stella fail to nurse the pale, aristocratic Rupert Coryot
back to health – to give him her frank young love? And
how could she suspect that his summer passion for her, a
Boer farmer's adopted daughter, would change in the
colder climate of his ancestral home?

Viscountess, lover, actress and mother, Stella flees from
the scorn and hatred of Edwardian high society to seek
fame in the theatre. But as the Great War shatters the
world she knows, she learns that her love will never die.

HISTORICAL ROMANCE   0 7221 3974 8   £1.95

A SELECTION OF BESTSELLERS FROM *SPHERE*

FICTION

A PERFECT STRANGER	Danielle Steel	£1.75 ☐
MISSING PERSONS	C. Terry Cline Jr	£1.95 ☐
A GREEN DESIRE	Anton Myrer	£2.50 ☐
FLOODTIDE	Suzanne Goodwin	£1.95 ☐
JADE TIGER	Craig Thomas	£2.25 ☐

FILM & TV TIE-INS

THE YEAR OF LIVING DANGEROUSLY	C. J. Koch	£1.75 ☐
STAR WARS	George Lucas	£1.75 ☐
FAME	Leonore Fleischer	£1.75 ☐
UPSTAIRS, DOWNSTAIRS	John Hawkesworth	£1.50 ☐

NON-FICTION

A QUESTION OF BALANCE	H.R.H. The Duke of Edinburgh	£1.50 ☐
THE DEATH OF THE DIAMOND	Edward Jay Epstein	£1.95 ☐
SUSAN'S STORY	Susan Hampshire	£1.75 ☐
SECOND LIFE	Stephani Cook	£1.95 ☐
YOU CAN TEACH YOUR CHILD INTELLIGENCE	David Lewis	£1.95 ☐

All Sphere books are available at your local bookshop or newsagent, or can be ordered direct from the publisher. Just tick the titles you want and fill in the form below.

Name _____

Address _____

_____

Write to Sphere Books, Cash Sales Department, P.O. Box 11, Falmouth, Cornwall TR10 9EN

Please enclose cheque or postal order to the value of the cover price plus:

UK: 45p for the first book, 20p for the second and 14p per copy for each additional book ordered to a maximum charge of £1.63.

OVERSEAS: 75p for the first book and 21p for each additional book.

BFPO & EIRE: 45p for the first book, 20p for the second book plus 14p per copy for the next 7 books, thereafter 8p per book.

Sphere Books reserve the right to show new retail prices on covers which may differ from those previously advertised in the text or elsewhere, and to increase postal rates in accordance with the PO.